AFTERSHOCK

DESIREE HOLT

◌

Decadent Publishing Company
www.decadentpublishing.com

This book is a work of fiction. Names, characters, places, and incidents are the products of the author's imagination or used fictitiously. Any resemblance to actual events, locales or persons, living or dead, is entirely coincidental.

Aftershock
Copyright 2014 by Desiree Holt
ISBN: 978-1-61333-681-6
Cover design by Fiona Jayde

Published by Decadent Publishing Company
www.decadentpublishing.com

Printed in the United States of America

~Dedication~

*Jackie. You will always be my Number One Guitar.
I hope you enjoy your role in the story.*

Chapter One

Remember they're excited. Jacked up about it. Cut them a little slack.

But not too much.

Rick Trajean, acknowledged leader of the hot rock band Lightnin', knew how jazzed they all were. Excitement snapped and crackled in the empty theater where they were rehearsing. Rick looked out at the seats and imagined them filled with a cheering crowd. His pulse accelerated and his breath caught in his throat.

Danny and Garrett are younger than Marc and me. This is their first real taste of celebrity.

Yeah, the other half of his brain said, *but they need to grow up in a hurry so they don't screw this up.*

Then we damn well better get to rehearsing.

Okay, so act like the top dog you are and pull them together. Time to set the mood and get everyone revved up.

The voice in his head was on full throttle, reminding him this was their future. Right here, right now.

Danny Chavez, the lead singer, had his earbuds in, listening to the most recent rehearsal of a new song. Newlywed Marc Malone, bassist extraordinaire, tuned his bass, back to everyone.

Lucky son of a bitch.

Not that Rick begrudged Marc and Emma one minute of

their happiness. If not for Marc and his family, Rick, along with his mother and his sister, would have been dangling in the wind when Rick's dad walked out on them. He just.... He just....

He just yanked himself back to the situation at hand.

"Okay, guys." He rapped his knuckle on the stool next to him. "Stop gabbing like a bunch of women. We have some hard, hard work to do."

"We got the idea, oh mighty leader," Garrett joked. "You can put away the whip."

Rick grinned. "I'm glad to see you acknowledge my exalted position."

Laughter broke the rising tension and all eyes focused on him. This was the first day of the rest of their lives, and Rick wanted to make sure there weren't any missteps. A month ago, they had been just a band on the rock-club circuit in L.A. Now they were about to cut a CD, were opening for best-selling Deep Blue River on national tour, and DBR's manager Butch Meredith, had them under contract. "You're the one who brought us here," Marc pointed out. "Gave us the drive and the discipline."

The others added their own affirmations. Emotion threatened to swamp Rick, forcing him to take a deep, steadying breath.

"Then let's get this rehearsal started. 'Low Down Man' is first up. I think a couple of the passages are still a little mushy."

"You like it because you wrote it," Danny teased.

"He likes it because it's good." Marc adjusted his bass. "Rick? I'm set to go here."

Garrett tapped the beat on the rim of a drum, Rick hit the downstroke on his guitar, and they swung into the opening bars of the song. He moved his body to the beat, foot tapping to the hard-rock rhythm. The heavy bass vibrated through his body along with the rhythm of the drums. Danny's voice had exactly the right sound of huskiness for the words, supported by Marc's rich baritone when he came in on the harmony. It continued to amaze Rick that after all this time he could still so easily lose himself in the music. Transport himself to a different place. They stopped two or three times when a particular passage didn't sound right or a riff was off, then took it from the top again.

Click, click, click.

The sound distracted him and he missed the next riff. Irritated, he lifted his gaze and looked out into the semidarkness.

And nearly swallowed his tongue.

A vision straight from his wildest fantasies marched down the aisle between the empty seats.

Holy shit!

He almost drooled at the curves her tailored business suit didn't hide very well. Thick auburn hair held by a clip swept back from her face, the rich cluster of curls tumbling past her shoulders. The style accentuated the planes of her face and highlighted her rich, full lips and the thick lashes framing her eyes. And her legs! Jesus! Emphasized by the high heels she wore, those legs seemed to go on forever.

As she closed in on the stage, she looked up at him, and every bit of breath left his body. His muscles tightened and, unbelievably, his cock swelled and pushed against his fly. Stunned by the intensity of his reaction to her, he blinked in an attempt to clear his brain. Not that it did him any good. Not even the obvious *Attitude* with a capital *A* tamped down his response. He opened his mouth to speak, only his brain seemed to have quit functioning.

Without his lead guitar in the mix, the music stopped completely and he heard the shuffling of feet behind him.

What the hell does she want?

He didn't have long to wait to find out. The mouthwatering vision climbed the steps to the stage as if she owned them and came to stand in front of him. Up close, he got an even better view of how well her tailored suit hugged her figure. How the jacket, so carefully buttoned, dipped casually at the waist before coming to rest on her hipline. His gaze was drawn to the upper swell of her breasts, just visible above the vee of her jacket. It was all he could do not to lick his lips.

But some invisible thread had morphed out of the atmosphere and connected them.

Warning bells clanged in his brain.

Trouble.

She smiled and held out a hand. "Sydney Alexander. Full Moon Promotions."

Full Moon. Oh, yeah. Butch had explained they'd handle the promo for the tour and someone would get in touch with him. But now? In the middle of rehearsal? Without calling first? What kind of a nitwit was she? Biting back a quick retort, he took the offered hand, then didn't know which bothered him more. His irritation that she'd popped in like this, or the sudden voltage that zapped him.

Well, shit.

"Rick Trajean. But I'm sure you know who I am."

She nodded. "Butch gave us photos of all of you. And, of course, I've seen the videos." She looked around. "Where's the best place for us to sit down and talk?"

Rick stared at her. "About what? In case you didn't notice, we're in the middle of a rehearsal. If I'd known you planned to show up, I would have arranged our schedule to accommodate you."

Her tongue wet her full bottom lip, colored a rich ruby red, and again Rick had to stop himself from staring.

Crap!

"This is important, Rick." She smiled at him. "I'm sorry I didn't call first, but I'm excited about this assignment." She looked at the others. "It has to do with the upcoming tour."

That smile. For a long moment, he stood there, trapped by an emotion he couldn't name. And didn't want to.

Then he glanced at the band. Everyone stared at the little tableau, eyes agleam with avid curiosity. Part of it, no doubt, because of Sydney herself.

He shook his head. "Understood. But rehearsal is at the top of the list for us. If we go out on the stage and we suck, that'll be the end of everything. So whatever you've got will have to wait."

He made his voice as firm as possible, but he wished his body would behave itself. Not like he hadn't seen a hot woman before.

She chuffed a sigh. "Fine. Fine. I'm anxious to get started, is all. I thought this would be the best time to get together."

Rick managed to pull his brain together. He had a very strong hunch this was Sydney Alexander's first major assignment with Full Moon, and she wanted to make her bones with Lightnin'. On the one hand, it ticked him off a little to have Full Moon send a neophyte to handle them. On the other, she had to have been with them a while to get this assignment. Plus, she might work extra hard to get the job done.

"Okay, rehearsal comes first, but yes, we need to talk about what the agency has in mind for us. I'll be the one you discuss it with, and I take it back to the band." He looked at his watch. "We'll be working about two more hours. I'm sure you must have some very important things to do in the meantime. Then we can meet and go over...whatever it is you have to talk to me about."

"Fine." She managed another smile, even while drawing the attitude around her like a cloak. Fire, so bright it scorched him, glinted in eyes greener than emeralds. "Two hours. Do you know where Coffee and More is?"

"Yes."

"We'll meet there." She turned away, then stopped and looked back at him, giving him that smile again. He thought his heart would stop. "Be prepared to spend some time with me. Okay? We have a lot to discuss."

"Yes, ma'am." He gave her his best slow grin. "Miss Sydney Alexander."

She marched down the steps and up the aisle, her skyscraper heels tapping harder with each step. Rick's eyes were drawn involuntarily to the sway of her hips and the smooth stride of those long legs. He couldn't decide if he wanted to pull her into his arms and taste those sinful lips or tell her to get lost. How could one woman incite such an emotional conflict in so short a time?

Well, he'd take care of their business in the appropriate manner. If nothing else, when it came to the band he was all business, all the time.

"Wow!" Danny said into the silence. "I'd like to get me some of that."

Rick spun around and pinned him with a look. "This has to do with our careers, you idiot. And you don't shop in the company store."

Danny, always irrepressible, seemed unfazed by Rick's attitude. "I'm just sayin'. You know?"

"Well, say something else." He shifted his gaze to Garret, his look questioning.

Garret held up his hands. "I'm set to work, boss. That's all."

Rick knew he didn't even have to check with Marc. He couldn't see any woman but his fiancée. He hoped whatever role Sydney Alexander played in their lives, his musicians would remember the tough climb to get to this point and not fuck it up in some stupid manner.

"All right. I'll meet with her and find out what this is all about. Meantime, we have work to do. Let's run through 'Hot Doggin'.'"

ଓଃ

Sydney picked up her café mocha at the counter and carried it to an empty booth, settled carefully on the bench seat, and placed her briefcase on the table. Her heart still thudded with the aftereffects of her confrontation with Rick Trajean. His picture had not done him justice. None of the pictures or videos she'd seen had. Tall and lean, with thick dark hair that curled to his shoulders. The sensual lines of his very masculine face were enhanced by the rough stubble of a dark beard. She'd had to clench her fist to keep from reaching out to touch it.

This man was walking sex, sensuality so raw and hot the air around him crackled with the heat. And lordy! Those come-fuck-me eyes, a color she could only call smoldering midnight fringed with lashes she'd kill for. How easy it would be to get lost in them.

She'd been around a lot of sexy men. That wasn't what bothered her. Rick Trajean reached deep inside her to ignite an explosion threatened to consume her. *Damn!* She didn't have time for relationships and certainly not with one of "her" musicians. She had a job to do. A goal. The Plan. Establish herself as one of the top PR agents in the business. The go-to person when you wanted success. A name people uttered with respect.

And this job should be her ticket to achieve what she wanted. She needed this success more than her next breath. No way would she put herself in a position to be the subject of industry gossip.

In her eight years at the agency, she'd worked with more musicians than most people listened to in a lifetime. They'd come in all shapes and sizes, many of them so blatantly sexy it made Sydney laugh. Their come-on lines were straight out of musicians-R-Us. Sydney, female as any other woman, somehow found it easy to look at the men as pieces of merchandise they were selling and not react to them at all.

Rick Trajean was different.

She'd had relationships in her life, some more exciting than others. But the effect he had on was like nothing she'd felt before. She didn't recall ever meeting a man who flipped her switches like Rick Trajean. When she walked into their rehearsal, a hot zap of sexual awareness—and something else, a sensation she didn't even want to define—jolted her. He pushed buttons she didn't know she had, tempting her with his presence alone. The atmosphere between them burst into flame, bringing a tug of emotions that slammed into her when she looked at him.

Not good at all.

I can do this. I want to. I have to.

Remember, Sydney. This is business, not pleasure. And important business. Don't you ever forget it.

Yes, important business. Her big break at long last. The internship at Full Moon had opened a whole new world for her. From the very beginning, as she watched experienced agents take unknown clients and mold them, her goal had been to develop the same skill. To find a band—a rock band, her favorite kind of music—and take it to the very top.

Pie in the sky? Maybe. But if you didn't dream big, why dream at all? For eight years she'd observed and taken notes. Learning from the agents she worked with when she became a full-timer.

Now she had her chance. She'd worked her ass off to get here. Closing her eyes for a moment, she relished the fact she at last had a client of her own to work with. All the contacts she'd cultivated over the years, all the connections she'd made, not to mention the power of Full Moon, would help her achieve The Plan. No idiot musician would screw it up for her. He had to know who was boss in this area. And that was her.

Much more than the normal dream of success, Sydney had harbored a very private reason for her passion. A hunger rooted in the days when a bitter woman gave shelter to a frightened child.

It wasn't Sydney's fault her parents were killed when she was ten years old. Or that her mother's sister, Janine, the sole relative who could take her in, had dated Sydney's father before he met and fell in love with her mother. Resentment and acrimony colored Janine's relationship with Sydney. She did her best to raise Sydney as a clone of herself, a hater of men, career driven at the expense of all else.

How often had Sydney heard the woman say to someone she'd "done her duty" by raising the child of the man who'd betrayed her. All the years of her youth, Sydney heard over and over how men were "no damn good" and how Beth stole the love of Janine's life.

"Gave up her own life, too," Janine spat. "Walked away from a promising career to do what? Be at the beck and call of a faithless man? You won't catch me doing that."

"But Mom did what she wanted to," Sydney always tried to point out.

"And what did she have to show for it? Take that as a lesson to be learned, Sydney. Watch out or the same thing could happen to you."

Sydney supposed she should be grateful Janine took her in at all, but the open hostility and constant rain of vitriol ruined any pleasure she might have found in having a place to call home.

Until Full Moon.

"Musicians? Publicity agent?"

She could still hear the scorn in her Aunt Janine's voice when she told her about it.

"It's a great chance for me."

"A chance?" The woman snarled. *"Stuck with musicians who are the worst examples of the male of the species? You'll be in trouble before you can blink. You should focus all your determination on a solid goal in the business world. Musicians are here today and gone tomorrow. And you could be, too."*

The agency specialized in public relations for single performers and bands. Selective about who they repped, they had created stardom for an impressive list of clients. While Sydney had stars in her eyes from the people she rubbed elbows with, the excitement of the business and the pleasure gleaned off every small task she conquered also infected her.

When the internship the summer following her high school graduation evolved into a part-time job while she attended the University of Texas at San Antonio, she jumped at it. Janine, sarcastic as usual, belittled it as a waste of time in a profession for useless people.

"I want to do this," Sydney had insisted.

"Fine, but not under my roof."

She took the woman at her word.

Since she hoarded and pinched pennies, she had the money to rent a not-so-tiptop apartment with three other girls and had never looked back. Not a penthouse apartment, by any means, it still couldn't have been better. Her new place put her outside Janine's sphere of influence. Every day, like today, the conversation replayed in her mind. Was she scared? Damn straight. But determined to be a success and nothing would stop her.

The head of the agency, Linc Forrester, gave her a full-time job as a college graduation present. Grunt work, she knew, but a chance to work up to a position as a recognized agent. And, thus, The Plan took shape. It consumed her every day, even as she tried hard to shut out Janine's words. Words with a permanent place in her head.

"You won't amount to anything. Not in the business you've chosen. You're too soft. The men will eat you alive. If that's the only goal you have, then you might as well settle for marriage like your mother did. You won't be good for much else."

Now, eight years later, on her own and away from Janine's hateful attitude, she'd actually moved ahead with The Plan. She had her first independent assignment with Full Moon.

Sort of.

She'd have to coordinate with whoever handled the promo for Deep Blue River, but Lightnin' belonged to her.

And she had big, big, big ideas for them. And herself.

The little girl who tried her best to please the angry, bitter woman still hidden in a dark corner of Sydney's psyche. Maybe she'd never disappear. Her presence created a constant fear of failure. If Sydney wanted to succeed, she needed to get past the scared little girl to the woman she'd become. And she had. Almost. Still, she wondered what it would take to make that frightened child vanish forever.

And prove herself to Janine, a woman she barely spoke to any more.

Enough! You have business to take care of. Forget about Janine.

And forget about Rick Trajean, in any manner except a professional one.

But, oh lordy. Something fiery and emotional had blazed

between them. What did she do with that?

You ignore it.

Yeah, right.

Determined to ignore the effect the man had on her, she took a sip of her mocha, savoring the rich flavor.

Then she opened her briefcase and took out the Lightnin' folder. Even though she knew its contents by heart, she went over the information one more time. The next couple of weeks she'd hit the pavement to promote them, tempting reporters, bloggers, columnists, everyone out there with any connection to the music industry. Put Lightnin' through their paces for their debut party, so to speak. To make it work, the band members— especially Rick—must acknowledge her authority and let her guide them. Forget about their groupies and starstruck, sappy females. Sydney held one position with them, businesswoman, and right now *they* were her business.

She studied the outline in front of her and chomped at the bit to put the pieces of the plan in place. The media releases were set to go. Linc had given her plenty of information to create them. She'd already arranged the event to introduce the band. A week in advance she'd fax and e-mail them, follow some of the contacts up with personal phone calls. Many were familiar from her prior role as assistant to the senior agents. She hoped that relationship and Full Moon's name would be enough to assure a good turnout. But you could never be sure, so follow up was important.

Okay, so maybe her unannounced walk-in today had been a mistake. She knew other agents did it, but probably after they were already established with the band. She'd get past this and do better next time.

She removed a yellow pad from her briefcase and began to make careful notes. So engrossed in her work, she missed Rick's approach.

"Those plans for us?"

Her hand jerked, the pen flying from her fingers onto the floor. Sydney looked up, her other hand at her throat, willing her pulse to slow down to a manageable rhythm. Not a dream, not a vision from her imagination but a hot presence with a voice that made her insides quake. And when his gaze locked with hers, a volcanic impact erupted inside her again. She opened her mouth but no sound emerged. Rick's rich baritone vibrated through her body. Shivers skated over her skin and danced along her spine. The first sight of him had rocked her and she thought she'd done a masterful job of concealing it. Only now, here they were, one on one, and the shimmery explosion that blasted at the door of her hidden emotions had strengthened.

Just listening to him made her nipples harden and her pulse beat hard and furious at every erogenous zone in her body. She had to squeeze her thighs together to control herself.

"Sydney?" he nudged.

"What? Oh, sorry. Hi. Thanks for meeting me."

"I asked if you were working on stuff for us." He nodded at the open folder and her pad of paper as he slid into the booth, a cup of coffee in his hand.

Forcing her eyes away from him, Sydney swept the papers into the folder and closed it. She turned the yellow pad upside down then plastered a smile on her face.

Business, Sydney. Be professional. You're in charge.

"Yes, as a matter of fact it is. I want you to know I've given a lot of thought to this and I've done a lot of research on what it will take to craft a successful plan. I've put together a strong campaign—television, newspapers, online blogs, personal appearances—to create and establish your image. Brand you, so to speak. That's what I wanted to talk to you about earlier. Why I came to the rehearsal."

Rick slid a small rectangle of pasteboard across the table to her with the Lightnin' logo on one side. When she reached for it their hands touched. Again Sydney felt that surge of electricity zip through her body and dance in the air. She looked up to see if Rick felt the same thing. If the glitter in his eyes was any indication, he did.

She didn't ever remember being so intensely aware of a man.

Not ever in her life. The reaction was so instantaneous it frightened her. Pulses throbbed and her breathing hitched. "Just making sure you were focused on us." The heat in his eyes scorched her. The tic of a muscle in his cheek showed he, too, fought to maintain self-control.

Holy crap! How is this happening?

No, no, no, Sydney. You can't let yourself respond this way to a man. Any man.

She pulled the card toward her and turned it over. On the reverse she saw Rick's name, cell phone number, and e-mail.

"The cell number is the best one to use," he told her. "You can always get in touch with me and schedule a meeting." Those hot eyes scorched her face for a long moment. "Please don't come to rehearsal again unless you're invited. When we're there, it's all about the music."

Sydney picked up the card, tucked it into her briefcase, and did her best to hide the way her hands trembled.

"I understand. I made an error in judgment today. It won't happen again." Even as she offered the semi-apology, she tried to put authority into her tone. "But I have a job to do, and I have to do it in a timely fashion or it won't work. And what I do will benefit the band."

If he would quit looking at her with such hunger. No, not simple hunger. More than that.

"I'm not an idiot, Sydney. But we're there to work." He blew out a breath. "Away from an audience, where mistakes can be corrected."

He had a point. But as a neophyte agent given the chance to test her wings, she could not fail. She'd been so intent on establishing her presence, her authority, it hadn't occurred to her she might interrupt the band's schedule.

Okay. Point taken.

"I hear what you're saying."

When she raised her eyes to him another shock zapped through her body.

I'm imagining it. I have to be. I can't afford one misstep here.

Her mouth lost all moisture, so she forced down a swallow of cold coffee.

Crap! I've got to get control of myself. Right now.

Okay, Sydney, take a breath and reload.

She managed to smile at him, doing her best to relax. "Look, I'm sorry we got off on the wrong foot. I'm just so focused on making you guys a success, I tend to forget what's going on outside my bubble. Sometimes even my manners."

"Okay, me too." One corner of his mouth crooked up in a semblance of a smile. "Shall we start over?"

She let out a breath. "Sounds good to me. I'm sure we can work things out so I don't interrupt your rehearsal time. It's just that all of this is so important."

"Believe me, it is to us, too." He leaned forward. "Now, how about you let me see what you've got in mind."

Showtime, Sydney. And make it good.

"One of the things Full Moon is tasked with, is the creation of a presence for the band even before the tour starts. My job is to build the excitement—the buzz. You know, the online gossip, the tease on the entertainment programs, the chatter about an emerging entity.

"I have a number of media appearances planned for you to get your faces out there. We have the kickoff all set, but I'll need to prep you a lot."

"Prep us." A statement, not a question.

"So you'll know what to say. You don't want to make a verbal misstep with the media." When he remained silent, she showed him the calendar. "We'll need to do a photo shoot with the band before then for the promo packets."

She went on to detail the other items on her list. Interviews with him as the leader. Meetings with some of the radio deejays in the different cities who would be key to getting their songs on the playlist. The type of questions they might be asked.

"Butch has okayed the order for merchandise to sell at the tour stops. We don't know how big the customer base will be, so we'll use the kickoff tours for other new bands as a guideline. The first two stops will give us a better feel for it."

Rick nodded, his gaze locked on her. "I understand. Butch did talk to us about it. You'll tell people what we're all about and pitch us to them for exposure."

"Right. But it encompasses more than the interviews. It's about the visuals, too." Sydney took a slow breath and pulled out an artist's sketch of their logo. She hadn't even talked to Butch or Linc about this but she knew it would work. If the band bought into it, she'd be halfway there.

"I'd like to jazz this up, give it some pop. Do the lightning bolt in silver and add some glitter to it."

She nibbled her lower lip while he studied the full color drawings. His expression gave nothing away.

Linc Forrester's warning when he assigned her to the band popped into her head.

I'm giving you this because I believe you're ready, Sydney. But be very careful. These aren't kids with stars in their eyes. They've been in the business a long time. Rick Trajean's got a good head on his shoulders. Use it. And yours, too."

"You really think jazzy T-shirts will make a difference?"

Sydney wet her lips. "I think they'll stand out on stage, draw the eye of the audience to you. Plus, it will make the shirts a lot more appealing to your fans. A lightning bolt represents massive light and power," she explained. "That's what I want people to think of when they see this band. I want the image to consume them." She paused. "If it works, I have some other ideas."

Rick leaned back in his seat, his dark eyes studied her.

"How do you really see the band, Sydney?" His tone of voice was uninflected. "How do you see us? I mean, if it's up to you to sell us, what is it you're selling?"

Sydney wrapped her hands around her coffee so he couldn't see how nervous she was. She'd been so sure when she put this together he'd—what? Nod his head and agree? Hand over the band to her to do with as she wished?

"I'm not sure what you mean?"

"I didn't say I disagree with any of this but, let me ask you a question. Did you ever see us at Aftershock, any of the club dates we did there? Or anywhere? Like any of the small concerts where we performed? Have you heard us live? Seen the reaction of an audience? It's not as if you popped onto the scene yesterday. And I'm sure there was a lot of chatter when Butch signed us."

Again there was a tense pause while he studied her. Had the conversation ended before it started? She tried to look away from him but it was impossible. At last, almost unable to breathe with the erotic tension, she forced herself to break the connection. Swallowed hard.

"I've seen the videos Butch has of you. Several times."

"But you've never seen us perform live, right?"

"No," she confirmed, reluctant to admit it. "Not live."

When Butch first signed the contracts for them, Linc told her she needed to see them before they finished their club dates. But one thing then another interfered so she'd depended on the videos to give her a feel for them. And listened to their music for hours. Another huge lapse in judgment on her part.

"Don't you think it would have been a good move before you started to lay out an image plan for us? Or interview questions?" He cocked his head and gave her a slow, careful look. She couldn't tell whether he tried to read her or undressed her with his eyes. Either way, a tiny shiver skated over the surface of her skin. "Answer a question for me, Sydney Alexander. Is this your first solo gig with Full Moon?"

Oh, God. Oh, God.

"I've been with the agency for eight years." She folded her hands and sat up as straight as she could, striving for a totally professional look. "I have a lot of experience, and I've made a study of the rock bands who've succeeded and why."

She'd lost her authority and scrabbled to get it back. If she just didn't feel the unwanted pull of sexual magnetism, the stream almost visible across the table. Or feel a sexual desire lodged deep inside her, so strong it wouldn't let go.

Rick leaned forward again, almost crowding her.

"Let me tell you something." His voice grew low, urgent, and hard-edged. "Lightnin' has a unique sound, a unique type of music, and a unique blend of voices and instruments. We've worked our asses off to develop it. The music we write reflects it and it's what's gotten us this far. We're working to make that better. I expect we have to clean up our wardrobe a little, but our music will brand us."

She felt skewered by his look and didn't like it. "But—"

Rick held up a hand. "So, if we're supposed to work together, don't get the idea you can call all the shots and dictate to us, because we'll have more trouble than either of us wants. We've been in the business a long time, too."

Yes, they had, and she reminded herself not to forget that. These guys were all in their early thirties. They'd more than paid their dues.

He sat back a little but when he spoke, his voice still carried an edge. "So if you're not willing to learn what it is you're selling, maybe we need to ask for another agent to handle this band."

Chapter Two

A stunned looked flashed across Sydney's face, as if she'd been blindsided. Along with it, he'd seen another emotion. Panic? No, it couldn't be. Not Miss Attitude.

If the situation weren't so serious Rick would have laughed, but he could tell by looking at her she'd paid her dues to have this chance, just as he and the guys had. He knew exactly what it was like to try and make someone understand you knew what the fuck you were talking about, and they should forget about arguing with you. He still needed that, in an industry that could eat him alive if he let it.

He hadn't meant those exact words to pop out of his mouth, but he found himself torn between the excitement of standing at the edge of the big time and worrying that he was dealing with someone who misrepresented herself or overstated who she was. He didn't want to blow the deal with Butch, but he didn't want to destroy what made the band great, either.

His biggest problem at the moment, though, involved more than Sydney Alexander knowing the real details of what she sold out there. He'd be more than happy to go along with whatever she and the agency wanted for them as long as she didn't screw with the core personality of the band. What made them unique. As leader, he had the responsibility to set the rules for this, to protect the band from changes that would remake who they were. To keep their integrity intact.

His biggest challenge was telling his dick to stop paying so much attention to the woman sitting across from him. And to try to figure out the tornado of emotion that had hit him the second their gazes locked. The impact of first seeing her still sizzled through his body, despite her attitude.

He'd certainly had his share of women although he was more selective than a lot of musicians were. He wasn't a groupie guy like Danny and Garrett. Groupies could be a disaster. One almost derailed Marc and Emma's romance. No, the women he connected with might be band followers, but they didn't have the lack of discipline found in groupies. They were women who loved the music as much as he did. They didn't collect musicians like bottle caps and he could engage them in conversation when they weren't in the middle of hot sex.

Not that he'd ever wanted to develop more than a casual relationship. Next to his family, the band occupied the top spot in his life. Period. Now it seemed as if all the gods he might have offended were having a big laugh at his expense. Because he couldn't remember ever having such a strong urge to rip off a woman's clothes and plunge his cock so deep inside her he couldn't tell where he left off and she began.

If the situation wasn't so serious to him, he might even laugh at himself. He should be trying to make sure this woman understood what she was selling. Instead he wanted to capture Sydney Alexander's face between his hands, tease her lips with his tongue before plunging it into her mouth, and crush her body to his so she could feel just how she aroused him. He wanted to release the clip and let her hair tumble around her face while she whispered erotic suggestions to him. No, he wanted more. He wanted to undress her piece by piece and feast on the lush body that made his mouth water and his cock throb.

Rub his scent all over her like some animal in heat. Claim her.

Great, asshole. Just what the moment calls for. Get your big head in the game instead of your little one.

With an effort, he banished the image from his mind. His

coffee had cooled, but he took a swallow to distract himself and get back on track. He shifted in his seat and surreptitiously adjusted his jeans so his balls weren't crushed. Remembering what was at stake, he forced himself to wait for Sydney's response. He half expected her to pick up the remains of her coffee and dump it over his head. He watched, keeping his face impassive, as she pulled herself together.

"I'm the agency rep Linc Forrester assigned to you." She cleared her throat. "When Butch Meredith signed your contract with us, he accepted me as the agent who would handle your band, and that won't change. You could have the best music in the world, but if you don't have some gimmick to make you stand out from the crowd, you'll be part of it instead of ahead of it." She glared as if daring him to disagree.

Rick ground his teeth. He didn't want to fuck up this chance for Lightnin'. The band was his life. They'd all worked so hard for this big break. When they signed with Butch, they knew they would give up a lot of control in exchange for the opportunity presented to them. And they trusted Butch. Rick realized he'd have to back off a little so he didn't damage the situation with Butch or put the band in a bad position. But maintaining their core essence was of key importance to him. And whoever sold their brand, needed to be tuned into that.

"Listen, I'm not trying to be a hardass. But it's important for you to take the time to find out who we are. So when you pitch us to the media you know in detail what your product is."

"Of course." She lifted her chin in a defensive gesture. "I've been *learning* for a long time.

Rick swallowed a sigh.

But you haven't been learning about us.

In spite of his good intentions he reached across the table and took one of her hands in his. Big mistake! Her skin was so soft, he wanted to rub his face against it. "Let's forget about the stuff in your folder for today. Come to a rehearsal, okay? A planned visit," he added. "Take the time to listen to us. Then we'll talk. Fair enough?"

He could almost see her battle between compromise and control. At last, she smiled and the brilliance of it speared through his body.

Holy shit!

"When?"

He frowned, running through their schedule in his head. "Day after tomorrow. Make it late in the afternoon and if we knock your socks off with who and what we are, I'll buy you coffee afterward. Or a drink. Whatever the situation calls for."

She blew out a soft breath. "Sounds good. As long as you're also willing to listen to my ideas after that."

"Done." He squeezed her hand before he realized it and dropped it at once. "Day after tomorrow at five o'clock."

He waited until she slid from the booth before pushing himself out. Following her out of the coffee bar he couldn't help focusing on the sway of her hips and her scent—a light floral fragrance—that had been driving him nuts. He took a deep breath to steady himself before opening the door for her to precede him outside.

Her car, a bright red little sports toy—and didn't that suit her to a tee—was parked near the building. He waited next to it while she unlocked the door and tossed her briefcase inside. When she turned to face him, he had to clench his hands into fists to keep from grabbing her.

Jesus, Trajean! Get your shit together.

"Well." She wet her lower lip with her tongue.

Rick thanked the gods he wore a T-shirt long enough to cover the bulge growing behind his fly. "So. See you in two days."

Her mouth curved in a tiny smile. "I don't know if *you'll* knock *my* socks off, but I hope to do that for you."

Lady, you already do. In more ways than one.

She held out her hand.

Rick took it in his larger one. The electricity that zapped between them stunned him. Sydney's eyes widened and a faint blush crept up her cheeks. A little gasp escaped her mouth like a puff of wind. They stood there, gazes locked, until at last she dragged her hand away.

"Okay, then." Her voice was breathless, choppy, as if she'd just run a marathon. "Good-bye."

Rick shoved his hands in the pockets of his jeans and stared after her little red car as it pulled out of the parking lot, wondering what the hell had just happened. And what, if anything, he did he intend to do about it?

ᘉ

Sydney tossed her briefcase onto a chair, her keys into the dish on the little table by the front door, and headed for her bedroom. *Bath. Right now.* At the office, Linc Forrester had played Twenty Questions with her about her Lightnin' meeting, and she had done some fancy footwork to convince him she had things under control.

Yeah, under control. Right. When just looking at Rick Trajean makes me so wet I'm surprised I don't drown in my own scent. When my heart does somersaults and some emotion deep inside me fights to break loose.

Still, Linc was pleased to know she had a second meet set up. She'd listened with as much patience as she could as he explained how he thought she should handle it and reminded her to give him a full report afterward. She wanted to tell him she didn't need a babysitter but deep down, when she wasn't being obsessive about it, she knew Linc's main objective was to keep Butch Meredith happy. Deep Blue River lit up the charts, filled concert halls, and showed up on everyone's television screens. Linc wouldn't want to screw up the deal by pissing off Meredith's new baby band.

Neither did she, but she'd planned for this since the day she first took the job at Full Moon. No, long before that. Way back in high school, she began to put The Plan together. The battle would not be easy, but she needed to do this so desperately.

And keep her emotions and her sexual response packed away. Preferably in some freezer.

Stripping off her clothes she turned on the faucets in the big spa tub in her bathroom and dumped in some bath salts. While waiting for the tub to fill she pulled on a shortie robe and headed to the kitchen to pour a glass of wine. She lit a cinnamon-scented candle, eased into the heated water, and started the jets. Then she leaned back, took a sip of the wine, and let out a slow breath.

Just what I needed after a real bitch of a day.

She hated that she and Rick Trajean had butted heads from the get-go, but she'd watched other agents work and knew how important it was to establish who was in charge when dealing with newbies. The band could take care of the music, the manager would handle the staging, and the publicity person created the image. That was the way it was done. Why couldn't they understand?

Another sip of wine and the liquid slid through her veins, easing the tension of the day. Closing her eyes, she let the fatigue slip from her body.

She had never seen eyes so dark, like bitter chocolate, yet so alight with heat. The man seemed to see into every corner of her soul. He'd wanted to shave but she loved the day's growth of beard shadowing his jaw. The rough stubble accented the masculine lines of his face, the strong curve of his jaw.

"I should shave first." His voice was low and rough, its timbre vibrating through her body. "I'll hurt your skin."

"That's okay." She touched his face. "It will make me remember you."

"I plan to give you something more than beard burn," he growled.

His arms tightened around her and his fingers threaded through her hair, cradling her head in his palm. When his mouth touched hers, the contact was so electric it snapped through her nerve endings. As rough as his beard was, his lips were as smooth. And his tongue! Oh, Lord, it slipped into her mouth and danced around like a live flame.

He pulled his mouth from hers with obvious reluctance, but in the next moment he pressed his lips to her neck, nibbling and sucking and licking. She could barely remember him easing them out of their clothes and onto the bed. But now she felt the cool smoothness of the sheets against her hot back as Rick covered her with his long, lean body. The hard thickness of his cock was a heated brand against her thigh, his balls just brushed against her skin.

His mouth blazed a trail along her collarbone before finding that erogenous spot behind her ear and teasing it with his tongue. One large hand slid along her rib cage until it reached her breast. His lean fingers were rough with calluses accumulated from years of playing the guitar and she loved the uneven feel of them.

Sliding her hands down the length of his back, she reached his buttocks and dragged her fingernails over the skin. He groaned and his heated cock flexed against her. She moved her leg just enough to trap him between her thighs and squeezed.

"Any more of that and this party will be over before it starts," he groaned. "I don't want to come until I'm inside you and the walls of your sweet pussy grab me like a vise."

His words made those very walls flex and convulse, hungry for his hard length to fill them. She was sure electricity was attached to his mouth sucking her nipples, sending jolts straight to her pussy. She tried to move against him, the feel of the hair on his chest against her skin so sensuous, but his strong hands held her firmly in place.

She wanted to cry out in protest when his mouth left its grip on her taut bud until he moved it to the other one. His finger and thumb closed around the pebbled flesh he'd just tormented and squeezed and rubbed it. Sydney was sure she was going to come from nothing more than his attention to her breasts. But before she could, his mouth was gone and his tongue traced patterns between her mounds, then trailed down to her navel.

He swirled the tip into the furled flesh, sending tremors racing through her. She arched up to him and moved her thighs farther apart. A current of air skimmed over the surface of her *body but as turned on as she was, it did little to cool her heated skin. She nudged him with her hips, silently begging him to drive his cock inside her and—*

Splash!

Sydney fought her way up under from the heavily scented bathwater, coughed up the fluid she'd inhaled and slicked her wet hair from her eyes.

What on earth?

The dream. *Holy crap!*

The pulse in her cunt beat furiously, demanding attention in the aftereffects of the fantasy. Fantasy? How had that happened? All she'd done was immerse herself in a relaxing bath, sip chilled wine, and focus on the flickering candlelight.

And dream about sex with Rick Trajean!

Ohmigod!

Ignoring the vibrations that pulsed through her, she punched off the jets, flicked the stopper, and climbed out of the tub. Disoriented, she nearly knocked over the wine, grabbing it just in time. With a what-the-hell shrug, she drained its contents and reached for the big bath towel on the counter. Water squished between her toes. A glance down confirmed she'd done a number on the floor when she attempted to save herself from drowning. Maybe the cleanup would remind her of the foolishness of daydreams.

But she couldn't get it out of her mind. With the force of a sudden wind, it slammed back into her brain, the image of their naked bodies, the feel of his hands and his mouth on her—

Stop it! This is business.

Yeah, try telling that to her traitorous body. Or to the unfamiliar emotions rocketing through her. Even as she smoothed lotion into her skin, she imagined Rick's hands stroked her, touching all the right places. His fingers slid into her, curling so the tips scraped her sweet spot, while his thumb teased her clit.

Well, damn it all anyway. She tried giving herself a lecture while she dried her hair and brushed her teeth.

He's just a guy. Nothing special. But most important, he's a client, so no dreams. Never. Ever.

But Rick Trajean was walking sex and her body ignored her words. She needed to get herself under control over the next two days, before she saw him again.

ଔ

"So what did she say?" Danny asked, as he helped himself to a slice of pizza. "She had a lot of nerve to barge into rehearsal the way she did. I hope you told her about that."

They'd gathered for dinner at Pizza and Pasta, the other members of the band anxious for details of Rick's meeting with Sydney Alexander. Marc had even brought Emma, his bride to be. Their romance had seen some rocky ups and downs, but now they were the icons for the happy couple, with their wedding not too far off. Most of the time now they beat a retreat at the end of the day to the home they shared. But everyone knew how important this whole thing was—the concert, the CD, the publicity. No one wanted to screw up, by themselves or with anyone else.

"She's the agent responsible for our promo with Full Moon." Rick chose his words carefully. "I guess she thought rehearsal was the best place to get us all together."

"But to just walk in like that?" Garrett shook his head. "Shouldn't she have told us she was coming? And what's with the attitude?"

Sydney Alexander definitely had that. Rick wondered if it was just an accident that her last named began with the same letter as attitude. The word fit her like a glove. But as the leader of the band it was his responsibility to smooth things over, keep the members reassured, and handle any glitches that came along.

Like Sydney.

"This is part of the whole deal with Butch," he explained. "He wants our name out there and some excitement generated before the tour kicks off and the first single releases. She has some ideas about how to promote the band." He took a bite, chewed thoughtfully. "I listened to her, she listened to me." Sort of.

"So is she all hacked off at us now?" Garrett wanted to know. "I can't figure out who messed up here."

"We both did. I shouldn't have jumped all over her, and she apologized for not prearranging her visit." Not. "She's only seen tapes of us, so I invited her to rehearsal day after tomorrow." He held up a hand against the expected objections. "We'll plan for it. Put a tight set together. Show her what Lightnin' really is."

"What exactly does she want to do?" Garrett wanted to know. "What kind of plans does she have? Did she tell you? Butch never really went over specifics with us."

"We touched on it." Rich mentally organized his words the way he did with his sister. "Full Moon wants to create a lot of buzz before the single hits and we hit the first concert date. They aren't novices. We both agreed Sydney needs to get a real feel for the band before we move forward."

"I'd like to get a real feel for *her*," Garrett joked.

Rick slanted a hard look at him. "Not funny, Gar. She's off limits. This is strictly business." He hoped he could remember that himself. He could still feel the tingle in his body from the brief physical contact with Miss Sydney Alexander.

"Yeah. We don't want to piss off Full Moon or Butch," Danny put in. "But we can't let them to make us into something we're not, either."

"Why don't you all relax until she comes back to rehearsal." Emma wiped a trace of pizza sauce from her mouth. "The agency wouldn't have assigned her to you unless they were sure she could do the job. Butch Meredith is a big client and they want to take good care of him."

"That's my lady. The voice of reason." Marc looped his arm around her, drawing her close, and kissed her.

"Not in front of the children, please," Rick joked. "Seriously, though. Emma's right. We have to trust Butch and the people he hires. So let's put on a good show for Sydney and make her understand what Lightnin' is all about."

Chapter Three

*S*ydney sat in her car in front of the old theater and checked herself one last time in the mirror in her sun visor. Rather than show up in a power suit today, she'd decided to play down her image a little, although not her determination. Now, after five changes of clothing she wore a pair of studded jeans with a billowy, tailored blouse. She'd redone her makeup and added tiny gold hoops at her ears.

And why do I even care? This is business, Syd.

Yeah, right. That's why you've fantasized about the hottest man you've seen in ages. Maybe ever.

She inhaled a deep breath and let it out slowly. Calm. She needed to relax. And have her shit together. This assignment would make or break it for her, and she couldn't afford to screw it up. Time to put her hormones into cold storage, at least until this was over.

Right.

She'd spent the past two nights going over all of her notes and once again researching the images and campaigns of similar bands on the Internet. Watching the videos. Making notes about them. Not that she hadn't been compiling this information forever. She hadn't just stuck to this decade, either, but went back to bands that had been propelled out of the herd and stayed in front. She wanted something different for Lightnin'. Out of the ordinary. Something that would make them stand out from the crowd. Capture everyone's imagination. She just had to make the guys see it.

And, down deep, she wanted the industry's acknowledgment that Sydney Alexander had plucked Lightnin' from the masses and created a star property, making them exceptional. A win-win, right?

Okay. Here I go.

Leaving her briefcase in the car this time, she stuck her iPad in her purse and strode into the theater. Checked her watch. Right on the dot of five o'clock. Good. She pulled open the door and the cool darkness of the lobby embraced her. The sounds of the band tuning up reached out through the inner doors.

She entered the main part of the theater to see they were, indeed, all on stage and waiting for her. As she let her gaze take them in she realized there was nothing to make them stand out. They looked like any other rock band at rehearsal, dressed in old jeans and T-shirts. Today what they wore didn't happen to be grungy, an acknowledgment that they were going to have an audience of one. Sydney respected the fact Rick wanted her to see them live, even in this setting. Still, she wasn't sure if it would change her mind as to the direction she wanted to take. She had seen plenty of rock bands live, many of them from the wings when she assisted a senior rep, and she always thought the videos, with all those special effects, captured the audience more.

"You haven't seen the right band yet," Linc Forrester told her once. "When you do, they'll make every nerve in your body burst into flame with their music alone."

Maybe. She wasn't so sure, but that was why she was here today.

Rick's gaze locked onto her as soon as she started down the aisle. Traitorous hormones tried to leap up and do a happy dance, but she ruthlessly suppressed them. A very difficult process, since the closer she got to the stage and Rick, the more his presence invaded her senses. Did he have to look so dark and dangerous? Be so damn sexy?

She skirted the front row and reached up a hand to him, trying to ignore the fact that he took in every inch of her. And that beneath lashes sinfully thick for a man, those eyes were filled with a smoldering heat that pierced her to her very core. God, she hoped no one else saw it. But then he blinked, the look was gone, and she wondered if she'd imagined it.

"Thank you for doing this." She planned to be as polite and businesslike as possible. "I really appreciate it."

Rick took her hand and the instant they made contact that same jolt of awareness burned through her. And maybe he held on a second too long before releasing her. He took a step back.

"We've put together a short set for you that we think best represents who and what we are," he told her. "We don't have proper lighting or anything so I hope you can use your imagination."

"No problem." She glanced over her shoulder. "Any place special I should sit?"

The band members stopped fiddling with their equipment and watched intently.

"About five rows back would be good. You won't be right on top of us but still close enough to get good sound."

"Okay."

She settled into her seat, pulled her iPad out of her purse to take notes, and sat back with an air of expectation. Rick wasn't looking at her now. Instead he engaged in quiet conversation with the band, maybe going over some last-minute details. Sydney wished now she'd gone to see them live at *Aftershock* right after all the contracts were signed. She hadn't needed Rick to point out that tapes didn't create the same ambience or the same connection to the music. But at the time, she'd thought she would just be, as usual, an assistant on the project.

Not a good excuse. Assistant or lead, I still should have made it my business to go hear them live. Although I'm not sure it would have changed my mind.

Well, she'd hear them now. And despite the videos, she

wasn't sure she knew what to expect.

They all moved into their places, Garrett up front and in the center, Marc stage right, and Rick stage left. The lights were harsh and the sound system meant just for their ears, but the moment they hit the downstroke of their first song, Sydney was mesmerized. The atmosphere of the old theater fell away at once, her attention captured by the energy of the musicians on stage.

Their music was emotionally charged, full of life and energy. Danny was the lead singer but both Rick and Marc had solos. And when all their voices blended she felt as if they sang to her alone. Not as professionals, but like the Sirens who seduced so many sailors. Rick, on lead guitar, was nothing short of amazing. Exhilarating. Transfixing. His fingers danced over the strings like an angel's wings, plucking just the right sounds.

As the band moved through the set Sydney found herself immobilized by the effect of what she heard. She could imagine them in the atmosphere of a darkened rock club, spotlights hitting the stage, the people on the dance floor and in the booths mesmerized by the intensity of their music. It didn't seem to matter what the tempo was. Fast or slow, it had the same spellbinding effect.

They closed with "Music Lady," the song Sydney knew Marc had written for Emma. As she listened, she blinked back tears. The notes vibrated through her body and the final chords rocketed through her much like the intense spasms of an orgasm. The last note faded but still she sat there, awestruck. Rick had been right. She'd needed to see them live. The videos were great, but they didn't capture the band's essence or vitality. Now she knew what Linc Forrester meant. She was so enraptured she'd never even thought about taking notes.

"Sydney? Miss Alexander?"

Rick's voice shook her out of her immobility. She looked at the stage and realized they were all staring, waiting for her to comment. She pushed up from her seat, walked down to the edge of the stage, and cleared her throat.

"That was...." She searched for the right word. "Incredible. And that's a very weak description. Your music really comes out and grabs people."

Rick gave her a lopsided smile. "Change your opinion of us?"

She shook her head. "No. Only reinforced it. You guys blew me away." She looked at the other musicians. "But I do have some thinking to do now."

"We're much better with the proper lights and sound equipment," Marc told her. "The right atmosphere."

"Oh, I think it says a lot for you that the dynamism of your performance comes through so solidly without it." She looked at Rick again. "I'd like to structure the promo around that very thing."

He shrugged. "As long as you don't mess with what and who we are. But I'd like to see what you've got before you get started and again before it goes out. See if I can add anything to it."

What if he means change it?

"I think it's important for us to work together," she told him in a slow voice. "But I'd also like you to keep in mind you are virtual unknowns and we need to make a big PR splash before you hit the stage on your first concert date." She dug up her professional smile. "I think we both want the same thing, don't we? Success?"

"I hope you're right."

"So when can we meet again? We don't have a lot of wiggle time here, and I'm anxious to get started."

"I have a suggestion." Marc set his guitar on a stand and walked over to Rick. "Emma and I are having a little get-together on Saturday night. Nothing fancy. Just the band and some close friends. How about you join us? That way you can get a feel for who we are and how our personalities and talent contribute to Lightnin'." He looked around at the others. "That suit you guys?"

Rick's eyes widened and he stared at Marc. Sydney wasn't sure which of them was more stunned by the invitation. The other musicians looked a little shell-shocked, too. She guessed a pretty tightknit circle of people attended their get-togethers. She made herself laugh.

"Thanks, Marc, but I don't want to intrude."

"You're not." Rick's comment surprised her. "Marc's right. You need to know who we are beneath the music."

"Well." She paused. "If you all are sure."

"We're sure."

Rick's voice was so rich it coasted over her like hot chocolate. Its deep resonance scorched her nerve endings and made her tremble. She dug her fingernails into her palms to keep focused.

"Then, thank you. Very much."

She walked back to her purse, pulled out her phone, and typed in the address Marc called out to her. She was proud her hands didn't tremble, even though an emotional storm raged inside her. Their music had set it off, so gut-deep with emotion it transported. Rick's come-fuck-me voice didn't help, either, seducing her senses whether he intended to or not. And now she'd be in a social situation with all of them and—

Okay. She'd go. Chat with everyone. Get a feel for them on a personal level. Make some adjustments in her campaign and then get on with business. Nothing would stand in the way of her success. Nothing and no one. And she'd stay as far away from Rick Trajean—on a personal basis—as she could.

Because she couldn't lose sight of The Plan.

She put on her professional smile. "Thank you very much." She looked at each of the men in turn. "You have a very unique sound. And you're right. I needed to hear it in person. I'll do my best to make sure everyone out there connects with it. I'll see you all Saturday. And again, thanks for the invite."

All the way up the aisle to the lobby doors, she could feel Rick's gaze on her. She never turned around, just kept walking. But when she reached the parking lot, she collapsed in her car and let out her breath in a long whoosh.

Holy crap!

The man's mere presence did things to her that other men couldn't coax from her no matter how hard they tried. She leaned her head back against the seat and closed her eyes.

Immediately his lean face appeared like a temptation in her brain. What if he felt the same? She hadn't imagined the chemistry between them the other day. How would she handle Saturday night?

I am definitely in a world of trouble.

 C8

As Rick put away his guitars, Marc walked over to him, blocking out the other band members.

"Am I wrong, or do I get the feeling you aren't happy with our promotions agent?" he asked.

Rick snapped the locks on a guitar case, maybe with a little more force than he needed to. He didn't know what to do with all the conflicting emotions battling inside him. His responsibility to the band had to take precedence over everything else. If only his dick would pay attention.

"Rick?" Marc prompted.

"What? Oh. Sydney." He set the case aside with a deliberate motion and picked up a second one.

"I don't know yet if I'm happy with her. I want to see what she comes up with first."

Marc quirked an eyebrow. "Didn't she show you her ideas the other day?"

"Yeah, but I wasn't too flashed out about them. She'd never seen us live, for one thing. That's why I had her come back here today. Listen to a planned set."

"And?"

Rick shrugged. "Can't tell. I'll have to see what she comes up with after this." He slanted a look at Marc. "You think it was smart inviting her over Saturday night?"

"Don't you? She'll get some up close and personal time with us." He grinned. "You looked like you wanted some of that up close and personal for yourself when she was here."

Rick scowled. "I'm focused on the band right now. Period. And my mother and sister. I don't have time for anything else."

"Jesus, don't take my head off. Anyway, it might do you some good to chill out now and then. All this intense shit in your life can't be healthy."

Rick set the other guitar case next to the first one. "Oh, so now you're concerned with my health?"

"Rick. Hey. I'm your friend. We've been tight since we were fourteen years old. Take a step back here, will you?"

Rick huffed out a breath. "Sorry. I just want everything to go off without a hitch for both the tour and the CD."

"It will be fine," Marc assured him. "Whatever artistic conflicts you and Miss Sydney Attitude have, you'll work them out."

"Miss Attitude." Rick laughed. "Good name for her. So you felt the don't-mess-with-me vibes coming off her, too?"

Marc looked at Rick then away then back again. "I think this tour is just as important to her but for different reasons. Give her a chance, okay? Butch is probably paying Full Moon big bucks." He chuckled. "And if you happen to get a little more personal with her—"

"Not gonna happen," Rick barked. "So forget it."

"Yeah, yeah, yeah. Listen. I trust you. We all do. We know the band comes first with you. Let's just see how things go Saturday night in an informal setting. Maybe Emma can chat her up."

"We'll see. Although if anyone can talk to her about the band it's Emma."

"No shit." Marc laughed again. "Remember when we met? She'd never listened to a rock band in her life. Been to a club. Nothing."

"I hear you." His own mouth curved in a smile. "Hell, she wouldn't even tell you her damn name for the longest time."

"So maybe someone who comes to Lightnin' from that angle can give her a perspective we can't. The audience reaction. What turned her on about the band."

"Okay, okay. I just—"

"Relax, man. If there's a problem, we'll all jump in to help,

40

okay?"

Rick nodded, but he sat on the stage for a long time after the others left. Sydney Alexander had no idea how he'd clawed his way up from a desperate situation to build Lightnin' and take it where it was. When his dad dumped all of them for a new life—yes, he'd walked out on Rick and Meredith, as well as his marriage—they all felt as if the rug had been jerked out from beneath them.

Then he met Marc, whose family had provided much-needed stability for all of them. Mrs. Malone had become a good friend to Rick's mother and included all of them in Malone family activities. When he and Marc put Lightnin' together, the two of them had worked to create a solid foundation. One that wouldn't have other musicians slipping in and out the way it happened with so many other groups. They wanted definite commitments from Danny and Garrett because their contribution would be critical to the magic mix they were creating.

From day one, they had all worked very hard, and now it was about to pay off. He wasn't going to let Miss Attitude or anyone like her screw with what their creation. But everything came with its own set of problems. There was Butch to consider and all the obligations that went with that contract. Money was being spent on them. Big money. If they made a mess, no one would ever touch them again.

He sure couldn't fuck it all up with sex. And whatever else seemed to link him to Sydney Alexander.

"Rick?"

He jerked at the sound of Marc's voice.

"I thought you left," Rick said.

"You looked as if you spaced out sitting there, so I came back." Concern cut deep grooves in Marc's face.

"Sorry about that." He blew out a breath. "I'll finish packing up and get out of here with you."

"Wait a second." Marc pulled him around so they faced each other. "Is there more going on here than just business details? Something we need to talk about?"

"No." Rick jerked his arm away. "There's nothing."

But Marc's gaze burned into him like twin lasers. "You can't lie worth a damn to me, Trajean. So give it up. Do you have the hots for Sydney?"

Rick shook his head. "It's nothing. Leave it alone."

"You know," Marc said in a thoughtful voice, "once you get past the attitude, she's okay." He winked. "And sexy."

"And off limits," Rick reminded him. "A surefire way to screw up this deal. On many fronts."

"Yeah, I know." Marc slowly wound a cord around his hand then tucked the ends in. "Risky business. But I wish you'd find someone to lighten up your life a little."

Rick stared at him. "Like I haven't had women before?"

"There's women and then there's *women*. Even if you hook up with Sydney, I trust you to not let it affect the business of the band."

Rick snorted. "Then you've got more faith in me than I do."

"On another subject, Meredith all set for college?"

"I sure hope so." His sister was due to leave in three weeks. "She's got enough crap packed for ten females."

Marc laughed. "You live with two women and you haven't figured out by now all the stuff they collect? Anyway, going off to college is a big deal. I thought my brothers were loading up to move to another country when they left."

Rick shrugged. "I'm not too excited about her being so far away."

"Far away? Rick, she's only going to College Station. Texas A&M is a three-hour drive."

Rick sobered. "I worry about her. That's all."

"She'll be fine," Marc assured him. "She's got a good head on her shoulders. And you and your mom have given her a good sense of herself. Now, come on. Let's get out of here." He paused. "And Rick? Cut yourself a break, okay? You've made this band your whole life. Live a little now and then."

Chapter Four

"*D*amn. No, double damn."

Sydney pounded the steering wheel. What rotten luck. Of all the times her car could pick to be a problem.... She turned the key again and listened for the motor to catch, but only heard a bad grinding sound. She was hot, irritated, and wanted to throw a temper tantrum. Finally, she yanked the key from the ignition and pushed the car door open. There was nothing for it. She'd have to call the auto service and get someone to come take a look at the damn thing.

The heels of her sandals clicked on the floor as she made her way back into the house. Sitting in a hot car in a hot garage was not her first choice of activity. Actually, her first choice would be zipping down the streets in the outfit she'd outrageously splurged on for a get-together she wasn't sure she should attend. She paced back and forth with quick, hard steps, frowning as she dialed the number for the garage and waited for someone to answer.

"Your little toy giving you trouble again, Syd?" Bill French's gruff voice held a trace of humor. "I told you the other day to bring it in for service."

The car was Sydney's baby, her present to herself five years earlier when Linc gave her a great Christmas bonus. Since it was now out of manufacturer's warranty, she took it to the garage owned by the father of one of the secretaries at the agency. She loved that he treated her almost as another daughter and she trusted him implicitly, a very precious commodity in her life.

"I know, I know. I'd planned on doing it next week." She started to chew on a fingernail before snatching her hand away from her mouth. "Can you get away to take a look at it? Or send someone?"

"I'll come myself. Be there in a few." He paused. "You do know it's Saturday, right? You're lucky I happened to be here this late."

"I know, I know. And I truly appreciate it. Thank you so much."

Bill chuckled. "You should think about getting a real car," he told her. "Anyway, expect me in about fifteen."

The breakdown put a definite crimp in her plans for the evening. She could always take a cab to Marc and Emma's, but she still had to get home. Call a cab at whatever hour she decided to leave. Fend off polite offers from the others.

She caught sight of herself in the hall mirror. Man oh man. She'd splurged on yet another new pair of jeans, plus a tank top and an overblouse tied at the waist. She couldn't believe it had taken her two hours to try on clothes and create the right thrown-together, casual look for tonight. Strappy sandals with kitten heels had made another dent in her wallet.

She blew out a breath.

She never spent so much time on an outfit for a special event.

But if she could win over the band—especially Rick—it would be worth every penny. The first step was getting them to accept her. No, scratch that. The first step would have been getting to the damn party but here she was. Stranded. And not looking forward to the phone call she had to make.

Bill was as good as his word. Fifteen minutes later on the dot, he was in her driveway with his tow truck.

"No saving the beast here, missy." He shook his head. "It's either the alternator or ignition. Whatever, I'll still have to get the part. I can get you a loaner by Monday."

"Monday?" she nearly shrieked, then dialed it back. "I'd hoped by then you'd have fixed the damn thing."

"If they have the part in stock." He studied her face. "You got big plans tonight?"

"I did," she said in a miserable voice. Maybe this was an omen, a sign she wasn't supposed to go.

"Well, honey, just tell him to come and pick you up. I never like when men don't want to pick up their dates."

She wanted to tell him it wasn't a date but that would only lead to more questions. She thanked him for coming over right away and watched as he drove off with her car on the flatbed.

Better call and let them know I'm not coming.

They'd think she was blowing them off or something equally rude. Flipping through the numbers in her cell phone, she found the one for Marc and Emma. No way could she call Rick for this.

"I'm really sorry," she told Marc when he answered. "I looked forward to some casual time with you guys."

"Been there, done that," he said. "But don't give up. Hold on a second."

"What? No, Marc. Wait, wait, wait."

From the muffled sound it was obvious he had his hand over the speaker on the phone while he talked to someone and she was pretty damn sure who. For a moment she was tempted to just hang up, but no. Then the band would get ticked off and she'd look like an idiot. Still, could seemed to be happening with Rick any less perilous?

"Hey, Sydney, you still there?" Marc's voice broke into her thoughts.

"Yes, I am. I'm here."

"Listen, Rick's gonna come pick you up. He said he'd be happy to."

Oh, I'm sure.

"That's not necessary," she protested. "I hate to inconvenience anyone."

"Not a problem. Besides, we're all looking forward to this.

Give me your address."

This was a mistake. She'd be alone in the car with Rick, not once but twice. In close quarters. Just the two of them. But she couldn't afford to irritate these guys, so she rattled off her address.

"Oh, not so far away. Expect him in about fifteen. See you when you get here."

She spent the entire time she waited having a conversation with herself. Being alone with Rick even for a short drive would be dangerous. She didn't do meaningless sex but she certainly didn't see herself at the start of a relationship with Rick. He was a client, for the love of God.

Well, okay, then maybe meaningless sex would be okay. They could do it, get it over with, and move on.

Wait. Maybe she'd misread all the signals and he didn't feel the same attraction she did. No, she'd seen it in his eyes. Sensed his reaction.

Crap! I must be losing my mind!

The piercing sound of the doorbell shattered her internal conversation. Taking one last look at herself in the hall mirror, she pasted her professional smile on her.

I can do this.

But the moment she opened the door and saw Rick standing there, her entire body went on full alert. The sleeves of his deep blue shirt were rolled up, exposing his muscular forearms and jeans that outlined his lean hips and long legs. His hair was neatly combed, the ends just touching his collar, and a smooth shave accentuated the strong line of his jaw.

Sex!

And oh, much more than that. Something she didn't even want to think about.

One corner of his mouth lifted in a grin as if he knew what naughty image he'd conjured in her imagination. But then their gazes locked and a thunderbolt couldn't have struck her harder.

For God's sake, Sydney, this is business, remember?

She took a deep breath and pulled herself together.

"Thank you so much for picking me up. It really wasn't necessary. I sort of feel like I'm crashing a private party, anyway."

His mouth curved in a smile, the first genuine one she'd seen from him. "Not at all. It's just a casual get-together and the band is glad you're coming. Informal is always a good way to get to know people."

Sydney hadn't expected the shiny black pickup sitting in her driveway. Her eyes widened as she stared at it.

Rick gave a soft laugh. "Not what you expect from a rock musician, right? It's my version of a hot sports car." He helped her up into the cab. "I'm a pretty utilitarian kind of person. This has a lot of bells and whistles, but it's as jazzy as I get."

She folded her hands in her lap and took in a slow breath as he backed out of the driveway. The interior of the cab, dark and filled with the faint scent of his woodsy aftershave, created the illusion of a private little world inhabited by the two of them. She was acutely aware of the nearness of him, his masculinity, the play of muscles in his arms as he handled the steering wheel. The sensation of intimacy was so strong Sydney felt it wrapping around her. Her breathing became uneven, her pulse ratcheted up, and the world outside the truck disappeared in the black velvet fog of the night.

Thank God this isn't a bench seat. I need the barrier of the console or I might forget myself and plaster myself to his side.

She cleared her throat, hoping to pierce the charged air. "So who all will be there?"

"Oh, you know. Just the band. Emma, of course. A few of our friends."

"And me."

"And you." He nodded. "Danny and Garrett brought dates, their flavors of the month, so don't expect adult conversation from them."

"Not you?" The words popped out of her mouth before she could stop them.

He laughed, a sound low and deep. "Are you afraid I might

have some angry female ready to rip my eyes out because I took off to pick you up?"

"No, I—" Heat crept up her cheeks and she wanted to cover her face with her hands. "That was a dumb thing to say. Of course you don't have a date. Or you wouldn't have been sent on taxi detail."

"I might have been," he teased. "Like I said, she might be poised on the front porch with her claws out."

"Now you're mocking me, right?" Or was he? Rick in a playful mood threw her off balance.

For a long moment he didn't say anything and Sydney wondered if she'd just stepped into it. Maybe he *did* have a date back at the party. Where did that leave her? The third wheel?

Syd, this is not a date.

"No one waiting," he said at last. "Not that there's any reason why you'd be interested, but I'm not seeing anyone." Another pause. "Right now."

"Does that mean you have someone in mind?" Why couldn't she just shut her stupid mouth?

"Still thinking about that one." He plucked a CD from the console and slid it into its slot in the stereo. "How about some tunes while we ride? We record our rehearsals to help us figure out what's good and what's bad. Most of this is new stuff so you get a sneak preview."

"Wow. Thank you." Yes. Music. A distraction to offset the charged atmosphere of the cab.

The notes floated out into the cab and filled the space. The compelling emotion she'd felt at rehearsal flooded her again. Sydney was gripped again by the dynamism of it. The fact that the songs were only rough productions on nonstudio equipment underscored how powerful they were. The bass pulsated through her body; the notes of the lead guitar pierced the air.

And the voices!

Ohmigod!

Talk about come-fuck-me voices.

She closed her eyes and let the sounds wash over her. She

knew Rick did this in an effort to let her see and feel the essence of the band but what it really did was reinforce what she imagined for them. Clash and flash. She'd just have to make them see it. Make *him* see it.

When the music stopped, her eyes flew open and she realized they were parked in front of a house. She looked over to see Rick smiling at her.

"We're here."

"Oh. Okay."

"So. What did you think?" The casual tone was underlined with tension. Even a little insecurity.

Insecure? Rick?

"I think you'll be a huge success." She gave him her best smile. "And I'm really psyched about working with you."

His dubious expression told her it wasn't quite what he wanted to hear, but he just nodded.

"Right. Okay, then."

He helped her down from the cab and kept his hand lightly on her elbow as he guided her to the door. She could feel the outline of each of his fingers like hot steel branding her skin, and a shiver skated along her spine. What about this man drew such a reaction from her? Made every one of her erogenous zones stand up and beg? God, she had to keep some space between them, but how was she supposed to do that?

Rick opened the front door and ushered her inside. Sound and laughter enveloped her. The house was small but a lot of love and work had gone into making it a home. The living room was alive with both people and color and more conversation drifted out from the kitchen.

Sydney stood frozen, not sure what to do next.

Then Emma was there, smiling at her, taking her hands.

"I'm so glad you could make it tonight."

"Thank you for the invitation. I appreciate it."

Emma gave her a wry grin. "I'm sorry about your car but Rick was happy to pick you up." She looked at him over Sydney's shoulder. "Right, Rick?"

"Yeah. Happy to."

Sydney glanced back at him, unsettled by the heat in his voice, but he smiled and urged her into the room.

"Let's get you a drink," Emma said. "Marc has a bar set up in the kitchen. And everyone is very excited to meet you. Come on."

Both the colorful kitchen and the living room were filled with people. Danny and Garrett greeted her, even giving her little hugs. Marc handed her a glass of wine and Emma steered her from group to group making sure everyone knew she was the publicity agent for Lightnin'. Sydney tried to sort out all the names and figure out who was with who. Some of the guys were musicians not currently on a gig, others just friends or family, like Marc's brothers.

Rick had been right on target about the girls Danny and Garrett had brought. Draped over the musicians' bodies in their abbreviated shorts and tight T-shirts, they might as well have had *groupie* stamped on their foreheads. They managed to disentangle themselves long enough to say hello. Then Emma was introducing her to some of her friends. The women all looked at her with a mixture of awe and jealousy.

Music played constantly in the background, a muted counterpoint to the continuous hum of multiple conversations. Sydney did her best to blend in but, at times, she felt as if she came from another planet. Danny and Garrett and some of the others were exactly what she would have expected—rock musicians who cared about their craft and having a good time. Period. And both susceptible and agreeable to her ideas.

But Marc and Rick seemed to be cut from a different cloth. She was surprised to see how committed Marc was to Emma. He acted like an old married man. And Rick. What was up with the serious face all the time?

It occurred to her for the first time since Linc handed her this assignment how sparse her knowledge was about the individual players. She had no idea what was beneath the music, the only thing she'd concentrated on. Until now she worked only in a position lawyers would call second chair. Much, much different than being the leader of the team.

I can do this. I've been waiting for this. I worked hard for it. And I know my ideas are good. I just have to make the guys see it.

Rick, who had stayed scant inches away from her since they arrived, now talked to one of Marc's brothers, apparently satisfied she was comfortable. Needing a breather, she eased out to the patio off the living room. While she sipped her wine, trying sort everyone out in her head, the patio door slid open again.

Emma smiled at her. "Finding it a little confusing?"

"Not so much." She sighed. "Well, maybe. Yeah, okay." She grimaced. "But these guys are my job, Emma. I have to do right by them. I've studied them, watched their videos, memorized the files on them."

"And that's good. But you've only seen what the public sees. Here?" She gestured toward the living room. "They're like all the other jerk musicians." She laughed, a sound of pure pleasure. Except for Marc, of course. Oh, and Rick."

Sydney ran her fingertip around the rim of her glass.

"How did you handle them when, you know, you and Marc first started dating? Were they what you expected?"

Emma laughed again. "First of all, Marc and I never actually did what you'd call dating. Did anyone ever tell you our story?"

"Your story? No, there was nothing in the file about the two of you except you are engaged."

Emma swallowed some of her wine. "The night we met was the first time I'd ever been in a rock club in my life. Really," she added at Sydney's astonished expression. "You wouldn't believe the uptight, buttoned-down life I'd led."

Sydney quirked an eyebrow. "You're kidding."

"Uh uh. Not a bit." Emma smiled. "Do you know that for weeks I wouldn't even tell him my name?"

Sydney's jaw dropped. "You're kidding. Why not?"

"Because I was afraid. I worried about everything. What if my friends saw me with a rock musician? And my folks? Forget that. They were the ones who'd buttoned me down in the first place. I tried to keep the two parts of my life separate."

Sydney studied the other woman. "How did that work for you? And didn't Marc get mad?"

"More hurt than mad, I'd say. But before long we were so into each other he almost didn't care."

Sydney couldn't contain her curiosity. "So what happened?"

"We had a big fight over a misunderstanding. And my best friend made me see what a jerk I was being." Emma took another drink of her wine. "So I got up my courage and went back to Aftershock, where they were finishing up their gig. Butch had already signed them to the contract and they were getting ready to prepare for the CD and the tour."

"Was he glad to see you?"

"Oh, yeah." She looked off in the distance, her eyes suddenly dreamy. "Because he didn't know my name he used to call me 'Music Lady'. When I walked into the club that night, the next number the band played was the song he wrote for me. That's where 'Music Lady' came from. I nearly broke down and cried."

"My God!" Sydney felt emotion wash through her. Her heart stuttered and tears threatened to spill from her eyelids. The impact of Emma's words made her catch her breath. "That's—that's—What a great love story. So you settled him down."

"Not so much. He was already pretty settled before I came along." She studied Sydney. "He and Rick are a lot more alike than you might think when you meet them. Marc's very close to his family. Always has been. And Rick's kind of been the man in his family since his dad walked out on them when he was fourteen."

"You're kidding me." Sydney hadn't thought it possible for her to be any more surprised, but apparently she was wrong. What a shock that must have been to Rick's life.

"Not a bit. The luckiest thing for them was moving to this neighborhood after the divorce. He and Marc became good friends and the Malone family sort of adopted Rick, his sister, and his mom. Rick's very protective of them and takes his responsibilities seriously. Even though his mom says they're in a good place now and he needs to live for himself for a change."

"Wow." Sydney's jaw dropped in astonishment. "I didn't know any of that."

Emma shrugged. "He doesn't talk about it with strangers."

"And I'm a stranger," Sydney guessed.

"For now, anyway. He's taken charge of the band the way he did his mom and his sister. It's his life. So if he gives you any crap, tread lightly. Let him get to know you." She touched Sydney's hand lightly. "I know the guys are excited to have someone assigned only to them. I don't know what your ideas are for their promo, but I hope you get to know the guys as people before you put a plan together. Their personalities are a big part of what makes up the band."

"I hear you."

"One more thing." Emma paused for a moment. "You need to kind of feel your way with Rick."

What Emma said explained a lot, but it didn't change the ideas Sydney'd formulated or her approach to the project.

"I'll keep that in mind. Thanks for sharing all of this with me." She started back into the house.

Emma stopped her with a hand on her arm again. "One other thing you might want to know. It's real obvious to Marc and me that Rick has some strong feelings for you. He's doing his best to hide them but when the two of you are within a foot of each other the electricity lights up the place. I don't know how you feel, but Rick's very important to us."

In other words, don't screw him over. Nice thought, but who's going to worry about me?

"Not a problem. I make it a rule not to mix business with pleasure. I'll be sure he understands that." She managed to smile. "In the nicest way possible, of course."

Now I just have make sure I remember it.

"And you aren't upset that I came out here to talk to you about this?"

Was she? It was easy to see the situation from Emma's point

of view. She had to keep that in mind.

"No. I understand where you're coming from."

"Good." Emma's face took on a serious look. "I'd like us to be friends, Sydney. I know you'll be with the band a good part of the time. I'm trying to arrange my schedule so I can be at a lot of the concert stops. You'll be busy doing your job, but it would be nice to connect on a personal level."

"I'd like that, too." Sydney didn't have too many female friends. Emma seemed like someone she could feel comfortable with.

"Enough with the serious talk. I think we could both use some more wine, don't you?"

Chapter Five

The moment she walked back into the house her eyes were drawn to Rick. His hooded gaze made every pulse point throb with need. The rest of the evening went by in a blur, but wherever Sydney moved, she felt his eyes riveted to her. Whether he was tipping back a bottle of beer or just in conversation with someone, his gaze found her and locked onto hers.

She was completely aware of him even as she tried to absorb all the sights and sounds of the group. The interactions of the people there. Get a feel for the band as more than musicians, the way Rick had wanted her to. She chatted a little with Danny and Garrett when they didn't have a female form welded to them. And with some of the other people who were more interested in how glamorous her job was rather than Lightnin'.

She had a good time but at the end of the night, although she now saw the band as real human beings rather than just a commercial commodity, she still hadn't found a good reason to change her ideas. Convinced she was right, she'd have to find some way to make them see her plan would work.

When the party began to break up and people were saying their good-byes, Sydney looked at her watch and was startled to see it was two o'clock. *Where had the night gone?* The hours had passed in a blur while she absorbed the atmosphere and the people.

"Ready to go?"

She heard Rick's deep voice at the same moment she felt his hand warm at the small of her back.

"Yes. Wow!" She glanced at her watch again. "I didn't realize it was that late."

"A sign that you were having a good time." He was so close she could feel his breath on her cheek like a whisper of a breeze when he spoke to her.

"Let me say good-bye to Marc and Emma and thank them."

"Right behind you," Marc said. He grinned and held out his hand. "Thanks for coming over, Syd. Is it okay to call you Syd?"

"Um, sure." And why was it no one in her life had ever called her that before? Never anything but Sydney. "Thanks for including me. I had a great time."

Emma gave her an impulsive hug. "We should get together soon."

"Oh. That would be nice." She saw a look pass between the men and wondered what that was all about. She'd have to wiggle it out of Rick.

"Good. I'll give you a call. Rick can give me your number."

"Looks like you and Emma really hit it off," Rick commented when they were back in the truck.

"Yes, we did. Although we barely had time for a short conversation."

"I think she's looking forward to having another female around the band who doesn't wear clothes three sizes too small and enough makeup for ten women. Emma's cool." He was silent for a moment. "She and Marc had what I'd call some challenges when they first met."

Sydney laughed. "I know the story. Emma told me. Wouldn't give him her name? He must have been really determined to keep pursuing her."

"He was." Rick tapped his thumb absently on the steering wheel. "And look how well that turned out."

Silence, but one loaded with heat and tension.

Sydney cleared her throat. "I enjoyed talking to people tonight."

Marc thought it would be a good venue for you to hang with them away from rehearsal. With all the other people there I'm not sure it turned out so well."

"Oh, no," she said quickly. "It was fine. I got an informal sense of who and what everyone was. Who people are friends with defines them too, you know."

At least I did when I wasn't thinking about you.

They were making polite chitchat but the sexual tension between them vibrated in the air. Her pulse accelerated and, despite the air-conditioning's chill, her palms were damp. She glanced sideways at Rick to see if he was affected, too. If his rigid posture offered a clue then he was definitely tuned into whatever was going on between them.

This is so wrong. It's bad news to mix business and pleasure. And I have a job to do. I can't be distracted.

That had been her mantra from the moment she set eyes on Rick Trajean at the rehearsal and a jolt of heat scorched her nerve ends. From that first contact, from the moment their hands touched, a powerful reaction arced between them. She knew it and tonight she was hyperaware that he knew it. But to act on this attraction was wrong on so many levels. The band was a client. Butch Meredith would be looking over her shoulder. She had a job to do and couldn't be distracted. And most important, at the moment, they had dramatically opposing views of how they saw the band and how she should market its image.

She'd had three glasses of wine, though. Enough to relax her, but not enough to wipe out the image of Rick standing in the living room, beer bottle in hand, while he talked to someone. His jeans outlined his long, lean legs and his incredible ass made her imagine what he would look like naked.

Holy shit, Sydney! Don't go there.

"I can smell your brain burning." Rick's husky voice broke the silence. "What's giving you such deep thoughts?"

Thoughts of you naked, as if I'd even tell you that.

Sydney folded her hands in her lap and tried to shut off her brain. "Nothing special. Just remembering some of the music I heard at the get together. Older stuff from the CDs playing."

"And?"

"And it seems the band has always had a great sound. Now it's richer, more mature. I think this will be a breakout tour for you."

"I sure hope so, but I'm done thinking about the tour tonight. And here we are at your place."

Before she could politely thank him and make a graceful exit from the truck he was around to her side, had the door open, and a hand held out to help her down. The moment their skin made contact the sizzle hit, almost knocking her down with its strength. Intense heat surged through her body and her heart rate sped up, doing a sudden jitterbug. Rick's hand tightened on hers and when she looked up at him, she saw he felt it, too. Regretfully she extricated her hand and dug her key out of her tiny purse.

"Thank you for the pickup and delivery service." God, and didn't she just sound so prim.

"You're welcome. But this service is door-to-door. I want to make sure you get inside okay."

"I'm fine. I promise you."

But he stood there waiting, and it was either be incredibly rude or let him walk her up to her little porch. She slid the key into the lock, pushed the door open, and stepped into her small foyer. When she turned to thank Rick and say goodnight, he was so close she was plastered to his body. Heat blazed in his eyes and a muscle twitched in his cheek. A shared look changed into something way too intimate. Those dark eyes, the color of bitter chocolate, looked right into hers and challenged her. She should move, but her body didn't want to obey her mind.

Then his hands clamped down on her shoulders and he lowered his head. His mouth was hot and hungry, his tongue greedy and devouring as he took her in a kiss that was more filled with passion and hunger than any she could remember. Ever. Still clinging to her purse and her key, she opened to him and trembled when his tongue swept over hers and coaxed it to dance.

"So sweet," he murmured against her lips.

But the kiss itself was far from sweet. It was hot and spicy. His tongue delved into her mouth like a heat-seeking missile. Sydney trembled as the kiss, so intense, so heated, seduced her and invaded every one of her senses. For a long moment she forgot to breathe. It was Rick who broke the connection at last. He lifted his head but his hands still gripped her as he ran the flat of his tongue over her lips.

"This is crazy." His voice had a gravelly sound.

She nodded. "Crazy." She struggled to get out the one word.

"Insane."

"Mad," she agreed.

"I think we need to lock the door."

He slid his hands from her shoulders and shut the door, turned the lock, and slid the dead bolt in place. Then he took the key and the purse from her and put them on the little table in the entryway before pulling her body tight against his.

Her hands shook as she slid them up along his arms to his neck and fisted them in his hair. His mouth scorched hers again, the heavy sensuality of it enhanced by raw emotion. Desire streaked through her like a tornado gone wild. Every inch of her body screamed for this man to touch her everyplace at once.

He lifted his head and locked her in place with his gaze.

"Syd, you have to know how much I want to take you to bed. I want to make love to you. Watch you come apart for me."

"Y-you do?" God, she sounded like an imbecile, but when he touched her, all rational thought deserted her.

"The first time I saw you, I wanted you." He gently nipped her jawline and strung kisses along the line of her neck. "Every time I'm near you, my cock gets so hard I'm afraid if I bump into something it'll break off."

"I don't—"

"Don't what?" He brushed the flat of his tongue across her bottom lip.

"The tour. The agency." She wanted so much to be sensible. But not as much as she wanted him. Still, some shred of sanity told her to make at least a token protest.

"They aren't here with us tonight." He licked the shell of one ear. "Tonight it's just Syd and Rick. No one else." His breath whispered over her mouth. "Tomorrow we'll worry about the agency and the tour. And everything else. Tonight this is what I want to think about. Because I want you more than I want to breathe."

She could feel the swollen length of his thick erection pressing against her through his jeans. His chest was a hard wall of muscle against her breasts that ached for his touch and her nipples, so hard they were painful. His hands and his mouth coaxed sensation from her.

I want this.

"O-okay."

He cupped her chin. "Which way?"

Sydney didn't pretend not to understand. "Upstairs. Second door."

He swept her up in his arms as if she weighed nothing and took the stairs two at a time. She wrapped her arms around him and nuzzled her face against his neck. Whatever earthy aftershave he wore invaded her senses and ramped up her awareness of him, if that was even possible. Nudging the door open with his foot, he carried her over to the bed and set her on her feet. As if he had the layout memorized, he reached over and snapped on the bedside lamp. Then he just stood and looked at her. The heat in his eyes scorched her skin.

"There's no going back," he said, but in his eyes it was a question not a statement.

"No going back," she agreed, as butterflies beat their wings in her stomach.

"Not tonight, anyway."

She nodded and clenched her unsteady hands into fists.

Hands that trembled from the unnamed emotion that tried its best to bull its way up from deep inside her.

"Not tonight," she said in a voice so soft she could barely hear herself.

"All right, then."

With a gentleness that belied the visible tension in his body, he unknotted the tails of the blouse at her waist and eased the fabric down her shoulders. Next came the tank. The soft material whispered against her body as he drew it over her head and tossed it to join the blouse. Although she still wore her bra, she was seized with an unexpected desire to cover herself.

"Uh uh," he said, as if he could read her mind. "I want to see everything."

Cupping her breasts in his large palms, he bent to take a nipple into his mouth, fabric and all. The bud tightened and puckered beneath the thin satin. Heat shot straight to her pussy, as if propelled by an arrow, and moisture flooded her bikini panties.

Rick's hand gently kneaded her other breast. His thumb rasped over the taut point. Sydney had to grip his shoulders to hold herself steady as need and desire surged through her in a hot, erotic flood. Her body shook with the force of it. His touch was so incendiary that fire erupted low in her belly and spread to every nerve and pulse point.

He teased her breasts mercilessly, until her knees were weak and she could barely stand. Lifting his head, he brushed his mouth over hers. With the tip of his tongue, he drew tiny circles at each corner of her lips then followed the seam, a slow lick that was as arousing as any other touch. He nipped at her lips, gentle bites he soothed with his tongue before slipping it onto her mouth again. As he slicked his tongue over hers, coaxing it to an erotic dance, he reached for the button on her jeans. *Pop!* Then the slow glide of the zipper, a soft rasp in the heated silence of the room. He eased the fabric down her hips to fall at her ankles and dropped his gaze to the triangle of pink silk covering her mound. One hand slid deliberately down her belly to cup her through the fabric of the panties. She heard him suck in a breath when he felt how wet she was.

One long, lean finger traced the length of her slit, pushing the silk in between her pussy lips and stroking her with a long, deliberate movement. Sydney dug her nails into Rick's shoulders, trembling, not sure how long she could stand. Heat washed over her in waves, set fire to her nerve endings, and ramped up her pulse. When she tried to squeeze her thighs together to trap his hand, he just gave a low, rusty laugh and lifted his finger away.

"Like that, do you?" His tongue traced the seam of her lips again. "So do I. You're so fucking wet already I can smell your scent. The best perfume ever."

She moaned as he slid his hand between her thighs again and his finger stroked steadily through the wet silk. When the tip touched her clit, she cried out and rocked against him. He banded one arm around her for support as he rubbed the swollen bundle of nerves in a steady rhythm. Inside her slippery channel, the walls pulsed with need and her body clenched. The power of her release built so fast it shocked her. When he bent and took a nipple in his mouth again, she erupted. Her hips rocked against his touch, the need to feel him inside her so strong.

She clenched her thighs around his hand, trapping him in her heat, silently begging him for more. She hung on the edge, out of balance, her release so tantalizingly out of reach. His fingers pushed hard against her throbbing clit, and he sucked the tender skin at the hollow of her throat where her pulse pounded so hard. Everything inside her exploded and she came and came and came.

Sydney was so weak when the tremors finally eased she wondered if she'd simply fold into a heap on the floor. But he wasn't done with her yet. Far from it. Easing her onto the bed, he knelt to strip her jeans and panties down her legs, pausing only to remove her sandals before discarding everything. He moved his tongue in a very lazy journey from her collarbone down between the valley of her breasts to the slight swell of her belly. He paused his journey at her navel where he spent long, tortuous moments tracing the furled flesh over and over with the hot tip of his tongue.

Pausing, he lifted his head and let his gaze travel over every inch of her body.

"God," he breathed. "You are so fucking gorgeous."

Sydney's breath hitched. Gorgeous. She had a hard time seeing herself that way. She thought of her figure as full of imperfections—breasts too small, hips too wide, thighs too heavy. But the way Rick devoured her with his eyes, she felt like a sex goddess.

"I could spend all night looking at you," he went on, "but there are other things I want to do more."

Exerting pressure on the inside of her thighs, he pushed her legs open, lowered his head again, and followed the line of her slit with his tongue.

Ohmigod!

She nearly levitated off the bed. Just that one erotic touch, that glide of movement set every nerve in her body dancing. Every inner muscle clenching. Tightening. Using his thumbs he pressed open the lips, fully exposing her, and repeated the movement. The long, slow, wet caress shot sensations through her body. How was it possible for her to respond like this again so soon?

But Rick was relentless. He lapped and sucked and thrust his tongue inside her. Dragged it out so it rubbed her sweet spot.

When he lifted his head to look at her, his lips shone with her juices and the hunger in his eyes burned into her. He ran his tongue over his mouth with a slow movement as he licked each drop of her liquid. Sydney thought it was the most sensuous thing she'd ever seen. She could barely breathe, her breath trapped in her lungs.

"Lie back," he murmured. "Let me do all the work here."

She did as he asked, fisting the coverlet as if somehow she could ground herself and not explode off the bed. He applied that talented tongue to her cunt again. And oh, he knew exactly how to use it, to caress, to suck, soothe when his teeth nipped her flesh. She was shocked when a climax began to build again low in her belly. One more tiny bite of her clit and a swirl of his tongue and the spasms rocketed through her.

Rick thrust his tongue back inside her where her walls could grip it as they throbbed and convulsed and quaked. Only the tight grip of his hands on her thighs and her death clutch on the fabric beneath her kept her grounded as he spun her into a velvet vortex, a place where fireworks exploded behind her eyelids.

When she finally came back to earth, her entire body trembled and a thin sheen of perspiration covered her body. As she struggled to draw a breath, Rick stood up and leaned over her, arms braced on either side of her. His mouth curved in a satisfied smile.

"You taste so good." He slid his tongue over her mouth, sharing her taste with her. "Better than any drink I can think of. I could get drunk on your taste, Sydney Alexander."

"I can't move," she said in a breathless voice, her lips curved in an answering smile. "I may never move again."

"Oh, yeah. You will. Give me a minute, and I'll prove it to you."

He lifted her so he could pull back the covers on the bed and arranged her so her head was on the pillow. Her limbs were just weak appendages of her body. He never took his eyes from her as he pulled his T-shirt over his head, toed off his shoes, and stripped away his jeans and boxer briefs. At last he stood next to her in the most glorious male nudity she'd ever seen. His lean rangy body was well-honed, his chest covered with a smattering of hair just a shade darker than that on his head. If she could have lifted her hand, Sydney would have run her fingernails through it, scraping along the hard wall of his chest. Long legs were bracketed by lean hips, but what made her mouth go dry as a desert was the long, thick cock that extended from its nest of curls, swollen and thick and ready for action.

Energy surged through her with unexpected force and she licked her lips.

She watched him pick up his jeans, dig out his wallet, and remove a condom, which he flipped onto the bedside table. His gaze devoured her, his cock hot where it brushed her thigh as he straddled her body. The look he gave her pierced straight to her heart. And just like that, arousal slammed through her.

"God, Sydney." His voice had a raw, raspy sound, like rough wood against a wall. "You haven't a clue how much I wanted you, right from the start. Or how I feel about you. I want everything. Your body. Your soul." He palmed her left breast. "Your heart."

Her heart? Oh, God! She was so afraid to misread what he said, afraid she'd get it wrong. Even though the look in his dark chocolate eyes told her he meant it.

Swallowing hard, she whispered back, "I want everything, too."

Jesus! He wondered if she realized just how perfect she was, dark hair spread across the pillow, lips swollen from his kisses, the scent of her musk driving him nuts. He wanted to lick every inch of her, explore every crevice of her body, do things to her he couldn't even begin to imagine. The smell of her skin and the taste of her lips were potent aphrodisiacs.

What the hell was going on with him? His head insisted this was a huge mistake, that it was the wrong time and the wrong woman to fall head over heels for. He didn't want to hear that little voice inside him. With a deliberate effort he shut it off. He wanted Sydney Alexander, more than he'd ever wanted any other woman in his life. Right from the moment he'd laid eyes on her strutting down that theater aisle.

Had he just told her he wanted her heart? Yeah, he had. And it scared him shitless to feel that way about someone.

"Let me touch you." She slid a hand between them to reach for his cock but he wrapped his fingers around her wrist.

"Not this time." That would definitely be his undoing. The

thought of her stroking him, licking him, taking him in her mouth sent a jolt of excitement through his body. As if he needed any more stimulation.

He wanted his mouth on her everywhere, but he couldn't seem to tear himself away from her lips. He began with just a light kiss, then nibbled her lips, soothed the little bites with his tongue before he delved inside again, savoring every nuance of her taste. Trailing his tongue along the line of her jaw, he stopped at the sensitive place behind her ear. When he gently bit her earlobe she let out a little squeak and tried to push against him.

Slow and deliberate, he traced a damp path to her breasts and sucked each nipple. When she moaned and writhed to his satisfaction, he slid further down her tummy to the soft curls on her mound. The tip of his tongue brushed her clit just for a moment before he moved to her ankles. He licked each place, carefully, from her ankle up the inside of her thigh and back down the other side.

By now, she was thrashing and begging him.

"Please, please, please."

He knew what she wanted. He wanted it, too. But he was determined to keep her on the edge as long as possible. Rolling to the side, he took her with him so she was on top. Her breasts pressed into his chest, her hard nipples like brands burning his skin. His fingers threaded through her thick hair as he covered her mouth again with his tongue, sliding easily into the hot wetness of it. He danced his tongue over every surface. Licked and tasted. When her own began to dance with his, his cock jerked in response and his balls felt as if tiny needles pierced them.

Rick eased her upper leg over both of his to press his knee against the wetness of her pussy. When he moved slowly back and forth, she pressed down against him, a silent demand for more. One hand slid along the curve of her hip, the indentation of her waist, along her ribs to cup a breast with his palm. The mound of flesh fit in his hand so nicely. He'd never been one for women with very large breasts, unlike Danny and Garrett. He went for the entire package, and Sydney's were perfectly proportioned for the rest of her. He rasped his thumb over the beaded nip. Felt her indrawn breath. He did it again, and her gasp made his cock flex.

Rick wanted to take his time with her, draw it out, make it last, but his control was so eroded he was getting desperate. His hands actually shook as he grabbed the condom on the nightstand, sheathed himself, and took a deep breath. He was determined to make this good for her, no matter how much it cost him.

Hooking his arms beneath her knees he pushed her legs back, opening her wide to him. Dipping his head, he gave himself a moment to taste her sweet pussy, assuring himself she was good and wet and ready for him. Her liquid was nectar on his tongue, and he lapped deeply.

Sydney watched him with slumberous eyes. Locking his gaze with hers, he nudged her opening with the head of his shaft, just touching it. The pulse at the hollow of her throat beat harder and faster, just from that minimal contact. He gritted his teeth as he reached for control before he eased into her a little at a time, until he filled her completely. Her walls tightened around him, a snug fit that made every nerve ending sizzle. He paused, giving her time to adjust to him, to get ready.

The feel of her around him was exquisite torture.

Holy shit! This was like the first time only better because now he knew what he was doing. No other woman had ever made him feel this way. Not ever. He needed to make this better than good for both of them.

Pulling all the way back he drove into her hard. Again. And again. She was with him every step of the way. They were like two animals in the grip of the mating instinct, each demanding power from the other. Nothing easy here. There was a shared desperation to reach that elusive peak and crash hard on the other side.

He increased both the power and the speed of his thrusts as

the muscles of her cunt gripped and squeezed him. The movement set up ripples through his body and he knew he was right there on the edge. Sliding one hand between them, he found her clit again and rubbed. He lowered his head to take one diamond-hard nipple in his mouth, bit down on it gently and moved to the other one. Never once did he ease up on the steady stroking motion.

Her cunt tightened even more. With her legs wrapped around him she dug her heels into his back and pulled him into her even deeper. Her nails clawed him, dug into his back. The moment he felt her climax unwind, he let himself go, and they fell over the edge together, shuddering and quaking as the spasms shook them. When the grip of the orgasm eased, he touched his forehead to hers and drew in great gulps of air. He wasn't sure if it was his heart or hers he heard beat so furiously but his pounded like a jackhammer in his chest.

He had no idea how much time passed before he thought to lever himself up from her and lower her legs to the bed. With great care he slid from the hot grasp of her body and headed toward what he hoped was the bathroom. Condom disposed of, he made his way back to the bedroom and picked up his jeans and boxer briefs. But instead of putting them on, he stood there with them in his hands, aware he was about to do something stupid.

The smart thing would be to get dressed, give her an affectionate kiss, and head for home. But smart didn't seem to cut it at that moment. He didn't want the night to end and he was sure that could only spell trouble. But he'd meant what he said about wanting her soul and her heart. Just as he wanted to give his to her. He was stunned by what he felt for her.

Sydney Alexander touched a place deep inside him. His heart. She was right there in his heart. Danger signs popped up everywhere. There was no room in his life right now for any kind of real relationship. The band, the tour, and the album deserved every bit of his attention.

He didn't want to care about those things. Not right now. If this turned into something very real, he'd figure out how to balance it later. And convince her at the same time, because he was sure she'd be coming from the same place he was. With deliberate effort he shut his mind to the voices in his head and tossed his clothes onto a chair. Sliding into bed again he pulled Sydney up against his body, spoon fashion, and rested a hand on her left breast. Her heart beat a rhythm against his palm and her sweet ass fit right into the curve of his body.

"I thought you were leaving," she murmured, her voice slurred with drowsiness and satisfaction.

"I thought so, too," he whispered.

He tucked her head beneath his chin and closed his eyes.

It's more than sex, Sydney. A whole lot more. What are we going to do?

Chapter Six

The bedroom was still dark but enough light from the early morning sunrise filtered in through the blinds for Rick to drink in one last sight of the woman lying in bed. He stood for long moments and stared down at the graceful curve of her shoulder, the silken mass of her hair, the swell of her bottom as the sheet draped over it. He had the profound feeling that last night had forever changed his life, and he wondered if she would feel the same.

The night was incredible. That was the only word for it. He could still taste her on his tongue, smell her on his skin, feel her body pressed against his. Now he knew what some guys meant when they said sex could be like a religious experience. He closed his eyes to recapture the snug feel of her pussy as it clutched his cock, milking it. That fast, he was hard as a rock.

Damn!

Sunday wasn't a workday for her, at least not until she and Lightnin' hit the road, so he had to restrain himself from waking her. He wanted one more taste of her, one more touch, one last moment to inhale the scent distinctly Sydney, more than he wanted to breathe.

Get it together, Trajean.

It would be better for both of them if he left before she woke. Give them some distance until they sorted out this thing that swept them up like a whirlwind. But he didn't just want to beat it out of there as if what they'd shared was nothing. Morning-after protocol had never been a problem for him with other women, but Sydney was different. What should he do? Wake her? Let her sleep? Leave a note? He couldn't remember feeling so uncertain since the first time the band auditioned for a club owner.

Finally he dug around in her kitchen until he found some paper. He couldn't exactly say *Thanks for the great sex but we better get back to business*. Not when she'd invaded every inch of his body and his brain. Made him feel things he'd never expected. When he fell, he sure hadn't thought it would be for a prickly female who guarded her emotions so carefully she tried to pretend she didn't have any.

He wouldn't give up on her, though. On them. Last night, layers of emotions had been exposed for him to see. He wanted her to know it meant a lot. That it was special. That this was just the beginning. It wouldn't be easy, but somehow he'd make her see what they had here. What they could build on.

Finally he scratched out what he hoped would be acceptable. Just the right tone. And left quietly. He needed to get home, get his shit together, organize his thoughts. He was sure he'd hear from her today or tomorrow about Lightnin' business. He didn't want the call to be awkward, but he had no intention of letting her pretend nothing explosive had happened between them.

As he drove home all he could think about was the hours they spent together, the connection. The intensity of what they shared. And where they went from here.

At home he stood in his bathroom, waiting for the water in the shower to heat up, sipping his third cup of black coffee.

What have I gotten myself into?

He studied his face in the mirror, as if he might find an answer there. Last night had been, well, unbelievable was one word that came to his mind. Unforgettable. Out of this world. But where in the fucking hell did that leave him? Meeting a woman like Sydney Alexander and falling into...he didn't know what to call it yet, was not part of his plans.

He saw how Marc's family functioned as a unit and had always wondered if he'd ever find the one right woman who could fit into the intricate pieces of his life. Someone like Emma, who literally came out of nowhere to complete Marc and enrich his existence.

But am I ready for that?

There was too much to accomplish. As the band leader he needed to focus all his energy in one direction. Lightnin'. Maybe if he'd been more of a player....

No, that wasn't who he was. Like Marc, Rick was kind of an anomaly in the music business, especially the rock world. He wasn't into the groupie scene. He wasn't always on the lookout for a woman to hang out with. Or someone to get laid with. Since the genesis of Lightnin', he'd been very focused. Very responsible. Very disciplined. At least he liked to think so. He'd had to be. In the cutthroat music business, you were as good as your last song. Your last concert. From Day One he had a very specific vision for the band and a plan for how to achieve it. As the leader he established the goals and made sure everyone bought into them. He insisted on the same level of commitment from everyone.

The climb up the ladder of the club circuit had been a very tough one, with disaster always looming if someone made a misstep. He was the one who drove Lightnin', managed them, directed them, and made sure they didn't lose focus. He was the one, along with Marc, who created their brand, a trademark that came not from glitz and fancy packaging but from music that hit the soul. Music that was used every bit of their creative talent and was performed with emotion. That was *real*.

When his dad walked out, leaving him, his mother, and sister to fend for themselves, Rick had to grow up fast. As a young teenager he was thrust into responsibility, the same ethic of hard work and accountability that he took with him as the leader of *Lightnin'*. He believed with all his heart he could take the band where they wanted to go.

Some nights, those first few weeks after his family shattered, he had laid in his bed wondering if he had done something wrong. Maybe if he was smarter. Better at everything. More responsible. But his mother and sister were falling apart, so he'd hidden that frightened kid and forged ahead.

Now, suddenly, his life was changing around him. Meredith would leave for college soon. His mother had received a great promotion at work and had at last developed real confidence. And the band had this major breakthrough. A two-year contract with Butch Meredith. A tour. A CD with a recognized label. He couldn't let anything derail that. It was his responsibility to see it all worked out the way it was supposed to.

He was finally within reach of success. It was his obligation to make sure nothing impeded the band's progress or damaged the situation in any way.

But here was Sydney Alexander, out of the blue, an arrow that pierced him right at his core. He wished he could say it was just really good sex, but he'd be lying to himself. Ever since she'd walked into that rehearsal, he'd been smitten.

Smitten? Do they even use that word anymore? Jesus!

All he knew was this *thing* that detonated between them was deep and intensive and life-altering. The kind of connection that kept a bubble of anticipation floating in his stomach. He knew she felt the same way, knew it in his bones. Otherwise, last night wouldn't have been so intense. So, well, connecting. He was pretty sure it would be harder to convince Sydney of the fact than to figure out what to do with it himself. When he looked at his face in the fog of the mirror he saw the eyes of a man in major conflict A man not quite sure which side of him would win.

ം

His muscles were taut beneath her fingers as she rubbed them along his back. The soft hair on his chest abraded her breasts and stimulated her nipples until they were sharp, hard points. What she wanted more was to feel him inside her, his thick cock taking up every inch of space in her pussy, his balls slapping against her as he plunged into her again and again. She wrapped her legs around him and pulled him as tight to her body as she could, thrusting her hips up at him.

Low in her belly, the tension of her orgasm began to unwind like a tightly spooled steel coil. Her muscles tightened, her pulse pounded as she—

Bzzzzzzz!

Get out of here, you annoying bug. Can't you see I'm having the best sex of my life?

"Let me turn you over," he urged. "I want to take you from the back."

Bzzzzzzzz!

Sydney reached out to smack the irritating bug and hit—her clock radio.

"Good morning, ladies and gents!" The cheerful voice burst from the speaker. "Ready for some hot rock and roll today?"

Huh? What?

Sydney sat up abruptly, shoving her hair out of her face. She looked around, disoriented. She had kicked off her covers and was spread out in bed, naked. Naked? Where was the T-shirt she slept in? The boxer shorts? The annoying voice still spouted in a far too cheerful manner. At last her brain kicked in.

The dream. Holy hell. The dream.

She flopped back on her pillows, aware her body still throbbed in anticipation. Stretching out her arm she slapped the Off button on her radio. That guy was just too disgustingly cheerful for her. She wanted the dream back. She wanted Rick—

Rick!

Holy crap!

In an instant the previous night came flooding back. The touch of him, the feel of him. His scent. The way he filled her, kissed her, licked her—

Get your act together, Sydney.

Right. Act together.

How on earth had she let this happen? Oh, wait. It wasn't so much that she *let* it happen. An unstoppable force had headed in her direction the moment she and Rick Trajean locked eyes and it just rolled right over her. No matter how many times she told herself this could not happen, ever, it didn't seem to matter.

I'll never fall in love.

Okay, she'd made it her mantra. Repeated it to her co-workers. Some had even laughed at her.

"It's not like you get a choice, Sydney," one of them teased. "When the right guy walks into your life, you'll know it and won't be able to turn away from him."

She finally had to accept the fact that the moment she and Rick Trajean were in the same space, some kind of magic happened. He'd fought it as hard as she, but the gals at the office were right. When it happened, you didn't get a choice. You could only fight it for so long.

Rick felt the same powerful tug she did. She saw it in his eyes. Heard it in his voice. Felt it every minute he'd made love to her last night. Lord, it seemed the minute they were in the same room, they set fire to the air and were caught in a grip of unnamed emotions. It was a wonder no one else had picked up on it yet.

Love? No, no, no. No. That can't happen. Ohmigod. The Plan!

But last night The Plan had been the furthest thing from her mind. Maybe she could use the three glasses of wine she'd had as an excuse. Or the emotional effect of the music, and—

And the man himself. No doubt about it. One touch of his hand or his lips and all her brain cells shrank out of sight.

God, he was magnificent. He knew just how and where to touch. How to coax and seduce. How to make her believe she was the only woman in the world. How to *feel*.

And that terrified her. The Plan didn't leave any room for something like this. She had things to prove. To accomplish. She could almost hear Fate laughing at her.

So where was he now? Her bed was glaringly empty. She

guessed he'd snuck out while she slept. Okay, good. Right? That meant he really didn't think it was so special. She'd take her cue from that. Maybe she could wipe the whole thing out of her mind and they could go on with their business as if the past twenty-four hours had never happened.

Yeah, right.

She needed a long shower, hot coffee, a stern lecture, and she'd be herself again. She sat up and swung her legs over the side of the bed. A scrap of paper on the nightstand caught her eye and she reached for it.

Didn't want to wake you so early. See you soon? Can't wait.
Rick

She stared at the note. Not exactly hearts and flowers but better than nothing. And just maybe he was as afraid of this as she was. Maybe he wondered how they'd behave the next time they were together. In public. With the other band members.

The band!

Oh, lordy. They had business to take care of, and she couldn't afford to not be on her game. She was sure Rick felt the same way. They couldn't let anyone else know what was going on with them. At least until they figured out themselves what it was and how to handle it.

But just for a moment she hugged a pillow to her body, inhaling the lingering scent of him and remembered the feel of his hands and mouth on her body. She closed her eyes and let last night unroll like the replay of a movie, reliving every word, every touch. Enjoying the intensity of the unfamiliar emotion that swept over her whenever she laid eyes on him. Just for a second she wanted to wrap it around her.

Just for a damn second, okay?

All right, Sydney.

Today was Sunday. No work today. Damn that alarm, anyway. She'd been so lost in the moment last night she'd forgotten to turn it off. But since she was up, she'd get her day started. She would take that long, hot shower, wash her hair, and hopefully scrub some sense into her brain so she could get back to being Sydney Alexander.

If that was even possible.

Because somehow, after last night, she was no longer sure who Sydney Alexander was. Because Sydney Alexander didn't give in to the intense attraction and emotion that propelled her into bed with Rick Trajean. Sydney Alexander didn't expose her feelings to anyone. Ever.

Right.

She wished, just for a moment, she had a close girlfriend she could call to share a pizza with. Someone who'd answer questions for her. But as driven as she was, she'd left no time in her life to form that kind of relationship. Even the men she'd spent time with—few and far between—had been more of an afterthought. As obsessed as she was with giving Aunt Janine a big "fuck you," she hadn't taken time for anything else. What she wouldn't give today for a friend to dump her confusion on and get some feedback.

With a sigh of reluctance she dragged herself from the bed into the bathroom. As she stretched she couldn't help wondering what Rick was doing today. Who he was with. Where he—

Stop it!

Dress. Go out and do something.

What was happening to her?

She started to turn on the shower but realized her body was sore in places that hadn't been touched in a long time, at least with such intensity. Instead she drew a hot bath and sprinkled in some scented bath salts. Fixing herself a cup of coffee from her Keurig she carried it into the bathroom and set it on the edge of the tub. Then she eased into the hot water and sighed with satisfaction.

Idly, she touched first one nipple then the other, recalling the feel of Rick's teeth on them as he'd climaxed. When she brushed a fingertip over each one, the pulse in her cunt set up a rhythm again, a signal of the resurgence of need.

No, no, no! Not good!

She picked up her mug and sipped from it as she sent orders

to her brain. She had to wash away his touch and the sensations it aroused in her. How was she supposed to stick to her plan, when all she could think about was being naked with him again? How magnificent he'd looked in all his glorious nudity. And whatever this indefinable *thing* was that stretched between the two of them, she had no idea how to handle it.

Damn it, Sydney. Cut it out.

With a deliberate effort of will she forced her brain to shut down while she soaked in the tub. When the water cooled off, she kicked up the lever for the drain and stood, wrapping a large towel around her body. Five minutes later, dressed in shorts and a T-shirt, she fixed another cup of coffee, retrieved her Lightnin' folder from her briefcase, and carried it all out to the patio. This was where her focus should be. The Plan. The Big Plan.

Only, after last night, it was damn hard.

The mid-May morning was pleasantly cool, with just enough heat from the sun. Spreading everything out on the patio table, she sipped her coffee and studied the sheets of paper in front of her.

Her brain had been on speed drive ever since Linc Forrester met with her and handed her the Lightnin' assignment. The name alone had her thoughts sizzling. Linc had provided a T-shirt with their current logo, a lightning bolt on a blue background, but her ideas were so much bigger than that.

Her sketches were all centered around a massive, jagged thunderbolt striking down from a cloud mass, surrounded by sparks of electricity. The band's name flowed across the bottom in script, all of it covered with a sprinkling of glitter. She had shown everything to Rick who frowned at first before buying into it, albeit with reluctance.

Next she went over her list of promo items. The new logo would be used on the T-shirts, smartphone cases, tablet covers, pendants, buttons, key chains, and numerous other items. The media would get all the items as gifts in packaged kits. A messenger would deliver them to the locals and others would be handed out at stops on the tour. The rest would be sold at concerts and through the Web site she was having designed.

According to Wikipedia, "Objects struck by lightning experience heat and magnetic forces of great magnitude."

Sydney had adapted that to a tag line that read "People struck by Lightnin' experience emotional forces of great magnitude." She'd repeated it out loud dozens of times just to test both the sound and the way it rolled off the tongue. She was sure it was a phrase the media would pick up and run with. Now, having heard their music live, she was even more convinced of it. She smiled to herself as she drank her coffee and looked over her notes, images dancing in her head. Yes, this was definitely going to work.

She leaned back in her chair with her coffee cup, enjoying the soft morning breeze. The Plan was still on track. If she focused on nothing but business, maybe she could control what she felt for Rick Trajean, personal feelings she didn't know how to handle. Park them in a corner of her brain. This week and next, she would prep the band for their media debut. Calls would be made. People contacted. The final details for media day ironed out.

She knew in her gut this would work. She and Lightnin' would explode on the music scene like—well—like lightning.

Damn straight.

ଔ

"So tell me all about everything." Meredith Trajean popped a grape in her mouth and hitched herself onto the barstool next to her brother.

Hungry and with a need to be grounded by his family, Rick had dropped in at his mother's unannounced and begged breakfast from her. Sitting at the breakfast bar, drinking coffee, watching his mother scramble eggs, and listening to his sister framed his life in a normalcy he badly needed, especially now.

The abrupt entry of Sydney into his life unsettled him, in more ways than one. Beneath the surface, he sensed a driven woman, one as focused on her goals as he was on his. Maybe more so, which kind of frightened him. Even further beneath lay the warm, passionate woman whose bed he'd shared last night. A woman who opened herself to him in a way he was sure she'd never done before with anyone.

He had no idea what falling in love was like, nor did he expect it to happen with the speed of light. But Sydney Alexander was breaking through his self-imposed discipline. This was way more than sex. He'd spent the most incredible night of his life with her. Could still feel the silk of her skin, the softness of her curves, her wet heat gripping him. In seconds, he was hard as steel.

Quit thinking about it.

If he didn't discipline his brain, he'd embarrass himself in front of his family.

What he really needed to do was figure out how he was going to handle this. He had the distinct feeling a relationship scared her as much as it did him. They both had goals and didn't want anything that would distract them from reaching them.

Besides, what if their night together was nothing more than the heat of the moment? The heady environment? That first spark of attraction? What if, the next time he saw her, she acted as if nothing happened? Pretended it was all just business? He hadn't called her because he wasn't sure yet what to say when he did.

"Hello. Anyone in there?"

He realized Meredith was waving her hand in front of his face and jerked himself back to reality. After all, wasn't that why he was here?

"I can hear you, brat." He grinned at her. She'd grown into such a lovely young woman. In two months she'd be on her way to the university and he wanted to send her off locked in a suit of armor and a chastity belt. Or maybe accompanied by an armed guard. It wasn't too many years ago he'd been a horny teenager with just one thing in mind.

"Not a brat any longer, big brother." She stuck her tongue

out at him in a playful gesture. "Anyway, I asked you about the hot chick you took to the band party last night."

Rick stared at her. How the hell had gossip traveled this fast? "Where did you hear that?"

She grinned. "I know all. It's about time you realized it."

"Daisy Nestor's sister was at the party last night," his mother answered as she scooped eggs onto plates. "Daisy was on the phone to *your* sister at practically the crack of dawn, wanting the whole scoop." She turned and set two breakfast plates on the counter. "I told Meredith not to stick her nose in your business." She grinned. "But as your mother, I reserve first right of interrogation. So. Is there a woman in your life you've been keeping secret from us?" She fetched her own plate but, instead of sitting down, stood so she faced him.

Damn!

Rick concentrated on buttering his toast. "She's not a hot chick. She's the rep from Full Moon, the agency handling our promo."

"So she's not hot?" Meredith prodded.

Rick sighed and shook his head. "She's very nice looking but, more important, she's smart and knows what she's doing."

At least he certainly hoped so.

"Very nice looking?" His mother raised an eyebrow. "You sound like you're describing a spinster."

"Or a bad blind date," his sister added.

He set his toast down carefully. This was not at all what he'd expected to walk into. He expected breakfast, not the third degree. Damn that Daisy, anyway.

"Okay. You would probably agree she's a hot chick. But to me she's the woman who is going to create our image. Our brand. And help make us successful. Marc invited her so she could get to know the band a little better, although that didn't work out quite as we expected."

"And you offered to give her a ride?" his mother asked.

"Sounds like a date to me," Meredith teased.

"She had a problem with her car. She called Marc's house

and he asked me to pick her up so she didn't have to cancel. End of story."

He took a swallow of his coffee, followed by a bite of toast. The expectant silence poked at him like a hot needle. He looked from his mother to his sister and back again, a prickly feeling dancing along his spine.

"What?"

Kate Trajean shrugged. "You might want to bring her around sometime so we can meet her."

"Mom." He shook his head. "She's not a girlfriend. Not even a casual date. She's part of the team Butch Meredith put together. Can we give it a rest?" He looked at Meredith. "And tell Daisy Nestor she gossips too much."

؃

"I like her."

Emma Blake carried the breakfast dishes to the sink and began to rinse them. She and Marc had stayed up after everyone left to clean up the debris from the party. Now it was past noon, but they hadn't been in any hurry to get out of bed. Slow lovemaking, followed by an unhurried late breakfast, suited them just fine.

"I like her, too," Marc agreed. "I haven't had as much time to talk to her as I'd like." He chuckled. "But, the first day she walked into rehearsal, you could see the sparks between her and Rick. At first it was animosity. You could see the two of them silently wrestling for control. Now it's something different and the intensity is even stronger."

Emma stacked the dishes in the dishwasher. "Do you think he's falling for her? Wow, I'd love to see him have a real relationship. He deserves it."

Marc shook his head. "I don't think he wants to let himself go in that direction."

"Sometimes you don't have a choice." She grinned at him. "Look at us."

He brushed his lips over hers, gave a light stroke of his tongue over her lower lip.

"Quit it." She laughed, and hit him with a dish towel. "Let's at least clean up before we get into any hanky-panky."

"Which, by the way, would do Rick some good if he let himself go."

"Rick has a strong sense of responsibility to the band," Emma reminded. "It's like family to him. Stability. Just as he saw himself as the head of the household when his dad took a powder, he's shouldered on the same role with Lightnin'."

"You're right." Marc refilled his coffee mug and leaned against the counter. "We started this band together but he's better at being in charge than I am. I don't want that to be an obstacle to a special someone lighting up his life."

"Has he said anything to you about her? About Sydney?"

Marc shook his head. "You know Rick. He thinks *feelings* is just a word in the dictionary."

"I hate that for him." Emma closed the dishwasher and hung away the towel she'd used. "He needs someone like her. Marc, when I looked at them last night, it was impossible not to see the sparks between them. More than sparks. A deep feeling of some kind. I just hope he doesn't think he has to pass on it because of business."

"There's fire in the air, that's for sure. He might have been pissed off at the way she marched into rehearsal unannounced but those sparks flying between them didn't have anything to do with anger."

"You think she feels the same way he does?"

"Oh, yeah. You can't miss it. You saw it last night. I wish I knew what happens next with those two and how it will affect the band."

"Rick's a professional," she pointed out. "And so is Sydney. They'll figure it out."

"I hope."

"I got good vibes from her last night," Emma said. "She seems pretty sharp. She's going to be an important part of life in the band for some time. And the campaign she puts together is crucial to what happens next."

Marc nodded. "I agree. She won't let anything derail that, just like Rick won't let a situation knock the band off the track."

"Oh, great." She laughed. "Two hard heads. What a pair."

"He invited her back to rehearsal to hear a set we put together for her. I wonder how they'll react to each other in that situation." Marc walked up behind Emma, put his arms around her, and kissed the side of her neck. "You and she seemed to hit it off pretty well. Maybe you could give her a call."

Emma spun around in his arms. "And do what? Interrogate her? Pry information from her? Play matchmaker? Are you sure that's what you want me to do?"

"Hold on, honey." Marc backed up and held out his hands. "Rick is perfectly capable of getting his own info. I just thought it might be nice, since she's probably going to be at all the concert dates and stuff, if you got to know each other better."

"Uh huh." Emma grinned at him. "I know your game, Malone. 'Fess up. You're as curious as I am about those two and you think I can figure out what's going on with some girl talk."

He grinned. "Close." His face sobered. "Okay. I hear you. But will you think about calling her, anyway?"

She laughed at him. "I'll figure out what's appropriate." She stepped forward so her body was pressed against his. "Meanwhile, can you think of something exciting we can do today?"

He lifted her in his arms and headed toward the bedroom. "I'm sure I can think of a great way to spend the afternoon."

Emma leaned her head against his shoulder. "I figured you could."

Chapter Seven

Sydney sat in the back booth at Coffee and More with a cup of chai tea as she reviewed her notes for perhaps the hundredth time. No coffee for her today, not even decaf. She was too nervous. Too on edge. Five days had passed since the party at Marc and Emma's and the incredible night she'd spent with Rick Trajean. Every detail of those hours in the dark was still etched on her brain, no matter how much she tried to block it. Or wipe out the place he'd carved out in her heart.

Yes, Janine. My heart. Go ahead and laugh.

She knew Lightnin' rehearsed every day. She had their schedule on her iPad and she was busy with their promo stuff. But it was hard to stay focused when every five minutes she checked her phone for a text or listened anxiously for her ringtone. Every day, she kept expecting him to call, or at least text. But nothing. Not a word. Had he just wiped that night out of his mind completely?

How stupid she'd been to let down all her barriers. It seemed he hadn't felt the same magic she did. She'd broken every one of her personal rules and what had it gotten her? Dumped. And a week of anxious days and sleepless nights. Well, she was done. With all of it. She was sure now that night hadn't meant as much to him as it did to her. That was what she got for making idiotic assumptions. No more. If her future wasn't tied so tightly to

Lightnin', she would have asked Linc to give the client to another agent. Replace her. Okay, so that wasn't very professional but neither was falling for a client and tumbling into bed with him. She wouldn't let it happen again. Ever.

The real problem would come when she saw him today, when they sat across this table from each other. How was she supposed to pretend Saturday night hadn't happened?

She looked at her notes again but it was hard to concentrate when her stomach balled with apprehension and her nerves were rubbed raw.

See, Sydney? This is why you don't let your emotions get out of control.

Janine's spiteful voice screamed in her head and urged her to forget about her momentary loss of control. Put it behind her. Words flooded her brain as if her aunt sat next to her.

You're just like your mother. A man comes along and crooks his finger, you tear off your clothes and give up your dreams. Not that I think you'll listen to me anyway.

Okay, she was listening now. Besides, how would she handle it if he had pursued her, convinced her they had something going here? It wasn't as if they could go public with it. Not when the fans out there were about to get their first taste of Lightnin' and every media eye would be focused on them, the agency, and her. Not to mention the sick feeling she had that everyone at Full Moon, from Linc on down, would lecture her about sleeping with a client. That was a big no-no at the agency. She was sure they'd look at her with disappointment.

Besides, what if they clashed on future ideas? On her handling of the media? On anything else in the promotion plan? She had to use all her skills and all her energy to maintain a positive working relationship with Lightnin', most especially Rick as the leader. She didn't to let messy emotions get in the way.

So yeah. Maybe it was just as well he hadn't gotten in touch with her. Business had to come first. This was her big chance as well as the band's. She would pretend Saturday night never happened. Her focus needed to be on Lightnin' and The Plan.

Not on Rick.

Okay. Good. Fine. It's out of my mind.

Liar.

Giving herself a mental shake, she pulled up the calendar on her iPad and checked all the dates listed in bold font. The first media interview was in two weeks and it was a big one. Everyone within shouting distance was invited. She would need to rehearse Rick on the best way to handle it and clue him on what the vultures would be looking for. She'd be under a lot of scrutiny to see how she handled Butch Meredith's new baby. One screw up and she'd find herself carrying someone else's water.

She had a CD with some of Lightnin's rehearsal music on it and she'd downloaded "Music Lady" as her ringtone. She thought maybe if Rick heard it, he'd see she was really into the band. *Or into him.* Now it played the opening notes next to her and she looked to see who the caller was. Hopefully not Rick canceling their meeting.

The display read *Butch Meredith*. Holy crap! Butch calling her? Pressing a hand to her stomach to calm the butterflies, she pressed Answer.

"Hello?"

"Hey, Sydney. This is Butch."

As if he wasn't at the top of her call list.

"Yes, Butch. How are you?"

"Good. Real good." He was using the same voice she'd heard calm jittery musicians and irate media. Was she in trouble? Already? Had Rick complained to him?

She did her best to sound calm and collected. "What can I do for you?"

"Just touching base. Rick tells me you and he are meetin' today about the promo plan. I wanted to see if there was anything you needed from me."

I hope not.

"I think we're good, Butch. But thanks for asking." She curled the fingers of her other hand into her palm. "I'll lay out some basics for Rick in a little while. I did try to take everything he said into consideration."

"I'm sure it will all be fine. If Linc didn't have confidence in you, he wouldn't have assigned you to the band. and I wouldn't have signed off on it. Just want you to know I'm here if you need me."

"Yes. Thank you. I appreciate it."

She disconnected, leaned back in the booth, and let out a long, slow breath. She had no idea what to make of the call but if it meant she had to dial things back a little, she would. For the moment. Still, she was convinced her ideas would work and if she had to work them in slowly, so be it.

She was bent over the table, taking a last look at her notes, when someone pushed a fresh coffee in front of her. She looked up to see Rick's smoldering gaze.

"Oh. Um, hi!" Her heartbeat accelerated, her mouth went dry, and a pulse set up an insistent throbbing between her thighs. She had to remind herself to breathe. She certainly wasn't about to tell him she was off coffee today.

Is he going to say anything or just pretend nothing ever happened?

She was so tense with anticipation, she was sure her body vibrated.

"You looked very intent." He slid into the seat across from her. "Working on the latest details?"

"I am." She couldn't stop staring at him across the table.

That was it? Nothing about Saturday night? Not even to tell her it was a big mistake? By now she was ready to agree with him.

Okay. So I read more into that night and the things he said than I should have. If he wants to pretend it didn't happen, I can, too. Let's get to it. Janine was right and I was a damn fool.

Still, she didn't imagine the sexual heat that still simmered between them. She'd just have to find a way to deal with it.

She swallowed and forced herself to relax.

"I had our graphics person make some revisions to the logo," she began. "Tried to pay attention to what you wanted to get across." She slid some sketches to him. "I hope you like the new version we've come up with."

The lightning bolt was now silver outlined in black on a silver background in a circle. Maybe she'd try to add a little glitter to it. She had graphics of how it would appear on different types of merchandise.

Sydney wet her lips, her throat dry, nerves still jangling and her body not getting the message to ease up. She forced herself to wait a long moment for Rick to react. To say something. But he gave nothing away so she moved forward.

"The logo will still make an impact," she went on. "It's distinctive yet still in line with the feel of the band. And I want to start working with you on the big media presentation. The big coming-out party, so to speak. It's almost around the corner."

Rick nodded his head, his face unreadable. "Yeah, Butch happened to mentioned that."

Oh? Butch did?

"What did he say?"

Rick's mouth curved in a crooked smile. "That you were a whiz with the media and I should listen to your tips."

Sydney felt the tension in her body ease just a little.

Thank you, Butch.

"Good. That's nice to hear. Because we'll be together a lot preparing for the media event, rehearsing how to handle and what to say. I'm expecting a really large turnout."

He lifted an eyebrow. "You think we'll make that kind of an impression?"

"I hope so."

"Okay. I guess the ball's in your court."

The strain eased just a millimeter. "Does that mean you're good with this logo? I want to be able to show it to Butch and tell him you're happy with it."

He nodded. "Much better than the other ones." His expression was dead serious now. "All I meant was for you to understand that our music has depth and emotion to it. It tells a story. We want that to be the focus."

"I understand what you're saying."

"Good. I'm glad."

She looked up and caught him studying her with a very intent look on his face. A look she couldn't decipher.

Say something, she commanded silently. *Anything. Anything at all.*

"I'll tell Linc and Butch so we can proceed with the merchandise order. We have to place it soon. We'll have stuff for sale in the lobby of the concert venue opening night. First time for the public to buy it. We'll tease it along with our media releases, so they'll expect it."

"Let's hope for big sales, right?"

"Right. Now let's talk about the upcoming interview."

Sitting across from him, trying to pretend their night of unbelievable sex and emotional connection hadn't happened was one of the hardest things she'd ever done. Somehow, though, she managed it as she went over every aspect of what he could expect when Butch introduced the group at the media conference.

"I'll need to brief the rest of the band," she told him, "but you'll be the primary spokesman."

Both their careers were riding on this, but she was comfortable enough with his smarts to feel he could handle things. With each passing minute though, disappointment flooded her veins. For the first time in what seemed forever she wanted to find a quiet corner and have herself a good cry. She had acted against her better judgment, so she'd just have to pay the price.

Their coffee was long gone when he finally leaned back in the booth.

"Enough. I'm done for today. We rehearsed for four hours earlier and I'm about wasted."

"Oh." She was instantly contrite. "I'm sorry. Maybe we should have picked a different time for this."

When he didn't say a word she looked up from her notes to

see his gaze locked on her, his eyes like twin lasers.

"Is there a problem?" She was proud her voice was so steady.

"Aren't you going to say anything?"

She dropped her trembling hands into her lap. "About?"

"About Saturday night, goddamnit." His words were clipped. "I was sure when I walked in here today you'd be ready to chew my ass. Or—" he spread his hands out "—or something."

Now a thread of anger spiraled through her. Was that what he expected? That she'd verbally attack him the minute she saw him? For what? The night itself or not calling her? She might want to but she prided herself on her professionalism.

"I thought the message you sent was loud and clear. Or rather the lack of one." Beneath the table, she clenched her fists. "You didn't call so I guess I know where we stand. It's apparent what we have is just a business arrangement."

Much steadier, fueled by her growing anger, she picked up her folder to put it in her briefcase. Before she realized what he was doing his hands shot across the table and gripped both of hers. And oh, God. The instant he made contact with her jolts of electricity zinged through her. Heat wrapped itself around her like a warm blanket and her pussy throbbed with need. Her nipples ached and her throat was as dry as her cunt was suddenly wet.

She dropped the folder, the papers scattering on the surface.

I am such a loser.

She tried to snatch her hands back but his grip was too strong. His gaze immobilized her, his eyes darkened to the color of bitter chocolate.

"I'm an ass, Sydney. Feel free to call me one."

Her heartbeat raced at what she saw on his face. Heard in his tone. "And I would do that because?"

"Because I walked in here today acting like nothing had happened, when we both know it did. Because I didn't call or even text you, although I wanted to every single minute since the other night."

Her lungs felt squeezed and her throat tightened. She

couldn't seem to get enough air. "It's okay. I understand." Again she tried to pull away. And again he just held on more tightly.

"No. You don't." His eyes were still focused on her face. "I knew we had something brewing between us. More than just hot sex. You did, too. Don't try to deny it."

"I—"

He shook his head. "I'm not done. Saturday night totally blew my mind. *You* blew my mind." He looked down at their joined hands. "And it scared the shit out of me."

"Why? Now I *don't* understand."

"Sydney, my whole life has been wrapped up in my family and the band. There's so much about me you don't know. Falling for someone just isn't on my to-do list for a long time."

She wished he would let go. His touch was scorching her and it made it difficult to think. "It's okay. It's not on mine, either."

"You hit me like a ton of bricks." He went on as if she hadn't spoken. "I thought if I ignored it, didn't call you, text you, get in touch with you, see you, this feeling I don't know what to do with would go away."

"And did it?" She couldn't stop herself from asking.

"Not for one second. I know this will sound nuts to you but I can't get you out of my head. Out of my dreams. When I rehearse, I pretend I'm playing the music just for you. How crazy is that?" He blew out a breath. "I'm not good at stuff like this, Syd. I've never been good at relationships and never looked for them. Which is fine because no one ever came along and smacked me in the face the way you did."

His fingers laced through hers, and now she was afraid to break the contact.

"And now?"

His gaze when he looked at her was burning and intent. But then he looked down at their joined hands. "Jesus, I'm making a mess out of this. Sydney, I have real feelings for you, stuff I've never felt for anyone before. It goes way, way beyond sex. And I'm embarrassed to tell you I don't know how to handle this."

Relief made her giddy and a tiny hysterical laugh burst from her mouth. "I'm glad to hear it."

"What?" A flush crept up his cheeks. "Are you laughing at me?"

"No, at us."

"Us." He frowned. "What the hell does that mean?"

"Oh, Rick. You can't imagine how I felt. There are so many reasons why I've never opened myself emotionally to anyone like this before. When you didn't call, didn't text, just ignored me, what was I supposed to think? Then, today, you show up for this meeting and act like nothing happened. I figured you saw this as a big mistake and wanted to pretend Saturday night never took place. I'm as much of an emotional mess as you are. What I feel for you scares the life out of me."

The strain on his face eased, and his mouth curved in a crooked grin. "We're a real pair." He leaned toward her. "Syd, that was the best damn night of my entire life, and I want more of it. A lot more. And more of you."

"Are you sure?" There was the insecure ten-year-old in her head again.

"Positive. But...."

"There's always a but, isn't there?"

He shook his head. "That was the wrong word. The reality is I wasn't sure I could trust myself—what I felt. The past five days have been kind of a test for me, to see if this feeling went away or not."

"And?" she prompted, almost afraid to hear what came next.

"And it not only didn't go away, it got stronger." He chuffed out a breath. "I want us to see if what we've got is solid, because it sure feels that way to me."

She swallowed hard. How to say what was on her mind? "I'll tell you first I feel the same way. And I've never said that to anyone else. Ever. I want to be sure you understand that."

"Okay." Tension seeped from his body. "Now *I* hear a but coming."

She looked up at him. "But we need to think carefully about what we do next."

"Like what?" he growled.

"Like keeping this under wraps. Not letting anyone know about it." She held her breath, waiting for his reply.

He scowled and released his hold on her. "Syd, are you ashamed of me?"

"No, no, no. Not at all." She picked up her coffee mug to give herself something to do with her hands. "But this could affect both of us adversely. If word that we're together gets out, how will the agency react? The band? Butch?" She waved a hand in the air. "The media."

He cocked an eyebrow. "The media?"

"Yes, the damn media. Rick, this is an industry of rumors. You have no idea how easily tongues can wag. Pretty soon people will be talking about how long Rick Trajean will be fucking Sydney Alexander, instead of talking about the band."

If she'd slapped him he couldn't have looked more shocked. Or hurt.

"Are you kidding me? I mean, there's always club gossip, but I figured at this level we'd be past that."

She shook her head. "We're never past it. Reputations can be ruined by vicious gossip. I don't want that for you."

"Me? What about you? Or is that really what you're concerned about?"

"What?" Her eyes widened. "No. Please. That's not it at all."

"Listen to me, Sydney." He took her hands in his again. "I don't want to lose what we've got going here. I didn't call you because I was afraid you'd just blow me off, but now I see how wrong I was. I want to move forward. To see what we've got here. Find out if it's as real as I think it is."

She swallowed. "We both have big goals, Rick. We can't lose sight of them."

"And we won't. But at the end of the day, this is what counts. Let's see where it goes. I can understand why you feel the way you do, about not letting it out in public. You're probably right but I don't have to like it."

"Me, either. I want to tell everyone. But trust me. I know

what I'm talking about here." She blew out a breath. "Besides, you can't promise me that it isn't just a momentary thing. We need to be very sure of each other before we expose ourselves to all the gossip. And trust me, there'll be plenty of it."

"I am sure, and I'd like to think you are, but okay. I agree this is brand new. It seems neither of us has been willing to take a risk like this before. So we'll take it in baby steps and keep it just between us. For now." He pressed a kiss to her knuckles. "And I promise to text you so much you'll shut off the damn phone."

She laughed at his words. "Let's not go overboard." Then all traces of humor disappeared. "I've been so wound up since Saturday. And look at us. Two adults who haven't a clue how to manage a relationship like this."

"Because we haven't allowed ourselves to have one before. Or met someone we wanted one with."

"Yes." She sighed. "I've been so focused on getting my career started, building my creds, getting the media to respect me so they respond to me. And establishing myself at Full Moon. I couldn't afford to be distracted."

"Me, too. With the band."

The look he gave her made her tremble. Her pulse stuttered and the damn butterflies were back in her stomach.

"You know we won't have a lot of private time to be together," he pointed out. "Not yet, anyway. But, Syd?"

"Yes?"

"Listen to what I say. Whatever time we do have will be damn good quality time." He turned her hand over and pressed a kiss to her palm.

Shivers skated along her spine.

"I was so afraid to believe this was actually happening," he went on, "but I'm more afraid to miss out on something real and special. So what's next?"

"We need to focus all our energy on the launch and the tour."

"Agreed."

"And you won't continue to fight me on every little thing," she added, smiling to take the edge off her words.

"As long as you'll agree to be open-minded and listen to me."

Relief surged through her. "Then we're good to go. You've got the list of dates. The next big thing is media day." She slipped out of the booth, taking her phone and briefcase.

Rick dropped some cash on the table and followed her. "Come on, I'll walk you out."

When they reached her car, she tossed her purse and briefcase inside and turned to face him. "Tell me again this is real."

"It's real," he said in a soft voice. "And it's going to get better. We can't be scared of it, okay?"

"One day you'll have to tell me why you're as afraid as I am."

"Only if we exchange stories." He scanned the parking lot before cupping her face and placing a gentle kiss on her lips. "I'll call you later."

CB

Rick watched her drive away. He could still taste her and feel her lips on his. The moment he'd walked into Coffee and More and seen her in the booth, he'd wanted to kiss her. Restraining himself to make it light and sweet had been a big battle. He was about to step off a cliff and didn't know how deep the fall would be. For five days, he'd wrestled with the need to call Sydney, talk to her, hear her voice. Reassure himself that Saturday night hadn't been a dream. That what happened between them was real and special.

The emotional devastation left by his father's desertion had never completely gone away. His mother had finally moved on and Meredith seemed to be flourishing. But the young Rick never forgot his father's abandonment, or his need at that young age to create stability in his life. The one lesson he thought he'd learned was never to open himself up emotionally to anyone.

Until now, he hadn't had a problem, because he hadn't met anyone who made him want to alter his decision. Sydney Alexander had blindsided him. Invaded every inch of his body and mind.

No, he hadn't called her after Saturday night because the power of what he felt for her scared the shit out of him. But five days without seeing her or hearing her voice and five nights of the most erotic dreams he'd ever had, taught him that he couldn't just walk away from this. All the way to the meeting today he'd argued with himself, trying to talk himself out of what he wanted to do. And sitting with her, working, pretending there was nothing between them, was one of the hardest things he'd ever done.

It made him realize, however, he couldn't turn his back on what was happening with Sydney, the feelings growing between them no matter how scary it seemed. He felt better, though, at the knowledge she was as insecure about it as he was. Who knew Sydney Attitude Alexander shared his self-doubts.

He'd played by all the rules to get this far, worked his ass off, and given all of himself to the band. Stayed away from the groupies, or any kind of possible relationship that could knock him off course. Then, just when he least expected it, here it came, turning his life upside down.

Okay, they'd keep their situation under wraps like she wanted. The more he thought about it, the more he realized how smart that was. They could do it. They were both adults. Neither of them wanted to detract from the launch of the band. If anyone noticed what was cooking between them it would be Marc, and he could handle his friend.

Right?

As he sat there sorting through his feelings, his cell phone rang. The readout showed Butch Meredith's name.

Great. He better get his head together before he answered.

"Hey, Butch!"

"I just wanted to touch base with you," Butch said. "You met with Sydney Alexander again?"

"Yes, just now." He was careful not to let his voice give anything away.

"How are things going? She taking good care of you?"

More than you can begin to imagine.

"Yes. We had a great meeting. We reviewed the stuff for the media event. I signed off on the revised logo so we're good to go with merchandise."

"Excellent." Butch's voice was warm with satisfaction. "And the prep for the media?"

"We went over it a little but we'll meet a few more times before the big day."

"Okay." Butch paused. "I know this is her first solo gig, but Linc Forrester and I discussed it at length. She's been a great second for the past few years. I know he wouldn't let her fly alone if he didn't think she was ready."

Rick hesitated before making his next comment. It was the one thing that had plagued him from the beginning, the one thing that could interfere with his personal feelings for her. "Maybe he thinks if she makes a mistake it won't have as much effect with an unknown like Lightnin'."

"Linc knows better, so get that out of your head." The words had a hard edge to them. "Full Moon handles the public relations for my other clients. They've done a damn good job, but they know if they screw up, I'll move my entire client list to someone else."

A weight lifted from Rick's chest. All right, then. Good to go. She had the backing of the agency and Butch's confidence. And she had him, even if they wanted to keep it to themselves.

"Sorry," he said. "I had to get it out there."

"And I understand." Butch's voice sounded more relaxed. "But I've got it covered. Trust me. Now, how are the rehearsals coming? You guys ready to hit the studio yet?"

Rick felt a thread of excitement curl in his stomach. "For real?"

"It's time. The tour kicks off in three weeks, and we want to get the single out ahead of it. I'd like to do 'Music Lady,' if that works for you. I know it's not one you yourself wrote—"

"No, that's fine," Rick broke in. "Marc will be thrilled." And Emma, too.

"I'd like you to talk to him and Emma and ask them if they mind including their story in the promo stuff. It's a real hook and the fans will eat it up."

"I'm pretty sure they'll be fine with that. Great, even." He let out a breath. "Wow! So it's really happening."

Butch chuckled. "I'll have Linc pass the word to Sydney. I'd like her to interview the two of them and maybe rehearse them a little for the questions they'll get." He paused. "I don't typically like to put someone's personal life on display like that. It's not my style."

"They don't mind sharing," Rick assured him. "I'll talk to them first."

"Good. Then if you think you've got the song down pat I'll schedule the studio time."

"Oh, we're set." He grinned, even though Butch couldn't see him. "Absolutely."

"I'll get back to you with the info. Hopefully later today."

After disconnecting, Rick just sat there holding his cell. The dream was here. At last. They'd be in a top studio with engineers used to recording hit songs. People who would know what to do with Lightnin's sound. And "Music Lady" had such a good backstory. Butch was right.

He grinned as he punched Sydney's number into his cell phone.

"Am I overstepping if I say you must miss me already?" He could hear the smile in her voice. "I'm not even home yet and here you are."

"Because I've got great news and you're the first one I wanted to share it with."

"No kidding? Tell me, tell me."

"Butch called. We're going into the studio to record 'Music Lady.' He's setting it up even as we speak."

"Ohmigod!" she screamed. "Let me pull over before I have an accident."

"Definitely don't wreck yourself," he told her.

"Okay, I'm set. Now give me all the details."

He repeated everything Butch had said then promised he'd keep her in the loop. "But I'm sure you'll get the word as soon as the date is set. You'll include it in your media plan, right?"

"Oh, of course." Excitement crackled in her voice. "Oh, Rick. This is great. The record can release before the tour. What great timing."

"Thank Butch for that. The man obviously knows what he's doing."

"What did the guys say?"

He laughed again. "I haven't told them yet."

"You called me first?" There was a pause. "You have no idea how much that means to me."

"Yeah, I think I do." A warm sensation crept through his own body. "Listen, we'll probably get together for pizza and something to celebrate. Want to join us?"

Another pause. "Um, I'd really love to, but I think maybe that's not the best move."

"Sydney, people will see us together. Hell, we're working together."

"But this is a little more personal. I'll pass this time."

"Okay," he agreed at last. "But I'll call you afterward."

"Absolutely."

He disconnected the call, her soft words echoing in his brain. Just the sound of her voice did funny things to him. He sat for a long moment, running everything through his brain. She was probably right. Marc and Emma would give them the eagle eye and everything they did would elicit some kind of comment. He wanted to wait until this thing between him and Sydney was more settled, not quite so new. When they could control it better around other people.

Time to make his calls. The band, first and foremost. Then his family. He needed to talk to Marc and Emma about their part in the upcoming media blitz so they could be prepared. Then he had to fill in Danny and Garrett Sydney's timetable. But first things first. Studio time. Swallowing the last of his coffee, he hit the button for Marc's number.

Chapter Eight

Sydney rose before the sun on the day of the big event. She'd had a restless night, tossed and turned, dozing in brief snatches. At five o'clock, she gave up and got out of bed.

She dressed with great care, determined to present just the right image. Part of the scene, but businesslike, yet not too uptight. She didn't think jeans and a Lightnin' T-shirt would have been appropriate, although later in the tour it might serve a good purpose. Instead she chose black slacks and a magenta silk T-shirt that brought out the color in her cheeks. Her hair was pulled back in a wide gold clip as usual and earrings resembling tiny lightning bolts dangled from her ears. Okay, so that part was hokey. She was allowed a little, right? And she'd been so excited when she found them, she'd also bought a pair for Emma. The woman had thanked her profusely, excitement shining in her eyes.

At seven she was at the office to check the boxes headed for the restaurant and go over her list yet again.

"Music Lady" was in the can, and everyone felt pretty damn good about it, especially Butch. The previous week, she'd taken time for a long visit with Marc and Emma, making sure they understood what a media feast the story would be, but they were cool with it. And everyone saw it as a chance to "personalize" the band. Take it into the public's homes and hearts, so to speak.

They'd find out today if they were right.

Renee Fischer, Linc's administrative assistant, laughed when they met in the break room.

"I thought Linc was the only one who slept here." She chuckled. "Took me years to break him of the habit."

"I just want to make sure today goes off without a hitch," Sydney told her as she took a sip of the hot brew.

"It will, sweetie." Renee gave her a hug. "Everyone is rooting for you, Syd. You've been with us longer than some of the senior agents. You're a member of the family. And we know you'll knock 'em dead today."

"Oh, God, Renee. Thank you so much." The confidence they had in her was overwhelming. She had to take a deep breath to compose herself.

"Hey, don't start crying." Renee chuckled. "It ruins the mascara."

Sydney hiccupped. "I'll keep that in mind."

Of course, that wasn't the only reason she hadn't slept well. Since the night she and Rick were together, her dreams had been filled with erotic fantasies about him. About the two of them. Dreams that had her waking up breathing hard and covered with perspiration, often with her hand between her thighs to ease the aching need.

That one night had been nothing short of combustible, the attraction a living thing between them. She hadn't been able to say no to him about anything, nor had she wanted to. She could still feel the touch of his hands on her body, his mouth on her skin everyplace. The orgasm that rocked her world.

His touch was still imprinted on her skin and even though she'd changed her sheets, she could swear his very male scent still lingered in her bedroom. No amount of discipline managed to erase him from her brain.

Not that she wanted to. Not after their talk at Coffee and More. A week of insecurity had almost made her walk away from him so it shocked her to find out he had self-doubts just like hers.

Since then they'd spoken every day, even if just for a few minutes. And every night he texted her *Good Night*.

She was pretty sure no one in the band caught any vibes from the two of them. Oh, maybe Marc. They'd been friends since they were fourteen. But he wouldn't say anything unless he thought the situation was somehow harming the band. And Sydney wasn't about to let that happen. This was too important to them.

She was more worried about providing fodder for the gossip sheets. The industry was rife with it and too often lies and truth blended together. She didn't want that for Lightnin' or herself.

This was her big shot at the top as well as theirs. Her chance to satisfy the need of that scared little girl battered by Janine's constant vitriolic tirades.

She swallowed a sigh, hoping she'd made the right decision as far as Rick was concerned. She had to work hard to block out Janine's bitter voice that always lurked in the back of her mind, like some vicious counterpoint, telling her she'd made a huge mistake. That he'd disappoint her. Meet some other woman on the tour and she'd be history. She managed to forcefully squelch that voice most of the time. Talking to Rick every day and seeing him now and then always reinforced her feelings.

Today, especially, she'd have to be very careful not to give anything away. The sharks and hyenas would be looking for anything they could use to feed the rumor mill. The night before, she and Rick had talked at length on the phone about being on guard regarding their own situation. They would both be vigilant today. She hoped it worked.

Linc stopped by her office to brief her on some of the people who'd be at the event. Those who were key to the success of her plan. The ones she'd have a hard time with. And who to be on guard about. He made mention of a couple she should pay careful attention to, but she already had them on her "watch" list.

"Be careful of Macey Shreiner," he told her. "She had some lucky breaks when she started her blog and wrote her first columns. Now the industry thinks she's a kingmaker."

Sydney shrugged. "She's no worse than some of the others we talked about."

"Yes, she is. Macey's a man-eater. If you rub her the wrong way, she can make a lot of trouble for you, all in the guise of reporting the entertainment news. Be careful, Sydney."

"I'll remember that."

"Good, because I have big plans for you."

Macey Shreiner. The woman was no stranger to the scene. Sydney had seen her at many other media meets. She wielded a lot of power, not just as a columnist for *Make Mine Music* magazine but also with a blog whose followers numbered in the millions. Every newspaper of note followed it to pick up morsels she scattered and to take the temperature of the scene. She could make or break a performer. She was also one of the most predatory females Sydney had ever seen. Her exploits were legendary, only tolerated because of the power she held.

She put a star next to the woman's name so she wouldn't forget to be on guard. Linc was right about the man-eater part. Stories of Macey's affairs with musicians were scattered over a lot of landscapes, as well as tidbits about the people who got in her way who she destroyed.

Sydney knew there was a reason she'd disliked the woman on sight.

No problem, though. She didn't plan to do anything to piss her off.

Now she took one last look around Le Bistro's large banquet room, the one she'd reserved for today. Another half hour and it would be full. She'd place placed a folder embossed with the Lightnin' logo on each chair in the long rows set up for the occasion. Inside was the bio sheet on the band she'd put together as well as the list of tour dates and the background on "Music Lady."

At the front of the room, on a platform, was the table where Lightnin' would sit to answer questions. Emma would be in the front row, available when needed. Sydney had met with her and

Marc and walked them through what they could expect. Marc was so comfortable in his own skin he took it all in stride. For Emma, this would be a big coming out party, especially since, before meeting Marc, she'd never even listened to rock music.

And how strange is that?

But by the end of their meeting the couple was relaxed and even looking forward to it a little.

Sydney had already tested the mics and checked all the materials. Three Full Moon interns would arrive shortly to help her with the media, make sure everyone was aware of the refreshments but also help her clear the room in a timely fashion. Now she only had one more thing to do and they were all set.

Her biggest hurdle involved composing herself when Rick arrived. Everyone would have eyes on them for a variety of reasons. Personal discipline would be key. When he walked into the restaurant, he was courteous and smiling, greeting her much as he did the band and Butch. But when he thought no one was looking, he glanced over at her and winked. She hoped no one but her saw the hunger that flared in his eyes or the way her hands suddenly shook.

The day's schedule played over and over in her head as she stood there and she tried not to imagine all the things that could go wrong. What if nobody showed up? Or the band wasn't impressive in the interview session. Or the media hated them on sight. Or—

Stop it, Sydney.

This might be her first solo effort but if she didn't get her act together, it could be her last. And she was damned determined to show her bitter Aunt Janine she'd chosen a good profession and could succeed at it.

"Look at me now," she whispered. "What do you think, you old bitch?"

One more time she scrolled through her phone to check the list of media contacts that had accepted today's invitation. Okay. So far so good.

Tote bag in hand she hurried back to the small private room

where the band was having lunch. Emma had also been invited since she was so intrinsic to "Music Lady," and Linc Forrester and Butch Meredith had also joined them.

Glancing at the lunch table where everyone sat, she could see the tension radiate from each of the band members. They might pretend to be blasé about it all but she knew their excitement level ran high. The buzz in the room was so electric Sydney could practically feel it zip along the surface of her skin. Linc Forrester was talking to the band now in his low drawl, explaining what the process would be and assuring them Sydney would hold their hands every step of the way. Reminding them they could depend on her.

I can't screw this up. I'll never get another chance. That's why I have to stop practically vibrating every time I see Rick.

Her mouth went dry when she looked at him now. As long as she didn't look in his eyes and open herself to that soul-shattering connection she could make this work.

Get it together, Sydney. People will be watching. Stick to it.

So what do I do with these feelings that won't go away? Why does everything have to be so hard?

Because it is. So do it.

When Rick had signed off on the final artwork, he'd thrilled her by saying he thought it was both tasteful and exciting, an improvement over what they'd been using. It helped that everyone else agreed, too.

Today would be the big reveal to the world.

She focused on the table where the band sat and saw Rick watching her. Uh oh. Bad move. Heat surged through her, the way it did every time he gave her that smoldering look. Her nipples hardened and the crotch of her thong dampened. Need coursed through her, threatening to throw her off balance. Would she ever be able to look at him without this reaction?

In a way, she hoped not. Just not where it was quite so visible. Not where the media sharks could focus on them and not the band.

Today, like every other time they'd been together, their

glances locked and the temperature in the room redlined. Even now, she saw the heat in his eyes. Electricity zapped between them like—well—like a lightning bolt. Sometimes it almost seemed as if he could see right inside her. The thought made her shiver.

She pasted a smile on her face and approached the table.

"We're all set next door," she told everyone. "These are for you guys." She gave each of the band members a media packet so they could see what she handed out. The dark blue covers had a silver lightning bolt, striking down from a cloud embossed with the band's name in script. Then she held out the bag to Rick.

"I've got Lightnin' T-shirts, too. Linc's secretary gave me your sizes. I'd really appreciate it if you'd would change into them. It will make a great visual for the media."

"You mean like matching uniforms?" She'd worried that he'd balk at this, but he grinned instead, and she relaxed.

"Yes, Rick. Just like that."

Butch took the bag from her. "I think that's a terrific idea. A perfect way to unveil them for the media. You guys go and get changed. In fact, let me show you where you can wait until we introduce you."

"I think the shirts will look great, too," Emma urged. "You know, it's all about impact." She turned to Sydney. "Right, Syd?"

Sydney nodded, grateful for Emma's enthusiasm.

"Yeah, come on." Danny laughed. "We'll be the boys in black and blue."

"Not a problem." Rick held her gaze with his for a long moment. Then, with a tiny smile, he turned to the band. "Come on, guys. Let's get with the program."

Sydney watched them file out of the room with Butch. A hand touched her arm, and she looked up to see Linc standing beside her.

"Everything will be fine, Sydney. They want this more than their next breath. I'd rather they rein themselves in than go crazy wild over what's happening and make asses out of themselves."

"Butch would never let them," she reminded him. "He'd tear up their contract."

Linc nodded. "And Rick will relax as soon as we get past the media blitz this afternoon. I know he's uptight, but this band is his baby, his and Marc's. He'll get past today's event just fine. No worries. Come on, let's go next door."

Sydney couldn't tell Butch that Rick's attitude had nothing to do with nerves and everything to do with his feelings toward her. Every time he looked at her, she had to dredge up her composure and not go weak in the knees. She needed to get a grip before she made a mistake. Butch and Linc might be all warm and friendly but they had a lot of dollars committed to Lightnin' and both men would have her under their scrutiny today. If she tanked, that would be the end of everything. Of her dream.

Of her chance to thumb her nose at Janine.

She eyeballed the room they entered. Two thirds of the chairs were already filled and uniformed servers stocked the table against the back wall now with coffee, soft drinks, and a variety of dry snacks. Nothing left to do but pray.

As if he could read her thoughts, Butch himself suddenly materialized at her elbow.

"So far so good, Sydney." He smiled at her. "The band is all set, waiting for their cue. I like the graphics, the shirts will market very well, and we'll have a good-sized crowd today." He nodded at the chairs and at the people still filing through the doorway. "Another few minutes and we'll be standing room only."

Sydney returned the smile. "I asked everyone I contacted to send me a confirming e-mail if they were coming and the response was even better than I'd hoped."

"Linc and I discussed who would be best to handle Lightin', you know," he went on. "We needed someone who would be dedicated to the project and also be able to work with the agent assigned to Deep Blue River."

"I worked on some of their promo projects," she reminded him.

He nodded. "And all those things made you the perfect

choice." He squeezed her shoulder. "Relax, Sydney. It's all good. We're here to help you ensure that it all works.

Rick was doing his best to remain unaffected by Sydney's presence. If nothing else, he owed it to the band to behave in the professional manner he always had. But hell! The damn woman just got to him. Ever since their last meeting he'd driven himself crazy analyzing every word that came out of her mouth to be sure what they had wasn't just physical attraction. He had never trusted emotions. Not since his dad left.

It seemed, however, with Sydney he didn't get to make the choice about their growing personal relationship. The reality of it, the intensity, still shocked him. But here and now was not the place to indulge himself. The band was the focus here. He and Sydney didn't need to do anything that would detract from that. He needed to get himself under control, for everyone else, if not for himself. They looked to him as the leader so he damn well better start acting like one.

The problem was being constantly on guard. He hadn't been able to stop thinking about every single minute of that night, the feel of her skin, the taste of her lips. Being inside her. Just talking to her on the phone made him hard as a spike. The erotic dreams plagued him and left him sleep-deprived and unfulfilled.

Get your shit together, Trajean.

The band and Emma stood in the waiting area in quiet conversation. One glance told him the T-shirts rocked. When the lights hit the lightning bolt, it would really sizzle.

Okay, Sydney, you were right. I bow to your wisdom.

He could just imagine her laugh if he said that to her.

The door that led into the big room opened and Sydney joined them.

"Looking good," she told them as she walked up to the tight little group. "The shirts will photograph well and that's what we want. "

"They look great, Syd." Emma grinned. "Your artist did a

fantastic job capturing the electricity of the lightning bolt. And we're ready, all of us, for this to happen."

"Thanks." She glanced over at him again.

He nodded and smiled, hoping his face was an impersonal mask, even though it was damn hard to keep it that way. "You got my vote first," he reminded her. "And, I gotta admit, you were right."

She made a show of wiping her forehead with her hand and feigning shock. "Holy cow! Is that a compliment?"

"You know it is. Don't make me repeat it too many times." He turned so only she could see his face and winked at her.

"You guys need me to go over anything once more, or are we all good?" Sydney asked.

"We're fine," Rick assured her. "We've got the drill. Answer the questions, don't just give yes or no answers, watch you for your signal we're talking too much."

"Chill out, buddy, will you?" Marc frowned at him, then turned back to Sydney. "You'll be there to call on the reporters so they aren't all screaming at once, won't you?"

"Absolutely. I'll be managing the entire thing." She blew out a breath. "So. Ready to take your seats? It won't be long before everyone is here."

"We're ready," Rick said.

He looked directly into her eyes and saw his own feelings reflected there.

Later.

Okay.

I want to see you.

If you can.

I'll try.

For a long moment they were the only two people in the area. He knew he should turn away. Anyone in the band might catch the silent, heated exchange. But she was the one to look away and the moment was gone.

"Guys? And Emma? When everyone who's coming is here, we'll open the door so you can make an entrance."

"Why can't we just go ahead and sit down?" Danny wanted to know.

"It's better staging not to have you up there waiting for them. Heightens the air of expectation." She flashed him a grin. "Sort of why, on a concert stage, you have the band take their places and tune up behind a curtain."

"Oh, yeah. I get it now."

"Emma, you're in the front row. You okay with answering some questions? Just like we talked about, remember?"

"I'm fine." Her eyes sparkled. "I think I'm more excited than the guys are."

"Impossible," Marc laughed.

"Okay, then. Let's knock their socks off."

Sydney took a deep breath and walked back into the main room, moving to the doors where people streamed in. She pasted on her professional smile—one she hoped hid her sudden attack of nerves—and made sure to greet as many people as possible. She spotted at least three television cameramen setting up in the corners or at the side of the room. Some of the entertainment reporters she recognized, many she knew through Full Moon greeted her.

"Speak to the ones you know personally." Linc's drawl sounded softly just behind her. "I've got the rest."

Her stomach flopped when Macey Shreiner walked in wearing her best *I'm the queen* look. Sydney wondered if she should go up and introduce herself personally or what. Then she saw Linc talking to her so she moved away. Later would be soon enough for their first confrontation.

Finally Linc signaled it was time to get the show on the road. She nodded to a hotel staffer to let the band in. She couldn't help but feel a thrill of expectation when they filed in and took their seats on the platform. As her gaze swept the crowd she saw curiosity stamped on a lot of faces and heard a low buzz about the logo.

Okay, Sydney. Here we go.

She stepped up to the mic set at one side of the stage, swallowed hard, and let out a slow breath.

"Good afternoon, everyone. I'm Sydney Alexander with Full Moon Promotions. I've met many of you before and always enjoyed working with you. Those of you I don't know yet...I hope to change that this afternoon."

A smattering of laughter washed over the crowd.

"We're here today to introduce you to a hot band about to break loose on the music scene. In a very short time their first single, 'Music Lady,' will be available for purchase and we hope to hear it a lot on the airwaves. There's some basic information about the musicians in the folder you have, but they'll be happy to answer any questions." She pointed to Rick. "Rick Trajean is the leader of Lightnin' so he'll probably field most of them." She glanced over the crowd one more time. "Okay, then. Let's get started. First question."

They came fast and thick. Rick's manner, which she'd been afraid would be brusque, was in fact smooth and easy. As was Marc's when the questions came up about the story behind "Music Lady." He even pointed to Emma in the front row. When she stood and waved to the crowd, Sydney let out another soft breath. It was all going well.

She breathed easier when she saw the effortless way Rick dealt with everyone. Of course, she should have known. The band was his life. He'd handled all contract negotiations with the clubs, with all the small venues where they performed, with each opportunity that came up. It seemed he had all the information catalogued in his head.

Sydney made sure no one was ignored, smiled when someone had to wait his or her turn, jumped in if there was a query Rick wasn't sure how to answer. Danny and Garrett had their turns also but most of the focus was on Rick and, after him, Marc. More than an hour passed before things wound down, much longer than she'd expected. That was a good sign. It meant the interest was there and they should get some good coverage.

If the interest level was high enough, especially for the reporters and bloggers who had national audiences, the release of the single in one week would get a huge boost in airplay and downloads.

She noted Butch and Linc studying the crowd from the back of the room. Their posture might have been casual but Sydney knew they were mentally cataloging the questions and responses. Who asked what. How she'd prepped the band to answer. How she juggled the reporters. She also noted the cameramen hoisting their big video cameras and moving around the room to get shots from different angles. Good. Maybe the segments would be longer than sixty seconds.

She could feel the energy surge in the room, sense the excitement about the band. Although many of these people had been in the game a long time, a new client of Butch Meredith's always drew a lot of interest. Especially since he was pairing them with his top talent, Deep Blue River, on their first tour.

Sydney continued to call on people and made sure everyone in the band got a turn in the limelight. When the questions became repetitive and sometimes idiotic, she called a halt and motioned for the band to come down off the platform. She asked them to just hang with her for a few moments while she gave the reporters access to Marc and Emma. The media lapped up the love story, recorders on to catch every detail they could. Marc stood with his arm around Emma's waist the entire time, obviously protective. When Sydney thought the questions were digging too hard into personal territory, she eased Marc and Emma away and grabbed one of the mics. Time to shut it down.

"Thanks so much for coming today, everyone. Lightnin' and I look forward to working with all of you."

Acknowledging that their access to the band was finished for today, the media moved on to Linc and Butch, especially Butch. Sydney knew exactly what they'd ask him: why he decided to contract Lightnin' and send them on tour with Deep Blue River. How and why he'd gotten them signed to that band's record label. Digging for dirt if there was any. That was, of course, always a priority with the media.

Sydney thanked everyone who came up to hand her a business card, and there were a lot of them. Another good sign. It meant there was real interest in following the band. They all wanted T-shirts, which she promised they'd get. Actually, what they wanted was back at the office set for delivery. Linc had taught her that you don't give them everything at once. Always angle for yet another contact, even if it's third hand. So, tomorrow, the messenger service they used would be out distributing the shirts along with a promo sheet on how and where people in general could get them.

She wanted to do a little happy dance of excitement at how well the event had gone. She knew how to take the temperature of the media by now, and today it was blazing hot.

Take that, Janine.

"You guys did great," she praised the band. "We'll get some excellent coverage out of this."

"Are we out of jail now?" Rick gave her a crooked grin, the first smile of any kind he'd given her all day.

She laughed, although the sound was a little shaky. "Yes. The mob scene is over." She glanced over her shoulder. "And here comes Butch to tell you what a fantastic job you did."

"I'm proud of you," the man in question said, a big grin on his face. "You acted and sounded as if you'd been doing this forever." Then he turned to Sydney. "Linc and I will try to monitor things until everyone's gone," he went on. "Some of the reporters want to speak to each member of the band, individually, in a less-formal environment. You'll need to set up a schedule around their rehearsals." He looked at the guys again. "But don't panic. Sydney will be right there with you."

"We don't freak," Marc said. "But having her there will keep things under control."

Butch nodded. "And that's going to be a big part of her job from here on out. Managing media access, making sure we get the coverage we should, and that it's all positive."

"The last thing any of us wants," Rick added, "is to say the wrong thing and have it come back to bite us."

"Well, here's your first test," Butch pointed out as a reporter approached. Right behind her was a cameraman hoisting his equipment on his shoulder.

Sydney guided them through the quick video interview, staying out of camera range but making sure they could see her. If they needed her, they could just signal. Sydney was flying on the ultimate high. She glanced at Rick, more relaxed now, engaged in conversation with Butch again. She thought she'd done a good job maintaining a professional attitude throughout the day where he was concerned. Not personal at all. But the sight of him in the Lightnin' T-shirt, the blue fabric stretched across his broad shoulders and sculpted muscles had her hormones doing a happy dance. Her breasts ached, and the throbbing in her cunt echoed through her body.

No, no, no. Eyes on the prize, Sydney. And right now, it's not him.

All through the event, she waited for Macey to make her move. Approach her or most likely Rick. She stayed as close to him as possible so the woman couldn't get him off by himself. The room was all but empty and the band was waiting to ask Sydney what came next when it happened. The tall blonde in designer jeans, high-heeled, strappy sandals, and a tight red top wiggled her way up to Rick.

"Hi." She held out her hand to him. "Macey Schreiner. I write the *On the Scene* blog. We're—"

"Sydney Alexander." Syd held out her own hand, forcing the woman to take it. "We haven't ever met formally although I've seen you at a lot of these events before. I'm the Full Moon agent for Lightnin'."

The handshake was polite, but it was obvious Macey Shreiner's attention was focused elsewhere. A fist knotted in Sydney's stomach but she mentally threw back her shoulders. No way would she let this woman get her claws into Rick.

"So." Macey smiled at him. "I'd love to have a long conversation with you about the band and what it means to you.

When are you free, so we can meet?"

He looked at Sydney, obviously expecting her to take the lead here, but something perverse made her wait to see how he responded. Macey was the epitome of the predatory female, regardless of how valuable a mention on her blog was. It was somehow very important to Sydney that Rick be the one to turn down a private meeting.

Macey just waved her hand. "Oh, I'm harmless. I just thought it would be nice to chat in someplace more informal." She plucked a piece of pasteboard out of the slim messenger bag slung between her breasts. "Here's my card. Call my cell anytime." She pulled out her phone. "And why don't you give me your number, so we can be sure to connect?"

Now Sydney stepped in. "All interviews go through our office, Macey. You've been doing this long enough to know that. I'll be happy to set something up for you. We'll work around the band's rehearsal schedule."

"Of course, of course." She winked at Rick. "We'll get together one way or another, right?"

"Sure thing. I'll have Syd set it up." His mouth curved in a crooked grin. "Did you get a T-shirt? Syd, you've got a shirt for Macey, right?"

A *shirt* for her? Yeah, she'd give her a shirt. She'd shove it up her ass. And what was going on? Was he *flirting* with her?

"You'll be getting one from a messenger," Sydney said, her voice so saccharine she even made herself sick. "Along with a full package of Lightnin' items, which we hope you'll use in public."

"I love doing things in public." Macey was looking at Rick again. "In private, too. Maybe when we meet you can autograph my shirt for me, Rick. I'll be sure to wear it."

"We'll see what we can work out," Sydney said smoothly.

"Great." Macey practically purred. "I'll look forward to it. You know, not to toot my own horn too much, but my blog can help push you to the top in a very short time span."

If the woman got any closer to Rick, her body would be imprinted on his.

"We'll call you," Sydney answered for him. "We really appreciate the fact you want to feature Rick and the band. I'll be sure to get in touch with you in the next couple of days to set it up." And then because she couldn't resist, she added, "We'll both meet with you. Part of my responsibility is to go along on all interviews."

If looks could kill, Sydney thought, as Macey shot daggers at her. But she was a professional and a graceful loser. For the moment. Still, the message in her eyes was clear: this was far from over.

"Whatever you say." She patted Rick's cheek. "See you soon. If I don't hear from Sydney, I'll just have to hunt you down myself, right?"

She clacked across the floor on her high heels, ass wiggling in a blatant attempt at a tempting movement.

A huge bolt of jealousy stabbed through Sydney, so intense it nearly brought her to her knees. She wanted to scratch the woman's eyes out. Insinuate herself between the two of them and tell Macey *Hands off.*

Wait, wait, wait! Wasn't she the one who said they had to really cool it in public? And how could she be so jealous when they'd only had the one intense night together plus a lot of phone calls? They were still exploring their situation.

He can explore me anytime.

And that thought would easily get her in trouble.

It was a lot harder than she thought to maintain control, especially when sharks like Macey came cruising. The devil inside her wanted to haul him off to a dark corner, while the angel reminded her she had a lot of people looking over her shoulder on this gig—Butch, Linc, the media, the rest of the band.

Remember the gossipmongers, Sydney.

And that was a big dash of cold water. She didn't want to be one of those women who fucked their way through the industry. She wanted respect for her work. Well, she was getting it. But it wouldn't replace the erotic dreams that invaded her sleep every night.

She turned back to him, trying to figure out what to say next, and caught him studying her face for a long moment, something indefinable in his eyes. Heat stoked with a liberal mixture of emotions.

"Everything else aside, thanks for today, Sydney." His words were impersonal and polite in tone but the softness of his voice gave him away. "This was terrific. I was in awe of the way you handled everything. I know we clashed in the beginning and we've had our differences about—other things. But you were great today. And I saw Butch smile a lot, so he knows it, too."

"I appreciate that, Rick." She could be just as professional as he was. "The success of the band is my top priority."

"Mine, too." He paused. "So what's with Macey Shreiner? You'll take care of whatever she wants without getting me in trouble, right?"

She swallowed a grin, thinking, *That bitch.* "Oh, yes, I'll take care of Macey. You bet. I'll check with Linc and see when he thinks a one-on-one interview would do the most good. I need to make sure she understands the rules without ticking her off. She's a force to be reckoned with. If she takes to the band, she can give you a huge boost."

"I'll talk to you later?"

"Absolutely." Then she realized Danny had walked up to them and struggled to keep her tone professional and objective. "Feel free to call me anytime with any questions at all."

"I will. Thanks."

Danny gave her a strange look before he said, "Yeah, thanks from me, too. Syd. This was great."

But as she walked away, she heard him say to Rick, "Something going on between the two of you?"

She slowed down so she could hear the answer.

"Of course there is, you idiot. I'm the leader of this band and she's our publicity person. If nothing was going on between us, today would never have happened."

Grinning, she headed toward the back of the room. Well, she thought, he told the truth. No one could say he hadn't.

Chapter Nine

Rick headed to the private room where he'd told the band to wait for him. He wanted a few words with everyone before they split for the rest of the day. They still had a rehearsal schedule to firm up. Butch had indicated he needed to speak with them, too, about the logistics of the tour. But what Rick really wanted to do was bite nails. Or something else. Anything else. Maybe Sydney's nipples.

Whoa! He needed to get those thoughts out of his head when they were in public like this. Today, he could see her point of view with a lot more clarity. The two of them were working together. He was her client. And under scrutiny from every single person, from here on out. But they were adults, entitled to their own private lives as long as they kept them just that— private.

He wasn't sure he even understood his feelings for her himself, at least the passion of them. It reminded him of Emma and Marc, whose connection to each other was so vivid they lit up a room. He'd thought he had his priorities so organized—the band, the album, and the tour. But when something like this hit him in the face, he couldn't turn away from it. Could he?

The thing with Macey Whateverhernamewas had been interesting. He could see what Sydney meant about the vultures out there. He must have been very naive not to realize that some of the media people were nothing but groupies with power. He swallowed a grin when he thought of Sydney's assurance to Macey she'd be along on all interviews.

Macey aside, he had the distinct feeling something was bugging Sydney, and he was pretty sure it wasn't him. This thing with Sydney was so strange to him and new, he hadn't yet figured out how to read her emotions. She had said one of these times they'd have to tell each other their life stories but he wondered if she'd let out all her hidden secrets. Give him a clue as to what drove her in this business and what made her so uncertain about relationships.

Maybe Emma had an idea what it was. She and Sydney had hit it off. Marc had even mentioned at rehearsal he'd urged Emma to call her, maybe have coffee with her.

Wound up in his own thoughts, he forgot to watch where he walked and bumped into Marc, standing just inside the doorway.

"Whoa!" Marc chuckled. "Didn't your mother tell you to pay attention to where you put your feet?"

Rick held up his hands. "Sorry. Just...thinking about stuff."

"Yeah?" Marc studied his face. "Should I take a guess at what this 'stuff' is?"

"No. Don't worry. Everything's fine."

"Yeah? Then how come—"

"Hey. Sorry I took so long." Butch hustled into the room, interrupting whatever Marc planned to say.

For which Rick was grateful.

"Hey, Butch." He managed a smile. "What's your real take on how it went in there today?"

"Better than I hoped." The manager grinned at everyone. "Tomorrow you'll wake up to a lot of buzz about the band. I mean *a lot*. Even more than I expected." He looked at each of them in turn. "You did good up there today. Every one of you. You guys have sharpened your sound and you handle yourselves well. I don't like to make promises I can't keep, but I have a very good feeling about this tour."

"We won't let you down," Rick told him. "We appreciate the faith you have in us and the commitment you've made. All the work that's gone into this."

"I think a lot of the credit has to go to Sydney Alexander." Again he looked at each of them. "Syd's been with Full Moon for eight years, cut her teeth with some of their toughest clients. She's making this happen for you. Don't ever forget that."

"But if you hadn't signed us, none of this would be going on," Danny put in.

"And I signed you because I know you have what it takes." Butch shoved his hands in his pockets. "I know you've done all your own equipment handling and relied on the clubs where you play to handle the sound for you. That changes now."

"Because we're not in a club anymore." Danny nodded.

"Right. The tour starts in ten days. The song will hit the airwaves and be up for downloads two days before that. I want one more session at the theater then we'll change the rehearsal site." He turned to Rick again. "Tomorrow I'm sending a couple of guys to your rehearsal. Mickey Farentino and Gordo Herman. Mickey will be your road manager. He's one of the best in the business." He grinned. "I stole him back from another band. A story for some late night chatter. Ditto for Gordo, for your sound. I assume you all know how having a road crew works?"

Rick nodded. "Yeah, of course we do. Not that we've ever been able to afford one."

"These guys know what they're doing," Butch assured him. "They'll come to the rehearsal, listen to you, get camera shots of all your equipment, and make up a list. You'll use Deep Blue River's sound equipment at the concerts, but Gordo is assigned exclusively to you."

"If he hasn't worked with us before, how will he know the best way to mix us?" Marc wanted to know.

"That's why we'll change the location. Tomorrow, Gordo will listen to you at the theater and make notes while Mickey familiarizes himself with your equipment. The day after that, he'll show up with a crew to move everything to where Deep Blue River is practicing. They'll get you set up and you'll have a week for him to work with you before we break it down."

"Do we need to get a truck?" Garrett asked.

Butch grinned. "That's what your road manager does. He'll take care of everything. He's got the tour dates, so he'll handle all your hotel reservations, too. You just have to show up where he tells you to."

Danny grinned. "Like having our own personal assistant."

"He's a lot more than that," Rick pointed out. "He can make or break the tour so we better be sure to treat him good. And pay attention."

Butch scrolled through some notes on his phone. "I thought about a bus for this tour, but we'll go with a luxury van. Comfortable for traveling and, with a fairly short tour, I think it will work the best. So one of the guys will drive the van and another one will drive the truck. Mickey will probably ride with you. Listen to everything he says and you won't go wrong."

Rick cleared his throat. "I want you to know how much we appreciate all this."

"You'll earn it." Butch nodded solemnly. "Let's talk about merchandise. The same crew that handles sales at concerts for Deep Blue River will handle yours. But I always give the band an accounting after each stop. The numbers help me analyze the impact on the crowd. Plus you get a percentage of gross."

Rick had been surprised to see that in the contract. He'd figured they'd have to prove themselves before they got to that point.

"Mickey will schedule your soundchecks," Butch continued, "so you and the River don't conflict. You need anything, he's your go-to guy." He made another note then put his phone away. "Sydney Alexander will travel with us to handle the media at every stop."

Rick stiffened and didn't realize he'd made some strange sound until Butch looked up from his phone.

"That a problem, Rick? I thought the two of you fixed

whatever needed fixin'.'"

"Yes. We're fine. No problem." The problem belonged to him and his dick. And an emotion that he had yet to put a name to. Working with her every day would put a strain on his self-discipline—on hers, too, he was sure—but somehow they'd manage. They had to. Because it was clear to him now he didn't plan to give up either her or the band.

"Good. Okay. She'll be by tomorrow to go over the rest of her plan with you. Other than that, we're good. Oh." He snapped his fingers. "One more thing. Mickey's got cash for you so you guys will have some pocket money. Rooms and meals will be paid for with a credit card or billed to me, but you should have walking-around money. And don't worry." He grinned. "It comes out of your income. I may be kind, but not stupid."

He shook hands with each of them then left.

"Wow!" Emma looked at them wide-eyed from the from the now-cleared lunch table where she sat. "It's really happening, guys."

"You coming along for the ride, Emma?" Danny wanted to know. "We can make room for you in the van, right, Rick?"

"I wish."

"She can't give up her day job just yet," Marc told them.

Everyone knew how meeting Marc had turned Emma's life around for her. She was still working for a textbook publisher editing manuscripts, but her real dream was to be a published romance author. Marc encouraged her to move forward with it. Now her first completed and polished manuscript was with an editor and they were waiting for a yes or no. Even if she was contracted, she'd need a few under her belt before quitting.

"We hope our share of the income from the tour, the record sales, and the merchandise will be enough to offset the loss of her salary," he added. "We'll see how it goes."

"But I'll be there for the weekend dates," she assured them. "We've been saving for plane fare."

Rick hated to admit how envious he was when he looked at

the two of them. Marc was his best friend. Had been for years. He was delighted the two had found each other and wished them happiness. It was just.... That's what he wanted with Sydney. God, could It really happen for them?

All the other women he'd met had been easy to walk away from, some more so than others. Not that he just tossed them aside. He was better than that. His mother and sister had taught him respect for women. But they knew the score from the beginning and they were fine with a temporary situation that had no future.

But if he looked at the truth, he'd never had the depth of feeling for any of them that he had for Sydney Alexander. He still had no idea where the hell it came from, out of the blue, when he was so determined not to let stuff like this complicate his life. One minute they were at each other's throats, the next tearing their clothes off and burning up the sheets. And imprinting themselves on each other.

He'd have to hold his shit together. He had a responsibility to the band, as he reminded himself one more time. But Jesus! How did he stop wanting her? Needing her? And not let anyone know about it.

"I can't believe how the media ate it up today," Danny said. "I mean, they weren't just being polite."

Rick laughed. "Don't get too full of yourself yet, Danny Boy. We haven't even heard the starter's gun yet."

"The T-shirts really were killer," Garrett commented. "Super smart of Sydney to have us wear them."

"It was a good idea," he agreed. "I know in the beginning I gave her a hard time about some of the stuff she wanted. But things have turned out well, and we've found common ground."

Marc lifted an eyebrow. A grin teased one corner of his mouth. "Yeah?"

"Yeah. We've figured out an easy give and take here. She worked her ass off to make today a success and we need to recognize that. Give her credit, you know?"

"Oh, yeah." Marc had a devilish glint in his eyes. "We sure

do. Common ground."

Rick just shook his head. He'd talk to Marc later.

"Okay," he told the band. "Tomorrow, same time as usual. If you've got any questions for the road manager or sound guy, write them down so we look organized. We don't want anything to slip through the cracks. Meanwhile, we rocked it, so go home or go out and enjoy the day."

They all walked out to the parking lot together. Rick lagged behind the others. He knew he should leave but for some reason his feet wouldn't take him to his car. Was he waiting to see if Sydney was still here? How dumb was that?

Get out of here, idiot. She's long gone.

But maybe we can wait until everyone's left and then—

And then nothing. Be smart. Go home. Call her.

He was a mass of conflicting emotions. A relationship bordering on deep was so new to him, especially one that had raced full tilt out of the gate. But Jesus! She just did it to him. Inside and out. On the one hand he wanted everyone to know this smart sexy woman was his. Had chosen to be with him. On the other he could appreciate her point of view, especially after the episode with Macey Whatever.

Meanwhile, he couldn't spend the rest of the day standing in the parking lot.

He unlocked his pickup and climbed into the cab, shoved the key into the ignition. Then he leaned back in his seat and drew in a long breath. Stupid jerk that he was, he hadn't washed the truck since the night Sydney rode in it and it still held faint traces of her scent.

He closed his eyes and visualized her as she was today, the cool professional. So smart. So sharp. Herding the chicks, as it were, so they all got fed, and doing it so well. In the midst of the controlled chaos he'd had to admire how smoothly she handled everything. Even that hungry bitch Macey Whoever. *Thank you, Sydney, for taking care of that.* No way was he going to be alone with that female.

Sydney was the first woman he'd ever met who could get

both his cock and his heart in a twist. He wanted to call her and ask if he could come over. Celebrate with her. Have some awesome sex! But he had promised his family a blow by blow and he knew they hoped he'd come by for dinner.

But later, afterward, he'd give her a call and listen to her warm voice. And imagine her naked in his arms. At least they could have that.

CS

Sydney leaned back in her chair and stretched out her arms, twisting to work the kinks out of her neck and back. A smart woman would be out celebrating today's success with friends at a familiar bar, toasting the event and praising the band. Of course, Sydney had no friends—pause to allow one short pity party—because she'd spent her entire adult life, from her freshman year in college, focused on only one thing—success. Achievement, to show her aunt she could rise to the top of her chosen profession, one Janine scorned as a "puff job." There hadn't been time to make friends. She had to learn everything she could, be the very best at each step of the way. That's how she got the internship and then earned agent status.

Since she seldom saw her aunt, she needed to find some way to pass along the news of her rise in the industry.

So, okay, no celebration with friends. She had gone home with plans to take a hot bath and open a bottle of wine. Toast herself and relive the high points of the afternoon.

She'd gone home, all right, but only to change into jeans and a shirt and get back to the office. Sydney was scheduled to meet with the band again tomorrow, to go over the results from today and discuss the next phase of the campaign. She hoped for a lot of coverage. Some of it would take a few days to emerge, but the blogs would be pretty responsive and there would be some local television coverage plus the area papers. Now she needed to make notes on the next stage of the campaign.

As she sat at her desk with her notes in front of her, she heard footsteps in the hall outside her office. She managed to sweep everything into a folder as Linc stepped into her office.

"Don't you have a home, Syd?" He shook his head. "And I thought *I* was the workaholic around here. Get out of here. Better yet, go out and celebrate with your friends. You did an all-star job today."

"Thanks." She smiled. "It felt really good."

"Have you checked your messages? My voice mail is full of people who think they can go directly to me to get some face time with the band. I forwarded them all to Renee. She'll send them a mass e-mail to let them know them you're the point person. Period."

"Good." Renee would see that everything got to its proper place and would keep tabs to make sure nothing fell through the cracks. "Thank you. And no, I hadn't checked. I guess I didn't think anyone would be calling the office this soon."

Or my cell. Damn, Sydney. Bad form there.

"I also left her a message you need new business cards ASAP. She can send one of the interns to get them done at the Quik Copy place in the morning while we order some better quality."

"But I haven't used up the ones I have yet," she pointed out.

"These will have your cell number on them. You can't keep writing it on agency cards like you did today. It looks too temporary and you're anything but." He leaned against the doorjamb. "You'll be on the move a lot from now on, kiddo. People will want to get hold of you instantly."

"I haven't really thanked you yet for this opportunity."

He laughed. "You may not be thanking me when you've had your fill of sleepless nights and bad food." Then he sobered. "Seriously. You earned it. So now, get out of here and enjoy your success. There won't be a lot of time for partying from here on in."

"I will. And thanks again."

An hour later she was curled up on her couch with a glass of wine and Chinese takeout, feeling sorry for her solitude and wishing she and Rick could be together. He had told her about his plans with his family, plans that couldn't include her. At least, not yet. So here she sat, alone, wishing for something she'd never thought she'd want.

All these years while she'd put her plan for success together, while she'd compiled every bit of useful information, molded her ideas into a cohesive project, she'd had her eyes on one goal. Creating the image of a band that would take it to the top. She wanted her name synonymous with the band's success. Didn't have time for entanglements of any kind.

Oh, she'd had a few casual relationships, but the guys always knew the rules right from the start. Kind of a friends with benefits, thing. That was all she wanted. All she had time for. Then along came Rick Trajean, getting under her skin and aiming straight for her heart. And no matter how she tried, she could not get him out of her thoughts or her dreams.

Setting the glass of wine down on the end table, she leaned her head back and closed her eyes. Tried to clear her head of everything but the meeting with the band tomorrow. Wished Rick was here beside her. Unbidden, a tall, muscular man with smoldering dark eyes emerged as if from a cloud to take possession of her senses.

He bent low over her body, let his tongue take a slow glide over her lips. Lean fingers brushed the hair back from her face so he could look directly into her eyes. The hunger she saw in his, sent a drumbeat through her blood, made her nipples tingle and her breasts ache.

"So beautiful," he murmured. "So hot."

He trailed kisses onto her eyelids and along her cheekbones to the sensitive spot behind one ear. A tiny nip at her earlobe was like a lit match to her nerve endings. She reached for him to pull him down to her, but he banded her wrists with one hand, his mouth curved in a slow, deliberate, sensuous smile.

"Don't rush things, Syd. We're in no hurry here."

But she was. She definitely was. She wanted to tear off her robe, strip his clothes from him, and urge him to plunge his cock inside her. She writhed on the couch, trying to send him signals. He just gave a low, heated chuckle and shook his head.

"I'm taking my time here. I want to enjoy every inch of you."

Easing himself down beside her, he used his free hand to open her robe and pushed the silk fabric aside so his eyes could feast on her breasts. Sydney didn't think she'd ever seen such hunger in a man's eyes before. It made the muscles in her pussy clench with need and want.

So slowly she wanted to scream, he brushed the tips of his fingers across the upper swell of her breast. Little points of heat ignited wherever they touched. He pinched each nipple with the same deliberateness, tweaking them to send vibrations racing through her. She wanted to reach for him but he still held her hands in a firm grip over her head.

With slow deliberation he used his tongue to draw a line across the top swell of her beasts then repeated the motion. When he took one of her nipples in his mouth and closed his teeth over it very lightly, she nearly bowed off the couch. He sucked and nibbled until she was sure she would lose her mind. She let her legs fall apart, not caring how wanton she looked. She needed him to touch her. Everywhere. In all the right places. She'd never desired a man so.

His tongue was hot and wet as it licked across each nipple then down through the valley between her breasts to her navel. He drew a slow pattern around it before letting his tongue delve into the furled flesh. She wanted to fist his thick hair and press his head lower, but he still held her wrists captive.

When he shifted so his head was between her legs, he released her hands, and she reached for him. The slide of his tongue along the length of her slit made her buck up against him. Every nerve was on fire and sizzling. The tremors in the walls of her cunt vibrated out to the rest of her body. He tasted *and teased until she thought she'd lose her mind.*

"More," she cried. "Please. More."

But he lifted his head a moment to look at her and she saw the glint of the devil in his eyes.

"I'm going to devour you." His voice was low and rough. "Every. Single. Inch."

And then, as his lips closed over her throbbing clit, he slid two fingers deep inside her pussy, moving them so—

Ouch!

Sydney's eyes flew open.

Holy! Damn! Shit!

Her fingers were deep in her cunt. She'd thrust so hard against them she'd fallen off the couch and hit her head on the coffee table, banging her knees.

Ohmigod!

She pulled her fingers from her body with a quick movement and looked around as if she thought someone watched. But she was alone in her apartment, no Rick, just another intensely erotic dream. She wanted to erase the entire thing from her brain but unfortunately her body screamed for satisfaction. She bolted for her bedroom, flopped back onto her bed, and grabbed her favorite toy from the nightstand drawer. With her legs bent and spread wide, she eased the dildo into her body. She was so dripping wet she didn't even need lube to ease its passage.

The thick vibrator glided in as if the walls of her cunt were made of glass. In seconds she had inserted it all the way and turned it on to its highest setting. As she held it in place with one hand, she used the fingers of the other to rub her clit, faster, faster, faster.

She closed her eyes and bam! There he was, a tantalizing image. His sexy face and chocolate-colored eyes, all framed with dark hair. The memory of his mouth on her, his tongue, His...his...his....

An orgasm roared through, convulsing her, She shook from

head to toe with tremendous force, the tremors so intense they squeezed the air from her lungs and made her heart nearly beat its way out of her chest. At last the quakes subsided and she threw her arms to the side, gulping in great lungfuls of air and trying to control the erratic thumping of her pulse. She left the dildo in place while the last little quivers in the walls of her pussy faded away.

And was hit with an unassailable fact.

It isn't the same.

No, it wasn't. The toy was a poor substitute for the feel of Rick Trajean's thick, hard cock inside her, driving her to the edge of ecstasy and over. Rick, with whom she'd had the most amazing sex in the world. Ever. Sex that rocked her world and had her dreaming about it like an addict.

Sex that was beyond the physical. That was filled with raw emotion.

An emotion that pierced her heart.

When her breathing and her heartbeat slowed to a manageable rate, she slid the vibrator from her pussy and forced herself to sit up. Her robe hung open from her shoulders, the fabric partway down her arms. Her hands shook as she drew the garment back around her body slick with perspiration.

The Plan was still at the top of her bucket list, but holy mother! This man had exploded into her life, blinding her senses and capturing her heart. They had yet to give voice to their emotions, or spend more than the one night together but the truth was inescapable. She continued to be amazed he felt the same way. And it scared her. But she couldn't ignore the truth of the matter.

She was hooked on Rick Trajean, no question about it.

Tomorrow she'd meet with Lightnin' again and go over the next items on her agenda. She needed to be cool, clearheaded, and self-assured. And not give off signals others could read. She hoped Rick could do the same. The fact that the intensity of this was new to both of them was both a treasure and a pitfall because they hadn't the experience to pull it off. They'd just have to be clever.

I'm smart. So is Rick. We can do this.

With a sigh she pushed herself off the bed and walked into the bathroom. She dropped the dildo into the sink to clean it later and turned on the shower as hot as she could stand it. Maybe she could scrub the stamp of his body from her skin enough to wash away the dreams.

The problem was, she didn't seem to be able to wash him from her mind.

Chapter Ten

"So you're good with everything?" Mickey Farentino asked.

Rick looked around at the other members of the band. "Yes. All good. God, more than good. Thanks for this."

They had finished reviewing the tour schedule and Mickey handed each musician a thin packet containing the logistics for the band and how he would make things happen. To Rick it looked as if all they had to do was rehearse and perform. And stay out of trouble.

One of the first things Butch Meredith told them was his bands walked the straight and narrow. No drugs. No excessive alcohol. No alcoholic beverages on stage. No wild behavior. Crowd control backstage so the groupies didn't get out of hand.

"I'll bring industry professionals and friends backstage from time to time to watch from the wings," he reminded them over and over. "We have the after-parties. I don't expect to have anything to hide from people."

Rick had assured the man from the beginning they knew how to behave. He might have to ride herd a little more on Danny and Garrett but he'd given them "the talk" and they knew what was expected of them. They had all worked too hard for this break to screw it up.

"Thank Butch," Mickey said now. "I've been with him for ten years. He lets you know up front what's expected. You put up or shut up. You screw up, you're gone. So. Questions?"

"I have one," Danny said.

"Let's hear it."

"If you're so good, how come you aren't still with the band you signed on for?"

"Danny," Rick began.

Mickey held up a hand. "It's okay. And that's a legitimate question. I've kind of become the go-to road manager for new bands on his client list. Teach them the ropes, so to speak, until they know all the procedures in their sleep. Then Butch will look for someone who's experienced to take over and run with you for the long haul. And," he added, "you'll have input there."

"Okay, then." Danny grinned. "I can get on board with that."

"Then let's get on with the rehearsal. Gordo—" he pointed to the man sitting behind and to the right of him "—will take notes on your sound while I do the same with the equipment you use. When we switch rehearsal places, you'll be using Deep Blue River's sound system. Butch has worked with their sound man for a long time. He catches on to new bands real quick so it's just a matter of plugging your stuff in and you're set."

"You can expect a lot of stops and starts the first time through," Gordo interjected. "Until you and I are both satisfied. That work okay?"

Everyone nodded.

Rick stood up. "Then let's get to it."

Mickey requested they play the set for the tour straight through the first time so Gordo could get a feel for the sound. He could note any changes of equipment while they played—different guitars, for example. They were almost finished when Rick happened to glance up and see Sydney walking down the aisle toward them. Only discipline kept his fingers from stumbling on the strings of his guitar.

She slipped into a seat about five rows behind Mickey and Gordo, set her briefcase next to her, and extracted a folder. Then she turned her full attention to the band. Sat back to listen. For the first time, he saw a look of intense concentration on her face, almost as if she studied the sound. Analyzed the words. Put it together in her brain.

Yes!

This was what he wanted, what he'd tried to tell her she needed to do. Only enormous self-discipline saved him from jumping down from the stage and running over to plant a kiss on those lips he dreamed about every night.

Jesus! He had it really bad.

They finished the set as usual with "Music Lady," Marc's voice true and full on the vocals. The sudden quiet in the auditorium was a sharp contrast to the pounding notes of the music. For a moment no one said a word. Rick tensed, waiting for a comment from either Mickey or Gordo. When they took a minute to confer with each other, his nerves decided to do a tap dance. Did they hate it? Surely they'd heard the music already. Butch would have seen to that. Would they have signed on if they didn't like it?

Sydney stayed in her seat, watching Mickey and Gordo intently.

Then Mickey stood up and walked toward the stage, a big grin on his face.

"Top notch," he told them.

And Rick let out a breath.

"I mean great. The videos didn't fully capture the electricity of your sound or its distinctive quality."

"You guys will be a snap to mix," Gordo called out. "Looking forward to it."

"Thanks," Rick said. "Appreciate it."

Mickey shook his head. "Don't think I'm just saying nice words. You guys have something very distinctive. A quality sound. I'll have to thank Butch for this gig."

He chatted with the band for a few more moments before he and Gordo left. They reminded Rick they'd be back later to pick up all the equipment and transport it to the new rehearsal spot then headed up the aisle to the exit.

Sydney still remained in her seat, waiting for everyone on

stage to put away their equipment before she rose and headed down to the front of the theater. Today she wore black slacks that hugged her hips and a long-sleeved blouse the same shade as her eyes. Her hair was clipped back as usual. Although it accentuated the planes of her face, he really loved it loose and spread over his pillow. Or curtaining the two of them and feeling it whisper against him as she leaned over him and—

"Rick?"

He was suddenly aware she was speaking to him. He still held one of his guitars and moved it in front of his body to hide the erection that sprang up at the sight of her.

Damn!

"Sorry," he said. "My mind was someplace else."

"I'm sure it is." She smiled. "I have some more things to go over with you. Your call if you want me to work through you or include the entire band in this."

He paused with the guitar still in his hands, his body immobile as he ran the suggestion through his mind. "Let's have everyone. Whatever you have affects all of us equally." Safety in numbers. This keeping it under wraps was tough and he needed the insulation. From the look in her eyes, she had the same problem. A thrill skittered through him.

"Okay, then."

They gathered on the stage where the seating could be more informal. Rick deliberately chose to sit where he could see her rather than beside her. The eye contact between the two of them would surely send signals to the others. Even so, he was hyperaware of her presence and of the little invisible shocks that ran up and down his skin. When everyone was ready, he nodded for her to get started.

Sydney wet her lips and took a deep breath, hoping to calm her jitters. At four that morning she'd given up the possibility of sleep, dressed and drove to the office. She trolled the Internet again and again as she waited with impatience for each of the blogs and online publications to go live. The butterflies were doing a tango in her stomach and she was so edgy she could barely swallow the cup of coffee she made. When the first results of yesterday's event appeared she was ready to dance around the office.

Linc had stuck his head in around eight on the way to an appointment of his own. "Do you ever sleep, Sydney?" He chuckled. "Never mind. Renee said we got great coverage of yesterday's mass interview. I looked at some of the stuff myself. Good work."

"Thank you."

"You're meeting with the guys today, right?"

"Right after Mickey and Gordo. Did you get a chance to look at the folder I left for you?"

She'd placed one hand in her lap, beneath her desk, and crossed her fingers. If Linc hated, it her whole program would fall apart.

"No, but I trust your judgment. That's why you got the solo gig. Good luck."

Now, with the band gathered around her on the stage, she reached into her briefcase and took out several articles clipped together. "First of all, I have some things to share with you that I think will put everyone in a good mood." She looked at each of the guys one at a time. "Did any of you check the blogs this morning, or any of the Web sites on the list I gave you?"

Marc chuckled. "Emma said she would as I was headed out. I told her I'd call after rehearsal. I didn't want to know what people said beforehand. If it was bad, it would be a downer, and if it was good, we'd be too distracted."

"You have nothing to worry about. I knew it yesterday and now I have proof." She unclipped the articles. "I printed these off the Internet this morning."

Rick held out his hand. "What are they?"

She passed them over. "Take a look. Go on."

The moment their skin touched, her pussy clenched, her blood heated, and only iron determination kept her hands from

139

shaking. Good lord! She made a huge production of organizing her notes so she could avoid looking directly at him.

"Holy shit!" Excitement edged Rick's voice. "Look at these, guys." He passed the clippings around so everyone could see them.

Sydney waited for their reaction as long as she could. "Well?"

When Rick turned and looked at her, a wide grin spread across his face. "Hot damn! They liked us."

"Well of course they did." She laughed. "And they're going to like you even more." She held up her cell phone so everyone could see her list of messages. "I've been getting calls all morning for more individual interviews. For access on the tour. For any information I can give them."

Danny threw back his head, shouted, "All right!" and pumped his fist in the air.

Sydney waited while they read all the articles, thrilled at their excitement. "Okay. So." She closed her cell and from her briefcase extracted sheets with the logo on them in different sizes. "I want you all to have a copy of this. Get an idea of the many ways the art can be used beside T-shirts. Can holders, patches, key chains, phone cases, all kinds of things. They've already been ordered from our merchandise suppliers. The idea will be to get as much product as possible into as many hands as possible."

"Who takes care of that?" Danny asked. "Do you?"

She shook her head. "We have people at the agency who process all this. They know how much of everything to order for each show, depending on the size of the audience. Also, our web person will put up a site and people can order through that."

They had a lot of back and forth about what went on the site, would they have a Facebook page linked to it—yes—and a Twitter feed—yes. Who would monitor it and how that would happen.

"So we really don't have any input into what goes out over the Internet from those sites, right?" Rick frowned. "I'm not sure I like that."

The reaction wasn't unexpected. He was, after all, the group leader and the guys looked to him for validation of everything. Their personal situation, whatever it was, had nothing to do with business decisions.

"I'm going to give you a list of some of the links you can take a look at," she told him. "The names on this list are bands we rep who are clients of the agency. We do their social media and you can get a feel for how they answer comments and questions. "Full Moon does this for all of its clients, as a matter of fact, and it's worked out really well. If you have anything special you want us to say, just let me know and I'll take a look at it."

"Wait a minute." Rick scrubbed his chin. "I'm not sure I like something so personal being taken out of our hands completely. If we have fans who Like us and comment, they want to talk to us, not some nameless geek."

Sydney lifted a large envelope. "Like I said, take a look at the links on this list." She handed a sheet to each of them. "Tell me what you don't feel comfortable with and we'll work to improve it. But your time is going to be taken up with rehearsing, performing, and interviews. There are only so many hours in a day. And it won't be some nameless geek. It will be me."

Rick shifted in his seat to look at her. "You? But when will you have the time?"

"I'm taking both my laptop and my iPad with me. I can work on it during downtime and it will also give you a way to see what's going on in real time. Does that work for you?"

His smile went right to her heart. "We'll give it a shot."

"Good. Remember, if you do have a problem with anything, we'll do our best to take care of it."

"What's next?" Rick pointed to the envelope she was still holding.

"Well. I've spent a lot of time studying photos of similar bands. How they appear on stage. How they present themselves to the audience. What sets the really successful ones apart."

"Hold it." Rick held up a hand. "I thought it was their music that did that."

She looked at each of them in turn. "A band can have the greatest music in the world, but if they don't make a visual statement, they might as well just be a studio band and create albums. They won't get the excitement of the crowd, the thrill of the sold-out performance. The presence on every video platform. Please, guys. I've spent a lot of time preparing for just what we have here. For a band who had the right kind of music that I could push to the top. Can you try to trust me on this a little?"

Rick looked at the others.

Marc nodded. "She's right, bro. Let's hear her out. If we hate what she's got, maybe there's room for compromise. We signed with Butch because we trust him. We have to give Sydney and Full Moon the same opportunity."

She tried to send him a silent message.

This is part of what we talked about, remember? Give and take.

She could almost hear him thinking.

"It's nothing extreme," she added. "I promised you and I heard what you said. Take a second and look and listen to my reasoning."

"Okay." He held out a hand. "Let's see what you've got."

Sydney handed out photos and drawings and tried to explain her concept. The significance of wearing the T-shirts on stage. Suggestions on how to add eye-catching impact to the performance on stage. Why the sparkle was important. All the things that could emphasize the name of the band and impress it into people's minds.

"We're creating a brand here," she said, trying to gauge everyone's reaction. "It's important to get it out there right from the start."

She waited, barely breathing while each of them studied the material. And, of course, they looked at Rick to see his reaction.

"Okay. Look." She pointed to the clippings. "We've got a good head start with these. Generated some excitement. Wearing the T-shirts was a good move, even though you might not have thought so at first. But now everyone wants one and when they write about the band that's what will be in their minds. So can you just think about some of this other stuff?"

"Okay," he said, at last. "But nothing extreme. Nothing I think alters who or what the band is. Agreed?"

"Let's wait until opening night and reevaluate," she told him. "You can be sure I'll always do my best to keep your objections in mind. Oh, and the clippings are yours. We have a service that takes care of that for our files. I'll keep on top of it, though, so you get them when they're fresh."

Sydney stuffed everything else back in her briefcase, aware on some level that the band members were headed toward the back of the stage. Except Rick. When she turned, he was right in front of her and she bumped into him. They were so close she could almost count his eyelashes. Her heart started its usual rhumba.

"I'm not being a hardass, okay?" His voice was soft and more relaxed than she expected.

Their gazes locked, and Sydney couldn't break away. At last she forced herself to blink, to focus on the business at hand. "I understand. Neither am I. Together we'll figure out what's best." She gripped the handle of her briefcase hard, the strap biting into her hand. "If I guess wrong, make the wrong decisions, it hurts both of us."

"I know," he assured her. "This is all so new to us. We've always done everything ourselves."

"And now you don't have to," she reminded hm.

"Thank you. From all of us." For a moment she thought he was going to forget where they were and kiss her. Instead, he gave her a wink and then turned back to the others.

Chapter Eleven

The excitement blazing in the air was almost visible. This was it. The big night. The kickoff. Everything would coalesce into the next ninety minutes on stage. For Lightnin', that time was reduced to thirty minutes, but it was their half hour to make it all work.

Wearing her permanent badge on a lanyard around her neck, Sydney leaned against a big, hard-sided travel case in the wings, in an attempt to stay out of everyone's way. The roadies still fiddled with the setup, making sure the band had bottles of water handy, the mics in the right places. Up on the catwalk at the back of the stage, the light crew was adjusting the equipment. Deep Blue River's roadies and guests were still in the band's dressing room. Sydney didn't expect to see them until Lightnin' finished their set.

Business was brisk in the lobby as people devoured the merchandise, for Lightnin' as well as Deep Blue River. The single had debuted two days before and, thanks to the early press, was getting great airplay and generating a lot of chatter. The office was keeping track of the downloads and so far they had racked up a significant number for an unknown band. At least, unknown outside the local area.

From beyond the heavy curtain, the sounds of the audience filtered back, a steady hum as people found their seats and greeted friends. Sydney was glad they were opening here, in their hometown, kicking off before a friendly audience. Every media person of note had a ticket and a pass for the after-party, thanks to Linc and Butch. Sydney had followed up with additional phone calls to her own contacts, just to add a personal invite and make sure they knew she was Lightnin's point person.

Okay, so most of the crowd tonight was here to see Deep Blue River. Linc handled them himself and had made them into an international household name. If Sydney did her job properly, it would soon be Lightnin' they clamored for.

Despite the fact she'd had very little rest, she was jazzed to the max. At three in the morning, she'd given up on sleep, made a pot of coffee, and sat down in the kitchen to go over her lists once more. She and Rick had managed to keep things professional between them despite being together every day, despite the fire that simmered between them in a steady, slow boil. They each did their own thing but whenever circumstance threw them together, like steel to magnets, their eyes sought each other and *wham!*

Now she took a long look at the band as they assumed their place on stage. With only marginal grumbling, they'd agreed to her jazzing up their stage presence a little. The T-shirts she'd given them had a scant dusting of glitter added to the lightning bolt. When the lights hit, she knew she'd been right to insist on it. Marc wore the leather vest she'd sent over and she thought it was perfect for him. Danny had opted for the leather pants.

"The ladies will love the way it cups my ass." He grinned.

Rick had swatted him on the back of the head.

All in all, she thought they looked incredible.

Especially Rick. The sight of him made her heart turn over.

Ohmigod, Sydney. Control yourself, okay? You were the one who set the parameters. So follow them.

Easier said than done.

She remembered the story Emma and Marc told her about the night they met.

"We took one look at each other," Emma said, "and that was

it."

From then on there wasn't anyone else for either of them.

But their situation was different. She and Rick had so much to lose if they gave in to this cauldron of desire and emotions bubbling between them. Accepting their connection was more than just sex was a big step for both of them. Hiding it from others grew more difficult each day.

But thank the Lord today had been busy and tonight insane. Setup. Soundcheck. Get the food delivered from the catering truck. Check off the stuff in the dressing room. Calm the guys even while she was a bundle of nerves herself. Monitor the Internet, especially Twitter, on her iPad. And, holy cow! People were going crazy with the tweets. Sydney hoped they increased tenfold after tonight.

All the family members had special seats in the audience, although Rick had asked if Meredith could watch from the wings. The almost-college girl hopped with excitement. A shorter, slender version of Rick, she had the same dark hair, brooding eyes, and infectious grin. Easy to like on sight. Sydney found a good place for her, sitting on top of one of the equipment cases. She could see everything and still be out of the way.

"I think I'm more nervous than the guys are." Emma's words brought Sydney back to reality. Marc's fiancée moved up beside her, hands clasped tightly together. Clipped to her top was the backstage pass Sydney had given her.

"You'll be fine." Sydney wasn't much of a touchy-feely person but she gave Emma a reassuring hug. "They'll be fine."

The media had gone to town on the Marc-Emma thing. Who didn't like a good love story, especially when it resulted in a song? Every column and blog had made mention of it and calls came in from the media at future tour stops requesting interviews with the couple. Marc was hesitant to take any attention away from the band. Sydney convinced him the story would bump up record sales and that was good for everyone.

When band emerged from the dressing room and took up

their spots on the stage, the butterflies in Sydney's stomach turned into the thundering hooves of horses. Linc and Butch were there with smiles of reassurance.

"This is it," Butch said, standing next to Sydney.

"Yes." She managed a smile, even though her insides were now jelly. "It sure is." She wondered if she'd ever reach a point where she could be as relaxed as he and Linc looked.

"Don't worry, Sydney." The manager squeezed her shoulder. "Your guys wouldn't be out there if I didn't think they could do it."

She hoped her brainstorm for the closing number paid off. Emma wasn't someone who was comfortable in the spotlight, but she'd do anything to help Marc. When Sydney had explained the impact her idea could have, they'd finally agreed to it. Now she just had to wait and see if she was right.

I am. I know I am.

The band went through its final tune-up before taking their spots. Then Rick nodded to the guy manning the curtain and hit the downstroke on his guitar.

Here we go.

The spotlights hit the stage, the band jumped in with a hot version of "Take the High Road," and they were off to the races.

Afterward, Sydney wasn't sure she even remembered all the details. She did know the set was flawless, the crowd was screaming, and the band was definitely on its game.

But all of that burbled along in the back of her mind as she listened to the music and the roar of the crowd. She couldn't believe how fast the thirty minutes went by. She had to check her watch in disbelief when she heard Rick announce the last number.

"We want to thank all of you for the great reception tonight," he told the audience. "We love you all. I hope you've downloaded and requested our brand-new single that has been out for two days. We're going to close with it because it's a special song to us. I'm sure you've read about it online and in the newspapers and magazines. Our bass player, Marc Malone, wrote it for his very special lady, who is here with us tonight. Emma, this will always be for you."

He counted off the time with his foot and they broke into "Music Lady." Sydney had heard the song in rehearsal and on CD but there was something so emotional about the way they played it tonight. Noticing movement to her left, she saw the members of Deep Blue River and a smattering of friends had also gathered to watch the last tune. A nice gesture from them. She swallowed a smile of satisfaction as she saw them actually getting into the music.

Marc's delivery was perfect for the song. His deep voice blended flawlessly with Rick's mournful sound on lead guitar, his own bass providing a body-shaking bass platform.

Music playing, hips swaying, dance for me, Music Lady.

Body moving, hot and grooving, Music Lady.

Sweet and sexy, that's her style. Make her stay a while. Music Lady.

There she is, Music Lady.

All I want, all I need. Music Lady.

He looked straight at Emma, standing beside Sydney, hands gripped together in front of her.

One long underscoring note on the bass before the last line.

...And she lives in my heart forever, Music Ladyyyyyy.

There was dead silence in the arena for a long moment. Sydney bit her lip, hard, wondering if they'd made a bad choice in using it as the final song. But then everyone in the audience jumped to their feet, yelling and clapping. And screaming, "We want 'Music Lady.' 'Music Lady.' 'Music Lady.'"

Next to her, Deep Blue River and the friends who'd been in their dressing room clapped as well. One of the guys let out a piercing whistle. For a long moment, Sydney couldn't move, couldn't breathe. She remembered Linc saying she'd know when a band stood out from the crowd. The music would make every nerve in her body burst into flame. That's exactly what happened tonight.

"Marc's looking this way," someone beside her said, shouting to be heard over the noise of the crowd. "I think he wants something."

Marc was turned toward the wings, his arm outstretched, his hand pointed in Emma's direction.

This was when they'd find out if the little shtick she'd coached them through would do what she hoped.

Sydney turned to Emma. "Here we go. Take a deep breath. You can do this. I know you can. They'll love you."

"Are you sure?"

Sydney nodded. "Listen to them. They want you, kiddo. Go give them what they want." She took Emma's arm and guided her gently toward the stage. "They love the band, and they'll love you."

Tentatively, Emma walked out of the wings into the spotlight. The noise increased to a deafening roar and the applause thundered through the arena.

Marc glanced at Rick, who nodded, and then he put his arm around Emma.

"Here she is, folks. My very own 'Music Lady'."

Emma waved to everyone, smiling, and the noise grew even louder.

Sydney grinned so hard she thought her face would crack.

"Great touch," Butch whispered in her ear.

Marc tightened his arm around Emma even more and smiled at her then looked out at the audience.

"Okay, everyone. If y'all can quiet down a little, I'll do the last verse again."

Rick picked out the segue as the roar subsided to a dull hum, then silence. Marc added the bass foundation to the melody and looked at Emma he sang the last lines.

She brings the light into my life
And she lives in my heart forever, Music Ladyyyyyy.

As notes of the song died away Marc gave Emma a kiss so filled with emotion that Sydney had to fight both tears and jealousy. The audience clapped, stamped and screamed for more, chanting, "Lightnin'! Lightnin' Lightnin'!"

But at a signal from Butch, one of the roadies pulled the curtain, the stage lights dimmed, and the house lights came up for the brief time it would take to reset the equipment. They had thirty minutes to get it done, no matter how much the audience yelled. Roadies hustled to make the changes for both bands, two crews this time. The members of Lightnin' laughed and high-fived each other, Emma still glued to Marc's side. The leader of Deep Blue River made it a point to shake the hand of everyone in their opening act.

"Ohmigod!" Meredith squealed and ran to throw her arms around her brother.

Butch hugged the guys and slapped them on the back. "Damn hot," he shouted. "You smoked it."

A Full Moon intern came rushing back stage in the midst of everything.

"Mr. Forrester." She tugged on Linc's arm. "You won't believe it. The lines are so long for merchandise, I told Jim and Chris to lend a hand."

Linc looked at Butch and *they* high-fived each other.

Linc laughed and said, "Cha-ching!"

"Told you so," the manager said. "Call your supplier and have them get on the stick. We may run short on the next two stops, but I know they can get us the additional merchandise by the time we reach Tampa. Go on. For an order like this, they won't mind a late call."

Linc already had his cell phone out and scrolled through his contacts. Phone to one ear, finger to the other to block out sound, he walked away to a far corner of the area where the racket wasn't quite so loud.

Sydney stood where she was, trying to stay out of everyone's way, when Rick broke away from his sister, came over to her, and lifted her in a huge hug.

"What are you doing?" she whispered in his ear. "People are watching."

"Good. I want them to know Lightnin' loves its promo person. You rock, Syd." He pressed his mouth to her ear for a brief moment. "And we rock together."

Then he stepped back but he never took his eyes away from her, twin flames searing right to her core. "I guess I need to start listening to you more."

His gaze lingered on her face for a long moment, his eyes filled with so much hunger and emotion it, nearly brought her to her knees. Even as she hoped no one watched, all her erogenous zones did a happy dance. *Damn.* She forced herself to drop her gaze before they set the stage on fire.

"We'll work together," she told him, taking a step away in an attempt to maintain some semblance of professionalism. "Your music, my public relations input."

"That we will," he promised. "And then some." Then he released her, laughed, and headed back to the band.

But even with space between them, the heat lingered, the powerful emotions they felt palpable.

She hauled in a calming breath as she watched Linc stride back to her, giving her a thumbs-up.

"Can they do it in time?" she asked.

"For the kind of bucks involved? Are you kidding? They'll work around the clock. They'll call as soon as arrangements are made in Tampa."

"Good. That's good."

"You did a fantastic job, Sydney," he told her. "Well done. I gave them your cell number and told them to deal with you directly on the Lightnin' gear from now on. You'll need to coordinate with them about getting the stuff delivered to the arena. I texted you their number, also, although in this bedlam you probably can't hear your phone."

"Thank you." *Yes!* What an affirmation. She was indeed going to be in charge. At least as far as Lightnin' was concerned.

"Don't thank me. You earned it."

"Absolutely." Butch walked up to them and gave her a hug. "That thing with Marc and Emma at the end? Brilliant. I knew you were the right one to handle them."

"Yeah, thanks," Danny said, his words echoed by Garrett.

Emma gave her a warm hug. "They don't know how much they owe you," she whispered.

Butch began to herd everyone toward the back of the building. The Malones and the Trajeans, obviously good friends, smiled and laughed with the family members of the others. The buzz of conversation rose again when they reached the dressing room.

"We've got about twenty minutes before Deep Blue River goes on." Butch raised his voice enough to get everyone's attention. "I need to get back to the wings. So let's spend a few minutes celebrating then talk a little about the after-party." He looked over at Sydney. "What are you waiting for? This is your gig. Come on. Mix and mingle. The media's gonna descend after the show and we need to be ready."

You'll meet a band that will make every nerve in your body burst into flame.

The words kept echoing in Sydney's head as she gave everyone a rundown on what to expect then took time to work the room, chatting a few minutes with each excited visitor. Tonight was the culmination of years of basement rehearsals and grungy bars. Of scrimping and saving and pushing everything aside except the music. They all deserved to enjoy it.

Butch's security guards controlled access to the area. Only those with passes were even allowed through the stage door. Danny and Garrett had their flavors of the month with them and various family members shared in the excitement. Rick stood with Meredith and a woman Sydney guessed was his mother. The pride they felt was evident on their faces.

She was stunned when Rick motioned for her to join them. She couldn't very well say no without looking like an idiot. Wiping her damp palms on her slacks, she moved over to where they stood.

For a moment Rick looked as if he intended to put his arm around her. Then he let it drop to his side.

"Meredith, you've already met her. Mom, this is Sydney Alexander, the brains behind all this publicity."

Sydney gave a soft laugh. "I don't think I'd go that far. This was a team effort."

"Don't sell yourself short," Rick insisted. "We owe you a lot."

"Yes, they do," Meredith added. Excitement sparkled in her eyes. "We saw all the coverage after the media party. We're all so excited."

His mother, a very pretty woman with the same dark hair and eyes, gave her a warm smile. "This is a big night for everyone, Sydney. And we're all aware how hard you've worked for it."

"Thank you, but the real hook is their music. Nice meeting both of you. I hope we'll be seeing you again on the tour."

Rick's eyes had been on her the entire time she spoke with his family. These were sharp women, and Sydney didn't for a minute think they'd missed the vibes that flowed between them. But that was for Rick to handle. Meanwhile, she still had work to do.

She continued to make her way from one band member to another, greeted family members, congratulated each of the guys on the performance. She was chatting with Marc and Emma, who were surrounded by Marc's family, when Butch rapped on the wall to get their attention.

"Okay, listen up, everyone. First order of business. Lightnin'? You knocked them out tonight. You delivered the goods I knew you had when we signed the contract. So give yourselves a great big hand." He waited a moment until the applause died down. "Another big hand for Sydney Alexander. She's smart, she's savvy, and she knew what to do to make this work."

Sydney was embarrassed to feel the heat of a blush creep up her cheeks. She smiled and nodded.

"She'll take the lead at the after-party," he went on, "so whatever she says, you do it. I'm there as backup if anyone needs me."

Sydney had worked with Linc on the prep, checking and double-checking the guest list. As soon as Deep Blue River ended the show, the caterers would unload vans and set up in the backstage area, off to the side and away from where staff packed up the equipment and loaded it onto a truck. Full Moon interns would be stationed at the foot of one aisle to check off names and hand out badges.

"It's the same after-party procedure that was in place when you did your guest shot with Deep Blue River," Sydney told them. "Only this time there will be a bigger crowd, more media, representatives from the record label. Individuals Butch wants to have face time with you." She looked at each band member. "I'll introduce you to everyone, be sure you get to talk to the right ones, and help answer any questions. We don't expect a problem but if there is one, just holler for me."

"We'll let it run for one hour." Butch picked up the thread. He laid out some simple facts for them, what procedure to follow if a media person approached them, what to say. "Then we're all heading to the Riverside Hotel. You'll roll out early in the morning so get as much sleep as you can."

The agency had reserved rooms for both bands and the road crews at the downtown hotel. Sydney would be staying there, too, so she could be close to the airport and her very early flight. She would be setting up interviews for Lightnin' for after the next show and also double check the list for that after-party.

Everyone would leave in the morning to get to the next tour stop by early afternoon. They had to set up and be ready for a five o'clock soundcheck. Plans were for Gordo to drive in the luxury van while Deep Blue River would fly, as usual, on a charter. Butch had arranged for cars to pick everyone up tonight so there wouldn't be any juggling of vehicles. He had also hired security guards to stand watch over the equipment truck until the crews pulled out in the morning.

"Any questions?"

Everyone shook their heads.

Then Rick took a step forward. "We just want to thank you, Butch, for this opportunity."

"You earned it." He winked. "And I expect you to keep on

earning it. You should know we almost sold out of your merchandise after your set, so we'll double up the orders for the next stops. Good job, everyone. Let's go listen to the River."

Sydney didn't think she'd ever had a night like this one. Deep Blue River rocked it out, giving in twice to demands for encores. All the musicians were riding the high of a successful performance, the merchandise for both bands had nearly sold out, and the media jockeyed for face time with everyone at the after-party. They all wanted the best story on Deep Blue River's new album and Butch Meredith's hot new band.

Sydney was everywhere, supervising what "her guys" were doing, making sure they got to talk to the right people but not too long with any one person. There'd be time in the future for longer interviews, even if they were conducted by telephone. Tonight was just for sound bites. As she moved through the crowd, she saw Butch do the same thing for Deep Blue River. She envied how relaxed the other band was, how much this had become second nature to them. Soon, she thought. Soon Lightnin' would roll into it the same way.

Nerves danced in her skin when Butch brought two people over to her, one hefting a video camera on his shoulder, and introduced them as from TMZ. She was sure they came for the opening of the River's tour. But the fact they wanted footage on Lightnin' meant the band had caught their attention. She gathered all of them for the interview but had Rick do most of the talking. The interviewer also wanted a snippet from Marc about "Music Lady," then they were done.

"Will they let you know when this will be on?" Rick asked.

"The office will monitor it and text me. I'll make sure you all get to see it."

She couldn't wait to see it herself.

I'm on my way, Janine.

The record people were high-fiving each other, not just on the launch of Deep Blue River's new CD and the response to the songs tonight but also to the crowd's reaction to "Music Lady." Sydney saw Butch huddled with them, watched each of them make notes on their smartphones. Tomorrow they'd all check for increased airplay and downloads and an alert from *Billboard* where the song charted.

The energy was so intense, it snapped in the air. It was wild, it was crazy, and Sydney basked in the results of her work. Put forth every effort to make sure people who wanted to talk to Rick got two or three minutes of face time. Was jazzed by the current of excitement when a reporter chatted with him then said she'd text requesting a full interview.

She did a mental happy dance when Rick admitted that her plan worked so far. People had *noticed* the band tonight. The media swarmed. She even pulled Marc and Emma aside to the quietest corner she could find so TMZ could do a bit with them. Then she was busy overseeing sound bytes from Rick and making sure the others got their day in the sun.

Sound Bytes asked for and got a quick Q and A with Rick and that, too, went off without a hitch. Sydney smiled up at him.

"It's gone really well."

He nodded, the look in his eyes blistering her nerve endings. Heat engulfed her entire body. But before she could figure out how to breathe again, the evening took a nosedive.

"Hope I'm not interrupting anything," a female voice drawled.

Dressed in another skintight outfit, Macey Shreiner moved in so close to Rick she all but crawled all over him.

"I've decided to follow the tour for the first two stops," the woman said in her sex-kitten voice. With a glance at Rick from beneath thickly mascaraed lashes, she added, "I want to make sure to get my one-on-one time with you, Rick. Talk about how you decided to put the band together and created the special sound."

"And you will," Sydney assured her.

Syd glanced at Rick's face and, for one very intense moment, their gazes locked. She hoped Macey didn't feel the flames of the heat roaring between them. Or the residual tension left over from their last meeting.

"Did you have a chance to get a drink yet, Macey?" It wouldn't do for the woman to feel the tension or detect the simmering sexual attraction. "Let me get one for you and we can talk about your piece for *On the Scene*."

She sent up thanks when Butch took the moment to deliver his little thank you to everyone, a signal to start shutting it all down. As people started to disperse, she felt Macey's eyes boring holes in her back.

Too bad. You aren't going to get your hooks into him. Not on my watch. Not ever, as a matter of fact.

Ohmigod, where had this streak of possessiveness come from?

For the next little while, though, she had no time to think about it as they continued to ease people out. Finally, everyone was gone and they could all head to their respective vehicles for the ride to the hotel. Sydney wondered if she'd even be able to sleep. As she helped usher out the last of the crowd and listened to the feedback, she could feel the success she wanted right there for her to grab.

Eight years she'd worked to get to this point, carrying everyone else's water, studying, learning, researching. By the end of this tour, they'd call Sydney Anderson the star maker. She'd take this band right to the top. Ideas spun around in her brain, bouncing off each other.

The little confrontation with Macey reinforced her belief that they needed to keep their personal relationship completely out of the public eye. And most of the private. They didn't need the slightest hint of gossip or everything she did would lose its impact. She'd be Sydney who slept with the bandleader instead of Sydney the star maker. And he'd wear the mantle of every musician who overdosed on fame and rolled into bed with any willing female.

Not on her watch. Damn straight.

She was still buzzed from the evening when she checked into the hotel. Lightnin' happened to be at registration at the same time and their excitement was palpable. Even Danny and Garrett came over and gave her a hug. They all rode up in the elevator together, the guys still high on excitement, laughing and bumping fists. Except for Rick, who was strangely silent.

They got off at the same floor she did and she discovered they were in the same section of the hallway. She was shocked to discover Rick's was right next to hers. She slid a glance at him, stunned to see him watching her, a ravenous look in his eyes. She couldn't mistake the desire in his gaze. Did he want her to join him? Should she ask him if he wanted to come into *her* room? What was the protocol here?

Unsettled, she fumbled with the key card and dropped it in her nervous haste to get inside. She wasn't aware he had moved until he was beside her, taking the card from her fingers. He slid it into the slot and, when the lock light turned green he pushed the door open.

"Here you go." He held the door back with his body and waited for her to enter.

"Th-Thank you."

She moved past him, rolling her suitcase in and turned to him. Before she had time to say a word he grabbed her arms, turned her to face him and pressed her against the door.

"I've been wanting to do this all day." His voice was heavy with a combination of emotion and desire. "I think tonight calls for a celebration, don't you?"

Speech deserted her and all she could do was nod. She wanted him, this man who had exploded into her life. More than she wanted her next breath. She was hungry for him with a passion that never seemed to leave her. Sydney cupped the roughness of his late night beard with her hands, loving the scratchy feel of it.

She tilted her face up just the least little bit to accommodate him as his mouth came down on hers. The minute their lips met, heat surged through her, as if someone had lit a match to her blood. She clutched at his shoulders to steady herself, knowing she should break away even as her body cried for more. She was drowning in him, his heat and scent invading her. And all she could think was *more, more, more.*

Rick traced the outline of her lips with the tip of his tongue, then the seam before pushing gently until she opened for him. Then his tongue thrust inside, slicking over hers before it curled to taste every inch of the soft skin. Her heart pounded and moisture pooled between her thighs. How was it even possible he turned her on so much so fast?

With his fingers threaded through her hair, he angled her head to take the kiss deeper. She moaned with pleasure as he plundered her mouth. That was the only word for it, and everything fell away. Nothing existed except her and this man who made her want things she'd never even thought of before.

Her brain barely registered when he shifted their bodies so he could close the door. He reached out one arm to turn the lock and she heard the faint clink as he the deadbolt moved into place. But he never lifted his lips from hers and she clung to him as if she'd never get enough of the taste of him.

In some distant part of her brain, she was aware when he lifted her into his arms and carried her deeper into the room. He only broke the kiss when he set her on the floor.

Moonlight slanted its bright rays through the open drapes, illuminating his face. Casting them in shadow. Accenting the craving blazing in his eyes. Beneath her touch, Sydney felt the tautness of his muscles, the slight tremble of his body, and she shook with need.

Locking his gaze with hers, he held her spellbound as he undid the clip holding back her hair. As it tumbled down, he ran his fingers through it, spreading it out over her shoulders like a cape.

"Like fine-spun silk." His voice was hoarse. Raspy. He lifted some of the strands and inhaled the fragrance. "Apple blossoms. I think it's become my favorite scent."

He trailed soft kisses across her cheeks and down to her jawbone across to a spot behind her ear that sent a jolt of lust through her. When he nipped her earlobe, then soothed it with a slick swipe of his tongue, she pressed her body against his. She could feel the thick hardness of his cock underneath the fabric of his pants. Almost on autopilot, she rubbed herself back and forth, the muscles of her pussy flexing with need and desire.

When he moved his mouth down her neck to the hollow at her throat and lightly sucked at the pulse beating there, she shoved her fingers through his thick hair, clutching his head to her body.

"I want to be naked with you," she murmured.

Oh God! Was that her talking? She'd never been this bold with anyone before.

"All in good time," he murmured. "I don't want to rush this." He lifted his head to place a gentle bite on her lower lip and followed it with a row of damp kisses down her neck to the open vee of her blouse.

Sydney arched her body up to his mouth, reveling in his touch. She felt desired. More than that. Cherished.

One of his hands moved to cup a breast through the fabric and his thumb brushed softly over her nipple. Even through two layers of fabric, his touch sent a charge through her body. He took what seemed forever tormenting first one nipple, then the other before, at last, he eased each of the buttons open, one by one, and tugged the material from the waist of her slacks. With a light touch, he brushed the fabric away from her body and skimmed his tongue over the upper swell of her breasts.

Every nerve zapped where his tongue touched her skin. She tried to hold his head close to her body, but he removed her hands and smiled at her.

"Slow and easy, Syd. Just hang on for the ride."

Hang on? The world already spun, and he'd hardly done anything yet.

Putting his lips over one nipple he sucked it into his mouth, thin satin fabric of her bra and all. He captured it with his teeth, grazed lightly before he moved to the other one. Finally he flicked open the front clasp of the bra, freeing her breasts. He'd seen them before, certainly, but tonight he seemed mesmerized by them, staring at them with a wild hunger in his eyes.

Sydney could barely remain standing. Just the look in his eyes was enough to make her shiver and every touch only made her weaker. His hands brushed her skin with a whisper of touch as he slid sleeves and straps down her arms. He discarded both bra and blouse and tossed them to the side.

When he sucked one entire nipple into his mouth, with no fabric as a shield, she felt the tug all the way to her pussy and squeezed her thighs together. She grabbed his upper arms to stabilize herself, digging her nails into the hard muscles beneath them. He suckled the nipple until she was ready to pass out from the pleasure before he turned his attention to the other one. By the time he lifted his mouth from her breasts, her entire body hummed with need.

"Hold your breasts for me." His voice was edged with harsh desire. "Do it, Sydney."

Without protest she cupped them in the palms of her hands and held them out to him like an offering.

"Good, good." His voice thickened. "Keep doing that."

Now he unfastened the button on her slacks and, with a deliberate movement, slid the zipper down. He traced his finger lightly over her navel before sliding his hand between her panties and her slacks to cup her pussy.

"Soaked." His voice was thick with lust. "Don't ever try to tell me you don't want this because I'll know you're lying."

He rubbed two fingers the length of her slit, pressing the silk fabric of her bikini panties into the hot, wet flesh. With each glide, he rasped the tip of her clitoris, the movement sending shockwaves through her body. She rocked herself on his hand and silently urged him to do more and do it faster. In a move of desperate need she grabbed his T-shirt and tried to yank it over his head.

Rick laughed, the sound low and sexy, but he took his hand from between her thighs just long enough to rid himself of the garment.

"Lick my nipples," he told her. "Bite them like I did yours."

Oh, yes. She could get with that part of the program. As long as he put his hand back where it was before. And he did, leaving her slacks halfway down her hips. She had no idea how she kept her balance, holding her breasts for him as he asked, and closed her teeth over first one nipple then the other. But nothing seemed to matter except the hot sensation building low in her body and the sounds of pleasure that rolled from his mouth. He sucked in a breath as she swiped at the hard buds with her tongue over and over. She could feel the thrumming of the blood in his veins beneath her touch. Empowered, she sucked his nipples harder and harder. In response, his hand between her thighs pressed more tightly against her cunt. His fingers stroked her slit and rubbed her clit through the now-soaked fabric.

She rode his hand, trapping it with her thighs, as she tormented his nipples and licked his hard chest. Everything in her focused on that central spot in her body where sensation piled on sensation. The more he rubbed, the more she sucked his hard little male tips. His breath sounded raw in the still air of the room.

"Stop," he growled, and used his free hand to tug her face away from his body. "No more. Not now. Come for me, Sydney. Come right now in my hand."

That was all it took to push her over the edge. She clutched at him as her climax exploded, and she poured into his hand. Her hips rocked as she rode out the spasms, the tremors in her pussy, the shudders that shook her body.

"You don't know how much I love to make you come."

She opened her eyes to see him smiling at her.

"But," he continued, "I think we have too many clothes on."

Chapter Twelve

 $\mathcal{B}$ rushing her hands away when she would have taken care of herself, he eased the slacks down her legs and helped her to step out of them. Then the panties. When he lifted them to his face and inhaled her scent, she trembled at the erotic sight.

His eyes raked the length of her body.

"Jesus, Sydney. The sight of you in those heels makes me so hard it hurts. One of these times, I'm going to bend you over the bed wearing nothing but those heels and fuck you from behind until you beg for mercy."

She sucked in her breath, the muscles in her stomach tightened; every place he'd touched her throbbed with a life of its own as her body responded to the imagery of his words.

He urged her onto the bed and lifted each foot one at a time, discarding the strappy sandals she wore. Then, slowly, he kissed the arch of each foot and trailed his mouth across the surface. Sydney had never known ankles could be erogenous zones until Rick laved each one with the barest touch of his tongue before he stroked it up the inside of her legs. Up one leg to where her cunt waited greedily for him to fill it and then down the other. Missing the part where she wanted him to touch the most.

Her breath caught in her throat, her lungs felt crushed, and every part of her body seemed to be on pause as he teased her with light kisses and little nips of his teeth. Easing her back onto the bed, he knelt between her legs and lifted them to drape over his shoulders.

"Close your eyes," he commanded. "Let yourself feel."

If she felt any more, she'd self-combust, but she did as he said. His thumbs caressed the lips of her pussy before pressing them open. One slippery glide of his tongue the length of her slit and every nerve fired, every muscle constricted. Nothing existed except for her body and the way Rick played it with his educated tongue. Over and over, he licked the wet flesh, stopping now and then to thrust it inside before resuming the steady, erotic dance.

Sydney dug her fingers into the covers to anchor herself as the heat inside her built higher and higher and the coil of need unwound faster and faster. When he slid two fingers into her hot channel, she dug her heels into his bare shoulders and tried to pull him closer. But Rick set the pace and he wasn't about to be hurried. The torture was exquisite. He glided his fingers in and out of her, sucking her clit into his mouth and brushing his tongue over it.

He took her so high she wanted that breathtaking free fall with desperation. Wanted to feel her body clench in spasm after spasm. At last, when she didn't think she could take the torment one more moment, he added a third finger and bit down on her clit. That was all it took.

She exploded, pushing herself at him as she drove herself on his fingers and his mouth. He eased her through it, sucking hard on her clit and thrusting his fingers in and out of her spasming pussy until the last tremor had subsided. Then he took a long moment to lick every inch of her sensitive skin, sliding his fingers free only when she went completely limp. Through slitted eyes, she watched him lift his head and ease her legs from his shoulders.

He rose to his feet, a dark silhouette outlined in the bright moonlight that fell across the room. The look in his eyes as hot as ever, he lapped every bit of her moisture from his fingers with excruciating slowness.

"When you fall asleep at night," he told her, "I want this to be the sight you take into your dreams with you. Me tasting you. Your juice on my tongue. In my mouth."

The image was so sensual her body began to catch fire all over again, despite the fact she still shivered from the orgasm.

Oh, God. I am so hooked on him.

"I want to touch you," she whispered.

Silently he reached a hand out to her and pulled her up to a sitting position.

"Just watch," he said.

"I want to feel you," she protested. "I *need* to touch you."

"Not yet. Touch yourself. Go on. Put your fingers on that sweet, soaked pussy of yours and rub yourself while I finish undressing. It makes me hot to see you touch yourself."

For a long moment, Rick thought she'd refuse. Her hand hovered tentatively over her slick flesh and her damp curls. Then she eased her thighs apart and ran one finger up and down the length of her slit. Once, twice, then in a steady rhythm.

Shit.

He was afraid he'd come before he even got his zipper down, just watching her. His gaze never left her, his eyes on that slim finger with its steady movement as he unsnapped his jeans. His cock was so swollen, he had to be careful sliding the zipper down not to do any damage. The moment he freed himself, his shaft flexed with need. As rapidly as he could, he got rid of his shoes and socks, jeans and boxer shorts, kicking everything to one side.

He wrapped his fingers around his cock and stroked with a slow up-and-down movement as he continued to watch her caress herself. One thick drop of fluid beaded on the slit right at the top of the dark purple head. With his forefinger, he spread it over the surrounding area. Then, on impulse, reached down and painted some of it on the finger she used to rub herself with.

Sydney opened her mouth on a tiny gasp and, on impulse, he

stepped between her thighs and clasped the back of her head, pulling it forward. Resting the head of his shaft on her plump lower lip, he rubbed it back and forth against the soft skin.

Sydney leaned forward and closed her mouth over his shaft then ran her tongue over the head. When she pulled back, her lips glistened with his precum, and she licked it away.

Jesus.

He tightened his grip on his shaft and nudged it toward her mouth again. This time, she pushed his fingers aside, replacing them with her own, and inched forward so she could take him deeper. An involuntary groan rolled from his throat and he thrust his hips forward. Her mouth was like hot, sweet sin, blistering him with its heat. When she slipped her other hand between his thighs and cupped his balls, he nearly lost it. Teeth ground together, he dug deep for every bit of self-control as he rocked into the burning wetness of her.

He knew he should pull out, knew he was too close to the edge but, holy shit, he wanted this. Badly. So he closed his eyes and gave himself over to her mouth and her hands, reveling in the feel and the sensation. Every nerve in his body was focused on the sensations she drew from him. When the familiar tightness gripped the muscles of his lower back and his balls, he stiffened and exploded into her mouth.

He forced his eyes open, needing to see her as he came in thick spurts. Her lips were closed tightly around his cock. Her fingers gripped the base and her throat convulsed as she swallowed again and again. He was close to a state of collapse, his legs so weak he wasn't sure he could stand. With the last of his energy, he withdrew slowly from Sydney's mouth, managed to lift her to her feet, yanked back the covers on the bed, and rolled onto it carrying her with him.

He lay back on the pillows and tugged her up until she was on top of him, straddling his hips, her head resting on his chest. He tried to find the right words to say, but his mind was a blank, wiped clean by her incredible mouth and her very responsive body.

Rick lazily stroked her shoulder and the curve of her back, loving the satiny feel of her skin beneath his fingers. Her soft breath tickled the hair on his chest, caressing his skin like a gentle breeze. He felt replete, barely able to move, yet at the same time still hungry for her body. He wanted to be inside her, feel her close around him. Feel her silky cunt grasp him like a hot, wet fist.

Unbelievably, his penis thickened again, hardening beneath her body. He needed to move while he still could.

Shifting her gently to the side, he stumbled off the bed to find his jeans, dug out his wallet, and extracted the condom he'd put in there optimistically just a few days ago. Then he was back on the bed and lifting her over him again. Centering the hot slickness of her pussy over his rapidly reawakening shaft, he used his hands to rock her back and forth. Her liquid heat burned into him. The blaze of it seeped into his body and rushed to every nerve ending.

The bright moonlight washed over her, framing her, reflecting off the graceful lines of her body. He was amazed at how fast he was ready again. Sliding one hand between their bodies he ran the tips of his fingers along the length of her cunt. His heartbeat tripped when he realized how wet she was again so quickly.

Rick grabbed the condom he'd dropped onto the bed beside them, shifted Sydney enough to free his dick, and rolled the latex on with an unsteady hand. Then, as carefully as if he was placing crystal on a tray, he eased her down onto his throbbing shaft. He heard the sharp intake of her breath when he filled her, felt her thighs squeeze against him. Linking his fingers with hers, he looked into her eyes, stunned at the raging desire he saw in them. She gazed back at him and, for a brief moment, he felt as if he could see into her soul. Saw things she kept hidden away.

Then she blinked and the thread was broken.

"Are you okay?" he asked. What would he do if she said no?

"Yes," she whispered. "More than okay."

She leaned forward and the silk of her hair fell around them like a dark curtain. She pressed her lips to his and rocked her hips gently.

"You feel so damn good," he told her, amazed he could say anything at all.

"So do you." Her words were still no louder than a whisper, her face cloaked by her hair that draped all around them.

Rick was torn. He could stay like this forever, but the need to come inside her body was that of a wild animal hungry for its mate.

"Move with me," he urged.

Releasing one hand, he slipped it between them to find the hot button of her clit. With slow movements, he rocked up to her until she caught the rhythm. His fingers stroked her so slowly that restraint was excruciating. At that same time, he didn't want this to be over. Wanted it go on and on.

But the grasp of her cunt around his shaft undid him.

"Ride me, Sydney. Ride me hard."

She took him at his word. With her hands braced on his chest, she rocked back and forth. As he moved with her, she increased the pace. Captured in the exquisite shroud of her hair, her soft voice whispering things to him he wasn't even sure she knew she said, he rubbed her hot button harder. Faster, in cadence with the rhythm of their bodies.

"God, you feel so good, Syd. So tight. So hot. I could stay like this forever and never get tired of it."

He thought she whispered, "Me, too," but he wasn't sure.

When he lifted his eyes to her face again, he saw only how lost she was in the rhythm of this erotic dance. Her breasts moved with the action of her body. In that one moment, the feeling he'd had from the beginning, that they were connected by something deeper and more intense than just body to body, engulfed him. This was more than just the best sex he'd ever had in his life. This was a forever kind of feeling. It both excited him and scared him.

She moved, her inner walls clutching at him and he groaned. He held on as long as he could but when he felt the beginning of her spasms he couldn't restrain himself. The sight of her with her head thrown back, mouth open just did him in. With her first contraction, he let himself go, jetting in thick bursts into the thin shield between them, his cock burned by the heat of her cunt. Over and over they shuddered together, cries of completion mingling, bodies moving as if in a choreographed dance. Until the last bit of liquid had drained from him and the spasms of her pussy finally subsided.

He lay perfectly still beneath her, trying to drag air into his lungs. His heartbeat was so thunderous it, shook his body. And when Sydney collapsed forward on him, he could feel the beat of her own heart as it blended with his.

There wasn't another woman he'd ever experienced this with. Ever. He tightened his arms around her, wanting to hold her there forever.

Brand her.

Make her his.

Sweet Jesus.

How did he get so lucky with her?

In the moonlit darkness the emotion between them was stark and real.

"Talk to me, Sydney. Tell me how you feel."

"I feel—beyond anything I've ever felt before." She whispered the words in the dark, her hair a curtain surrounding them, as she bent so her face was closer to his. "I feel special. Cherished." She ran a small hand over the taut planes of his stomach down to where they were joined. "I love the texture of your body, your scent, the taste of your kiss."

"Don't ever stop feeling that way." It was hard making his brain work when his body was screaming for release, but he knew she needed the words as much as the physical contact. "You are so very special. I want this forever, Syd."

In the moonlit darkness the emotion between them was stark and real.

He held his breathe and at last she said in a low, soft voice, "Me, too."

He hated to move after that, but he needed to dispose of the condom before they pushed their luck. Very carefully he lifted her from his body and freed himself, then slid from the bed. By the time he was back in the bedroom she was sound asleep, sprawled against the sheets, delicate lashes lying softly on her cheeks.

Now what?

More than anything, he wanted to crawl back into bed and fall asleep with her in his arms. But someone would look for him in the morning, and he had no intention of putting Sydney in an embarrassing position. He finally understood the need to keep this between themselves. Besides drawing focus away from the band, it could put her in an untenable position. Maybe even affect her job. He didn't want that. So until this tour was over and they could figure out how to go public, they'd steal whatever moments they could.

With great reluctance he dressed quickly and eased the door open. He was thankful none of the band was in the hallway as he let himself into his room. Stripping off his clothes, he crawled into the cold, empty bed. He knew he should shower, but he'd wait until morning. At least tonight he could sleep with her scent all over him.

He'd worry about tomorrow when it got here.

೩

The sharp notes of a trumpet blared, rattling Sydney's brain and pushing through the fog of sleep she was wrapped in. Still groggy, she relaxed when it stopped, only to jerk when it sounded again.

What on earth?

Then she realized it was her cell. She pried her eyes open to see the thing practically dancing on the nightstand. Through squinted eyes, she saw Full Moon on the screen readout. Her first reaction was apprehension. Was something wrong? Last night had gone so well. Hadn't it? When she checked the time and saw it was only six-thirty, her anxiety escalated. Why would someone from the agency be calling her at this hour?

Pushing herself to an upright position, she shoved her hair out of her eyes and picked up the phone. Absently, she noticed she was alone in the bed. Hadn't he wanted to stay? In the same instant she understood he'd done this to protect her. So no one would see him slip out of her room when people were up and about. She smiled and hugged his concern to her like a warm blanket.

When the ringtone blared again, she finally pressed Answer. And mentally crossed her fingers.

"Yes?"

"Sydney?" Renee Fischer's excited voice sounded in her ear. "Are you asleep? Wake up! Oh, my God! This was as long as I could wait to call you."

"What's wrong, Renee? What happened?"

"Nothing's wrong." The woman's laugh slid through the phone. "I checked the overnight chatter on the Internet the way I always do after a show and Oh! My! God!"

"What? What? Tell me."

"Holy cow, Sydney. Can you say overnight sensation?"

"Huh?" She wished her brain would kick into gear.

"The band! Lightnin'! Holy shit. The Internet is full of them. The Twitter feed is moving so fast I can hardly keep up with it. Everyone who Liked their Facebook page is posting and someone's video of Marc and Emma hit YouTube and went viral already. Sydney, you're a goddamned genius."

"What?" She swung her legs over the side of the bed. "Renee, give me a sec here."

She dropped the phone, raced into the bathroom to splash cold water on her face then picked it up again.

"Okay, now repeat every word. Slowly."

Even hearing it the second time, she could hardly believe it.

"And the download number at iTunes is rising every hour." Renee's voice vibrated with her excitement. "Like I said, we have a damned overnight sensation on our hands. Listen, I already woke Linc up to tell him, and he's calling Butch."

At that exact moment a foghorn sounded, letting her know another call was coming in.

"That may be him now. Let me take it and call you back."

"Okay. Hurry. I'm checking the online editions of the newspapers and the blogs. I'll send a report to your iPad."

Sydney disconnected Renee's call and cleared her throat. "Hello?"

"Sydney, I love you." She could practically hear the grin in Linc Forrester's voice. "I can't remember the last time I had this happen with a client."

"Um, thank you, but the band actually did all the work."

"Oh, yeah, I know. But that thing with Marc and Emma? Like I said last night. Goddamn genius idea. Remind me to give you a big raise. No, wait. I'll remind myself."

"Uh, thank you, sir." She wished she didn't sound like quite such an idiot but not all her brain cells were firing yet.

"Renee sent stuff to your iPad. Butch is giving the band another hour to sleep before he wakes them with the news. I'll get back to you after that. We'll have to make some adjustments here."

He clicked off, and she sat there holding the phone.

Overnight sensation! Did she dare hope? Maybe last night had just been a fluke. Maybe it wouldn't happen again tonight.

Maybe you should take a shower and pour some coffee in you and get to work.

Sydney stood under the shower for a long time and let the stream of water pound her awake. Her brain tried to absorb everything she'd just heard but her body was doing a happy dance as she remembered everything from the previous night.

The thing that shook her the most was the realization that this thing she had with Rick was real, not just a dream. It was beyond a hot physical attraction. Every touch, every look, every caress was an expression of a much-deeper feeling. And he felt it, too. The things he'd said, the words they'd exchanged in the dark. That astounded her the most.

From beginning to end, the night had been enchanted. That was the only word to describe it. From the anxious anticipation during the day to the frenzy of last-minute activities to the unbelievably excellent performance of Lightnin' to the magical moment on stage with Emma and Marc, Sydney had been riding a high. So many emotions assaulted her she could hardly sort them out.

She hoped no one had caught the vibes between her and Rick earlier in the evening. The quick glances. The heat pulsing between them. How was it possible something so strong could take root and blossom in such a short period of time?

During the after-party, they were too busy to think of anything else. When she reached the hotel and checked in, she was still giddy with excitement. Then there was that business with the key card, and his nearness and his touch had just undone her. In the erotic moonlit darkness, everything she felt for him, emotions she didn't want to give a name to, had rushed to the surface.

She could still feel his mouth on her lips, on her breasts, between her legs. His tongue as it teased and tormented every one of her erogenous zones. Remembered the sensation of his cock in her mouth and in her body. Her pulse accelerated and throbbed low in her pussy, and her nipples suddenly ached.

She wanted this man. Badly. And for more than just a tumble in the sheets. He wanted her the same way. They couldn't have made love the way they did last night without that kind of emotional connection.

Turning off the shower, she took one of the big bath towels and blotted her body with it, unwilling to scrub away the memories of the night, the imprint of Rick's body, the feel of his hands and mouth.

Ohmigod! I've got it bad. Business, Sydney. Business.

She ordered coffee and muffins from room service while she dressed. There was work to do before she caught her ride to the airport. She knew the band's pickup was scheduled for nine. Glancing at the clock on the nightstand, she saw that it was already eight-thirty. If she hurried, she could check all the social media and the media coverage and give them a report before they left.

Dressed and with her first cup of coffee in hand she opened her iPad. The first thing she read was Renee's long message. Then she scrolled through Twitter, stunned at what she saw—the notice that the hash tag #Lightnin was trending. Next she checked their Facebook page, dumbfounded at the number of Likes. And, finally, while she nibbled a muffin, she pulled up each of the Web sites on Renee's list, one after the other. The coverage of Deep Blue River was expected. What wasn't was the amount of space devoted to Lightnin'.

While some columns and blogs did give them only limited coverage, far more than she expected focused the article on her band. *Her band!* Headlines like *Hot New Band Explodes on Scene* and *"Music Lady" Sure To Zoom Up the Charts*, had her motor revving. Five of the writers had given a lot of space to "Music Lady" and the bit with Marc and Emma and even included a photo of the scene on stage.

Damn! It was way better than she'd hoped for.

Her hands shook with excitement as she logged into the iTunes store to check on the downloads herself and nearly fell out of her chair. She had to look twice to make sure what she saw wasn't part of her imagination.

Nope, there it was. Number Four on the rock tunes chart at iTunes.

Of course, both Butch and Linc would have seen it by now. She was sure they both slept with their smartphones. She picked hers up to send a message back to Linc, but as she held it in her hand a chime sounded and she saw an incoming text from Linc.

Up 2 # 4. iTunes. Mega media coverage. Grt wrk. I knew I made the right choice here. Tld the guys. Cl them.

She hugged the phone to her body, wishing she had her printer with her so she could make a hard copy.

Another chime. Linc again.

Butch ecstatic. Sys to meet hm in Lobby of htl at 4 and ride to soundcheck with him.

Her heartbeat tripped and stuttered before it settled into a more rapid beat. This was so great. Butch was going to give her position some teeth by having her arrive with him.

She was disappointed that there was no new blog up at *On the Scene* but maybe Macey was still writing it.

Maybe she's still in bed with whoever she dragged home with her last night.

Catty, catty, Sydney. Besides, who are you to talk?

Determined not to let the moment be spoiled, she pushed all thought of Macey and her blog out of her mind. She wanted to scream like a kid and dance around the room, and when she was finally back home she would do it. Now, however, she had to put on her professional self and make sure she didn't lose the momentum she'd gained.

But first she had to call Rick. See if the band was still here. Linc said Butch called them already but she also needed to touch base. Besides, she had updated information about the single.

Telling herself to stay calm, she punched in his cell number. He answered on the second ring.

"Morning, Sydney." The heat in his deep voice blazed across the connection.

Her heart did a happy dance while her hormones joined it.

She cleared her throat, reaching for some semblance of sanity. "Morning. I know Butch has already talked to you, but I wanted to give you the good news from the overnights."

"We saw them. I checked my iPad first thing this morning after Butch called and just now again."

"Oh. Good, good." She couldn't contain her enthusiasm. "But you should check Twitter and your Facebook page, too. My God, Rick. It's unbelievable. And we got great coverage of the shtick with 'Music Lady.' We need to keep it in the show."

She imagined his smile. "You're right. We talked about it this morning. Emma's going to come to the next two stops with us. Then I guess it will be up to you to figure out what to do when she's not there."

"Yes. Okay. We can talk about that later. Listen, there's Wi-Fi on my flight to Houston so I can keep up with the social media. Sometime today we should compare notes and see if you want to change anything I'm posting. The office has someone on the Twitter feed doing the usual thanks and great and all that stuff. I'll keep monitoring what's out there and text you when I get to Houston. Number four overnight on iTunes is beyond great, you know."

"No kidding." His voice vibrated with the high she knew he was riding. "Hot damn! Uh, hold on a sec." His sound was muffled, but she could hear him talking to the others. "The guys all send you hugs. Listen, we've gotta get going here but we can celebrate in Houston, right?"

There was no denying the double meaning in his words.

"You bet. And Rick?"

"Yeah?"

She screwed up her courage. "Last night was beyond wonderful."

"Sydney." His voice dropped. "Me, too. See you in Houston."

"Have a safe trip and enjoy the success. It's only going to get better."

Swallowing the last bite of muffin, she washed it down with the rest of the coffee, shut off her iPad, and collected her things. On the flight to Houston, she'd monitor all the social media sites and troll for other media coverage. She was rethinking her other plans for the band's image, too. Rick was right about so many things. Listening to them live and getting into their music was a much better indicator of what to do with them than some abstract plan, no matter how many other bands she studied. They were unique. What she needed to do now was make some adjustments with regard to the exposure based on last night's success.

The flight to Houston would be a short one, just a quick hop that would get her there in time to check in at the hotel before hooking up with the distributor their merchandise firm used. She planned to get a count on the Lightnin' items and see how fast they'd gone. Since the beefed up orders wouldn't reach them until Tampa, she wanted to try and figure out how to stretch what they had.

After that, she'd spend her time contacting the local media, make sure to touch base with the radio stations. Butch would be all over it for Deep Blue River but she had a hook for the band—Marc and Emma—for as long as she had them.

Tonight they'd appear in a massive arena in Houston, nearly twice as big as last night's venue. This would be the largest crowd Lightnin' had ever played to. She hoped they could still pull off the Marc and Emma thing at the end of the set like last night but she couldn't see why it wouldn't work. The audience ate it up. A bigger crowd would just love it more, especially with the coverage it got.

She locked her suitcase and pulled up the handle, slid the strap of her messenger bag over her head, and took one last look around before she left the room. The next airport shuttle left in fifteen minutes. Linc would take care of her room charge on the agency's master account so she only had to herself get down to the lobby and wait.

Giddy with excitement, Sydney did her best to look contained and professional as she rolled her suitcase out of the elevator. Bright sunlight bathed the entrance and the lobby so she figured she'd wait on one of the stone benches outside for the shuttle. She had just seated herself and pulled out her smartphone when the doors swished open again. The commotion behind her made her look over her shoulder—and freeze.

Apparently Lightnin' was running late on their departure because they were just now walking outside. Marc spotted her first.

"Sydney! The woman of the hour." He picked her up and spun her around. "We love you."

She laughed at his enthusiasm. "And I love all of you, too. But all the accolades belong to you guys."

"Not so." He shook his head. "We didn't get that coverage by accident. You had good ideas. Right, Rick?"

Sydney glanced over to where Rick stood. At the look in his eyes her body went liquid and, for a moment, she couldn't breathe. Oh, damn. Did her eyes telegraph the same message? She stepped away from Marc's arms and tried to gauge the band's reaction to the two of them. Lucky for her, they were too jazzed from last night's performance and today's news to pay attention to anything else.

Rick gave her a crooked grin that went straight to her heart. "Marc's right. Thanks for working the media the way you did. For your ideas. For taking good care of us. For everything."

With a supreme effort she tore her gaze away from his and managed her own smile. "Thank you. I'm enjoying every minute of it. Can't wait for tonight."

He looked as if he wanted to say something else, even took a step toward her. But a van pulled up with Gordo at the wheel and the band hustled to get themselves inside. In the midst of it all, the airport shuttle arrived so whatever else Sydney and Rick might have said to each other was dead in the water. At least for the moment.

Sydney waved at them as she got into the shuttle. "See you in Houston."

She was glad the other passengers seemed to be occupied with their own business because she was in no mood to chat with anyone. Her stomach still had the nervous jitters and she wondered if she should have had that third cup of coffee. After she cleared security at the airport she had more than an hour to takeoff so she stopped and got an herbal tea. Probably what she should have been drinking all along.

Sitting at a small table in the food court area, she pulled out her iPad and opened the list of things she needed to do once she landed in Houston. She had to keep focused on her to-do list. Everything was part of The Plan.

Everything, except what she felt for Rick Trajean.

As she sipped her tea, her phone chimed and she saw Linc had sent her another message.

Check On the Scene. Blog up. What's with you and Rick?

Her and Rick?

Hands shaking, she brought up Macey Schreiner's blog on her iPad. By the time she finished reading, her tea threatened to come back up on her and she had to swallow hard against the nausea.

Tidbit from On the Scene.

Hot new band explodes on the music landscape.

They came to see Deep Blue River and got struck by Lightnin'. Last night's concert was already sold out with word that star rockers Deep Blue River would be introducing the material from their latest album. But like everyone else, On the Scene *was interested to see if Butch Meredith's new baby band would live up to its early hype.*

The answer?

All that and more.

With leader Rick Trajean on lead guitar and his raspy vocals setting the mood for the band's sound, they electrified the audience with their high-energy opening number "Take the High Road" and from then on it was a wild, wild ride.

The band sizzles. It rocks. Its music reaches out and grabs you by the throat.

But the clincher is "Music Lady," the closer that brought tears to everyone's eyes. Written by bassist and band co-founder, Marc Malone, for his fiancée, Emma Blake, its emotional message held the audience in thrall.

Loved it when Emma joined Marc on stage and he sang the ending again, just for her. Released as a single, the song is already zooming up the charts.

And what's with the sparks we saw flying between Trajean and Full Moon publicist Sydney Alexander who's handling the PR for the band? They were both very careful to pretend nothing was there, but On the Scene *predicts fireworks.*

You read it here first.

Stay tuned.

Sydney closed her eyes and pulled in a deep breath. Let it out slowly. This was not happening. It was not. This was exactly the kind of thing she'd told Rick she was worried about. She'd thought they'd done a good job hiding their feelings but not good enough, it seemed. Angry because she hadn't gotten a guarantee of alone time with Rick, that bitch Macey Schreiner tipped her venom out of the ink bottle.

Had others caught a hint of things? Or just Macey, who wanted Rick's body.

Sydney didn't want to ask herself whose image was a priority here, hers or Rick's. Rock musicians—all musicians—got away with a lot of things because the public almost expected them to be a little wild. They could weather a storm. It was her own image that gave her a stomachache. What would people say about her? That she got her gig with Lightnin' because she slept with the bandleader? What other kind of innuendo would they throw out there? How would Linc react? And Butch?

We'll just have to be more careful. I can't give him up.

No, that was no longer an option. Not now. Not after last night.

But she couldn't let Janine be right, either.

Choosing her words carefully she texted back to Linc.

Excited the Emma-Marc thing is catching on. Rick and me? Just a good working relationship.

She hoped nothing would derail the momentum.. Or her job. The scared little girl frightened of her aunt's temper wanted to claw her way up from where Sydney kept her hidden. If she broke free, the past eight years would all have been for nothing. She could not let that happen.

Another chime from her phone. Butch.

Thumbs-up on Marc-Emma. Good hook. Glad you and Rick are okay.

Before she could reply another text came through.

Counting on you, Sydney.

Swallowing the nausea she texted him back.

Thanks. All is good. On to Houston.

The plane ride took less than an hour but to Sydney it was

interminable. Rick must have seen the item. Everyone had an iPad with 4G these days and, as excited as the guys were, they'd be hooked into Twitter and Facebook to catch all the latest updates. Not to mention checking the blogs and columns. What would the others in the band say about Macey's little teaser?

And Rick. What would his reaction be?

She didn't know if she wanted to see him and get his reaction or push back time so she could avoid the confrontation.

Houston traffic, as always, was a bear and Sydney tried to sit back in the cab and relax. In her mind, she rehearsed what she'd say to Rick when she saw him.

I told you this kind of thing would happen.

No, no, no. That would immediately set him off.

I hope this doesn't upset you. Macey writes whatever she wants.

Not that either. It sounded too much like she was just brushing it off.

Let's not let it become a big deal if we can help it. We can even joke about it. Make believe we're just having a little fun and the woman took us too seriously.

Except they hadn't really discussed it with the woman. And if it turned out the vibes between her and Rick were obvious enough for others to see?

Shit, shit, shit!

She hopped out of the cab the moment it pulled up at the entrance to the hotel, paid the driver, nodded at the valet, and grabbed her suitcase. She had to get to her room and strategize in private. She was smart. Better than smart. Surely she could figure out how to defuse the whole thing. She had barely let herself into her room before her phone chimed with a new text. She looked at the caller ID. Butch again. Swell. Forcing herself to relax she opened the message.

Just curious if there's anything to that little teaser bomb Macey dropped in her column today.

No, and there wasn't going to be.

Not a word. She wants his body. You know Macey. Stir up

trouble and step in when it boils over."

Great. Not against such, but the guys have to keep focused right now.

No kidding.

No problem. Did u chk airplay?

Yes. ML #4 on most request charts since 5 this a.m.

Sydney breathed a sigh of relief. They could focus on that and the really good coverage and kick the other to the curb. She hoped.

Grt. C u at 4.

She dropped her phone on the nightstand and flopped back on the bed. She'd give herself five minutes to agitate over the situation and then get to work. She had a lot to do before meeting Butch.

Chapter Thirteen

Rick did his best to relax on the drive to Houston. For a change, the interstate wasn't crowded and the weather was clear. The guys were busy with their iPads, eager to catch the latest updates on the concert and their single. He did okay until Danny reached forward and tapped him on the shoulder.

"So, Rick. About what that Schreiner woman said. Sure there isn't something you want to tell us?"

"Yeah, Rick," Garrett echoed. "How about the real skinny?"

Rick half turned from where he sat in the shotgun seat. "Knock it off, you two. The joke's over."

They'd ragged on him since Garrett found *On the Scene* on his iPad and read the part about Sydney aloud. Then everyone else had to pull it up and they hadn't shut up about it since. Why couldn't they just let it go? Crap. Butch had probably seen it, too. What would he think about it?

Maybe Sydney had called it right. If they acknowledged this thing between them, it might create a problem for everyone. Even put him in an uncomfortable situation. Not to mention what Sydney must be feeling after she saw the comment. But he just did not want to believe that.

He would never do anything to hurt her or put her situation in jeopardy but last night had make him want her even more. In every way possible. He had never taken time to think about the type of relationship he'd like to have with a woman or the kind of woman he saw himself with. He'd been too focused on his family and the band. But Sydney Alexander rocked his world.

They were two intelligent people. They could resolve this so they could be together. Right? Because he wasn't giving her up. He was well and truly hooked, his body and his heart. He would go out of his way to take care of this—of her—and make it workable because he wasn't walking away. Meanwhile he had to concentrate on getting the band ready for tonight. And focus on how he'd behave when he saw Sydney today.

He closed his eyes and deliberately blocked the teasing out of his mind.

"Hey, Marc, look at this?" From behind him Rick heard the excitement in Garrett's voice. "Rick, you got your iPad still on?"

Now what?

He roused himself and half-turned in the seat. "What have you got?"

"Didn't you say Marc and Emma went viral?" Danny passed his iPad forward. "Look at the number of hits it's up to."

Rick took the tablet and stared at the screen. Sure enough. Just like Butch had told them, someone had taken a video, probably with their phone, of the final number plus the scene with Marc and Emma on stage.

"It's got more than two hundred thousand hits so far," Danny added. "Holy shit! Marc, you're a hot superstar."

Marc laughed. "Only a little one and only for the moment. I need to text Emma. She flew into Houston this morning, and I don't know if she's checked all this stuff out yet. Anyway, this is about the band. It helps us all."

"Whatever," Garrett said. "It's got us way out there, so I love it. You should keep it in the show."

"Holy shit!" This from Danny. "We're trending on Twitter!" He gave a huge laugh. "Trending on Twitter. Us. Can you believe it?"

"Rick, I know you were worried about what Full Moon would

post on the social media," Marc broke in. "But I've been checking the postings and when you see it all, you'll feel comfortable with it."

Of course he would. Why had he ever had any doubts?

He glanced over his shoulder once more, his mouth curved in a half-smile as he saw everyone texting, thumbs flying on keyboards. He'd sent his own messages to his mom and Meredith and told them he'd call when he got to the hotel. He didn't want to carry on a private conversation in the van where everyone could listen in.

But when they pulled up to the entrance of the hotel, a phone call was the last thing on his mind.

"Don't anyone get out yet," Gordo told them. "I mean it. Give me a minute here."

Rick stared at the scene. It was jammed with people, some of them screaming, all of them waving cameras. Two men who appeared to be hotel security officers were doing their best to keep everyone away from the van, but they appeared to be fighting a losing battle.

"Hold on," Gordo said. He picked up his cell and speed dialed a number. "Yeah. Uh, Butch? We got a little problem here. Uh huh. Yeah. Uh huh. I don't think anyone did. All right. We'll do our best."

"What's going on?' Rick asked. He could hardly believe this riot was for Lightnin'. It had to be a mistake. Where was Deep Blue River? These was probably their fans out there.

"Butch wasn't kidding when he said you guys caught fire overnight." Gordo grinned. "He got the word the video went viral at a hundred thousand hits? Its five times that now and still climbing, along with someone's smartphone video of the opening number."

"So this is for us?" Rick stared out the window, incredulous.

"Sure is. Welcome to the maniac world of rock and roll." He began honking the horn.

"So what's the plan?" Marc asked.

"If I let you out here, there won't be anything left of you.

Butch is at the delivery door in the rear with two of the security guards he just hired. And cursing himself for not preparing for this. We'll have to sneak you in the back way."

Rick didn't know whether to be afraid or excited. He'd tried to soft-pedal the optimism about the contracts, the single, the tour. Tried to prepare himself if it all flopped. The realization they were on the verge of a breakout with their first major release and their first tour was more than he'd ever hoped for. But this was beyond anything he expected. So much of the credit went to Sydney. The band had performed, but she'd come up with the gimmicks that captured the audience and the media.

As the hotel employees continued to hold off the screaming fans, Gordo eased the van out of the circle. In what seemed like seconds they circled the block, drove down an alley, and pulled up to a loading dock. Rick spotted Butch waiting for him. Next to him were two men in jeans and polo shirts with some agency logo on them. They looked prepared to take on whatever came their way from the mountains of Afghanistan to the streets of Houston.

When the van came to a stop at a short flight of stairs, one of the men hurried down and opened the doors, motioning for everyone to get out.

Butch grinned like an idiot. "Looks like you guys caught the brass ring first time out. I think I need to rearrange our logistics a little."

He shook everyone's hand as they headed up to the loading dock, toting their own personal gym bags. Then Butch and the two guards hustled them inside the building, down a hallway, and through to a freight elevator. As they rode from the ground floor, Butch handed hotel key cards to everyone.

"You're all checked in. I've got your rooms together on the same floor. These guys will make sure you get inside without anyone knowing. Then we can draw a breath. At least for a little while."

"Where's the River?" Rick wanted to know.

"Their charter arrived about an hour ago. We knew to take

them in the back way, but we just weren't prepared for this for Lightnin'." He chuckled. "Can I pick a winner or what? Oh, and beginning tomorrow, no more travel by van. At the rate you guys are already bringing in the money, coupled with the River's sales, I chartered a bigger plane to carry both bands to all the tour stops. The equipment will still go in the truck."

"Holy crap!" Garrett's voice nearly squeaked. "If I'm dreaming, don't wake me up."

"I still don't have the overnights from *Billboard* on sales and play requests but, gentlemen, I'd say you're off like a rocket." He turned his gaze to Rick. "You can thank Sydney for the way she managed all the preconcert hype and the logistics of the after-party. And for coming up with the Marc-Emma thing."

"No worries there," he assured him. "We all know how hard she's worked."

"Good. Good. Let's get you up to your rooms."

Butch rode up in the elevator then walked down the hallway with them. Rick unlocked the door to his room and, for some reason, everyone followed him in. He turned to look at the rest of the band.

"Keep this in mind," he told them. "We're only as good as our last song or our last appearance. We've established a high level of expectation and we need to reach it every time. No goofing off, no groupies all over the place, none of that shit."

"But, Rick—" Danny began.

"That goes for all of us." He grinned at Marc. "Except for Marc and Emma, who are practically an old married couple. So. Everyone got it straight?"

They all nodded.

"I couldn't have said it better myself," Butch told them. "Relax. Order room service. Gordo will come and get you when it's time to head over for the soundcheck." He started to leave then turned back. "Oh, and another change in routine, starting tonight. I'll have fresh T-shirts for you at the arena so bring with you whatever else you'll need. You'll be hanging out there after the soundcheck. Dinner's catered in and you can relax before the show. See you later."

Rick closed the door and looked at his band members. "Anyone want to shout, do it now." Then he laughed and pumped his fist in the air. "We are on the way."

They decided to eat in their own rooms. That gave them alone time to make their phone calls, send any texts they wanted to, and decompress before tonight's show. After a long conversation with his mother and sister, Rick threw himself on the bed and closed his eyes, just giving himself over to the excitement of the moment.

This was it. What they'd worked so hard for. Planned for. Hoped for. He could hardly believe it. If he could just figure out how to handle this thing between himself and Sydney, life would be damn near perfect. Because while she could deny it all she wanted to, there was definitely something going on.

ೞ

By the time Sydney met Butch in the lobby at four, she was sure her cell phone was on the verge of self-destruction. The thing had rung all day, one call after another. Her only respite had been on the plane. Every media outlet in the area, including nationals with local reps, wanted tickets for tonight's show and passes for the after-party. She even had calls from Tampa about the next stop on the tour.

She added the names to her growing list and made sure to give them the verbal strokes they needed. The only one to set her teeth on edge was Macey Shreiner.

"I want face time with Rick," she demanded. "Alone. And I want it tonight, after the show."

Over my dead body.

"Tonight just won't work, Macey." She used her best PR voice. "I'd make it happen if I could. But I can arrange a meet in Tampa when we'll have more time."

"You wouldn't be trying to keep him to yourself, would you, Sydney?" The sly bitchiness in the woman's voice made Sydney grit her teeth.

"Not at all. We're on a very tight schedule here. That's all."

"I want him for a full interview before anyone else gets him," she insisted.

"I'll do my best. But you know Linc and Butch control some of that."

"Make it happen, Sydney. Call me with a time and place."

The call disconnected, leaving Sydney sitting there with her jaw clenched and a desire to bitchslap the woman. Too bad that wasn't possible.

She sent all her notes to Butch on his phone to update him and ask for any suggestions, but he'd simply texted back *Gd jb*. At four o'clock, dressed for the evening in what she called her work outfit—black slacks, a blouse in a vibrant color—tonight, it was sapphire blue—hair clipped back in what she hoped was a professional look, she met Butch in the lobby. In the cab to the arena he gave her the details of the mob scene that greeted the band at the hotel.

"Whew!" She laughed. "I'll bet they didn't know what hit them."

"Absolutely. You know, they're damn good or I wouldn't have signed them, but without your game plan and hard work, no one would even know who they are. The Marc-Emma-'Music Lady' thing is brilliant. Even I couldn't have predicted it would catch on the way it did. I can't say it enough times." He was making notes in his smartphone as he spoke. "I'll talk to Emma and see if we can arrange to keep her on the tour with us."

"I know her salary is important to them," Sydney pointed out.

"Salary?" Butch added another note. "That's the easiest fix of all. We can't lose the magic they bring to the stage."

"A lot of it has to do with their story and the chemistry between them," she reminded him. "It's so strong, it's almost visible."

"It also helps when people hear that story and discover she's not a groupie or tour follower. This is going to come out wrong, but she validates Marc."

Sydney nodded. "I understand what you mean and I agree. That's why I'm so excited about the way it's caught on." She patted her tote. "I have tonight's guest list and backstage badges for everyone. Linc recommended getting one of the security staff to check people in."

"That's standard operating procedure, as I'm sure you're aware. I know all the regulars on the event staff," Butch went on, "so I'll be sure to introduce you to them. What about the merchandise? And thanks for checking on Deep Blue River's, too."

"Sure." Sydney scrolled down in her Notes section. "I coordinated with the office and the local distributor. The stuff should be at the arena now. After soundcheck I can take a look at the lobby setup for both bands. I took pictures with my camera last night so I'd remember the way you like things set up."

"You're proving to be quite the valuable person." He was silent for a moment and Sydney could feel his hesitation about something. "Syd, don't take this wrong but is there something going on with you and Rick?"

"With me and Rick?" she parroted.

"Don't misunderstand me. I like you both and I'd like to see you happy. But if there's a relationship brewing, you need to keep a lid on it and be very discreet. This is a cutthroat business. Macey Shreiner's already got her claws out and there could be others. I don't want to see her destroy your career when it's really just getting started."

Neither do I.

"Understood."

"This business can be very cruel to women who have relationships with musicians, couples like Marc and Emma aside. So if there is anything...?" His voice trailed off. "Better to tell me now and be prepared."

She closed her hands tightly around her briefcase, absorbing what he said. Maybe she should go ahead and tell him now. Be prepared, like he said. Or should she discuss it with Rick first?

This was his manager, after all. But before she could say a word the ringtone sounded on Butch's phone, he answered, and the cab pulled up to the back entrance of the arena.

Butch climbed out, paid the cabbie, and stood aside so she could slide across the seat. Hand at her back, he guided her to the stage entrance. They presented their security badges to the security guards who stood inside like formidable sentries. The two of them plus the band, the sound crew, and both road crews had special badges with their photos and names on them. Guests had passes stamped with the name of the agency, the concert date, and *Guest*. Linc had asked Sydney to coordinate the distribution of the guest passes at all stops. A new package would be waiting for her at each hotel where they stayed.

As she and Butch climbed the steps up to the wings, she noticed two more security guards on each side of the stage. Just in case someone found a way to sneak in during rehearsal, she assumed.

There was a certain routine prior to every concert and Sydney had been through it countless times but always as an assistant to one of the agents. Now it became her responsibility to touch base with the road manager then make sure the distributor she'd spoken to had delivered the merchandise. Check the sales setup in the lobby. Double-check the guest list and field last-minute calls for passes. Make sure there was enough security around the stage. Fans could get really wild and obnoxious.

Lightnin' was on stage at the moment, prepping their instruments for the soundcheck, but the undercurrent of excitement running through everyone was palpable. The exhilaration of the morning's publicity, coupled with the mob scene at the hotel, had to have them riding an incredible high.

Mickey Farentino stood in the center of the stage, holding a clipboard and wearing a mic and headset. When he spotted her, he walked over to shake hands.

"So far so good, Syd." He laughed. "Although I think the guys are still in shock from the mob scene at the hotel."

She grinned. "Me, too."

"Lotta smarts in planning that thing with Marc and Emma." He winked. "Looks like Full Moon assigned a real promo brain to my guys."

Was that the heat of a blush creeping up her cheeks? Lord, she hoped not.

"Thanks, Mickey. I'm going to do my very best for them."

"Well, gotta get back to making sure everything is ready for the soundcheck."

Putting on her best public smile she took a moment to greet each of the musicians and fill them in on her media activities for the day.

"She's got it covered." Butch walked up beside her. "The numbers are still climbing on the single, by the way. iTunes changes every hour. And you're still trending on Twitter. I expect a lot more interest in you guys than we otherwise might have had."

"Just as long as she's there so we don't trip over our tongues," Rick said. He had his back to Sydney, tuning his guitar, but after he spoke, he turned around.

And, as always, his eyes sought hers. *Bam!* Heat pierced her like a thunderbolt. If she hadn't already been nervous, she would be now. In a moment so brief she wondered if she imagined it, he telegraphed a message.

Tonight. I can't wait.

"That's Sydney's job," Butch told them. "And she seems to be doing it damn well. Take all your cues from her."

For a moment, Sydney floated on the cloud of praise. Rick shifted his gaze back to her and again, that hot, emotional jolt shook her. She forced herself to look away before what she felt was written all over her face.

If I'm going to do this, I need to do it right. I can keep what's happening between Rick and me under control in public. I know I can. I have to.

"Thank you. I appreciate the confidence." She cleared her throat. "Full Moon makes it a practice not to schedule interviews before a concert starts," she told them. "You have too much to be concerned with and shouldn't be distracted. But I have two reporters who really want some time with you between your set and Deep Blue River's. Butch, that work for you?"

He nodded. "The River's good to go, so I can make myself available in the dressing room and give you a hand if you need it."

"Good. Thanks."

"Additionally," she continued, "I'm sure we'll get a lot more people videoing with their cameras. Especially when you get to the closing number."

Butch looked around. "Emma not here?"

"She's still at the hotel," Marc told him. "I thought it would be better if she got some rest and had a quiet place to eat. Can you make sure the security guards will let her backstage?" He chuckled. "I'm not sure they paid attention to what I said."

"No problem. Call or text her to be here by seven and tell her to come to the stage entrance. I'll be sure to leave word to let her in." Butch touched Sydney's elbow. "Let me give you a quick visual tour. I know it's nothing new to you but you haven't been in this particular venue before. Each one is different." He pointed to a glass-enclosed structure to the left of the stage, high up toward the ceiling. "Sound and light men. During the soundcheck they and the band have earbuds and lip mics to communicate with each other. If adjustments need to be made, that's how they'll pass the information." Then he waved his arm to the left. "Dressing rooms. I'll show you where Lightnin's is when we're done here. I want to get started because Deep Blue River will be here in an hour and the roadies will need to rearrange equipment. Let's go out into the audience to listen to the soundcheck."

Sydney took a moment to look out into the vast arena, imagining it filled with thousands of people. The place was half again as big as the arena they'd played last night.

Wow!

This is the big time, Sydney. Get ready for a wild ride.

Then she followed Butch down the steps and out into the empty hall. They took seats about halfway back.

"Best place to judge the sound," he told her.

This is my deal now. I'm in charge. Holy shit!

The enormity of it hit her with sudden force. Until now, she'd been on automatic pilot, followed the routine she'd learned when she assisted the senior agents. But last night, she'd been so nervous, the difference hadn't really hit her.

And now? Ohmigod.

Here she was. Sydney Alexander. Publicity agent for a Butch Meredith band. Right next to the legendary manager himself and being treated like an equal.

She had the nervous feeling she should be doing something besides sitting there. Slouched in the chair next to her, Butch was scrolling through texts, answering them, checking e-mails. And all the while looking more relaxed than she was sure she would ever be. Discordant notes drifted out from the stage as the guitars were tuned, underscored by erratic drumbeats and cymbal clashes. All part of the tuning-up process. Nothing new to her. Only the scene and the anticipation of what was to come made it different.

She pulled out her phone to start doing something with it—anything!—when she heard a squeal from the speakers, saw Rick nod to Garrett and he struck the opening chords of "Take the High Road." Even with all the starts and stops to allow Mickey to make adjustments the pulsing energy of the song raced out into the open auditorium.

She knew the history of the song from Rick. He and Marc wrote it at a time when the band was at a low point, disappointed in the club dates they were getting and trying to find their own original sound. Pseudo experts were coming out of the walls telling them they had to change that sound, do this, do that, make themselves copycats of other, more successful bands. But they had stuck to what they felt good with, refining it and making it work.

Don't sell yourself short; doubt's a heavy load.

Believe in yourself and take the high road.

It was a very high-energy song, a great set opener. Last night it had grabbed the crowd and brought them to their feet. She knew it was on the list for the album, and she had a feeling if it continued to get this kind of reception, it would be the next one up in the studio.

At the end of an hour they were all apparently satisfied the sound was properly balanced. Sydney watched Gordo climb down out of the booth and walk up to Rick, chat with him and the rest of the band. Then Mickey strode out on the stage with the rest of the road crew. Time to break it down.

"You're welcome to stay and listen to the River's soundcheck," Butch told her. "You might want to hang out with the guys in the dressing room, though. Help keep them from jumping out of their collective skin."

"Thanks, but I think I'll check the lobby setup first. Like I said, I can do it for both bands. What time is dinner being delivered?"

Butch looked at his watch. "In about thirty minutes. I want them to have plenty of time to digest their food before they hit the stage."

"Okay. I'll wander back there shortly after that."

Sydney wanted to be sure she had her act together before she dove into what she knew would be a whirlpool of testosterone, with Rick paddling the boat. She absolutely could not afford to give off any vibes someone else could pick up. How she planned to accomplish it with the heat they generated still escaped her, but maybe focusing on the merchandise setup would settle her mind.

In the lobby she found a beehive of controlled activity. Workers from the distributor carried in cartons of merchandise on dollies. Security guards with no-nonsense expressions made sure no one in the crush of the crowd outside made it through the door each time it opened. Last night Full Moon interns had taken care of the displays and the sales but they didn't travel on the tour. Over the years, Butch had accumulated crews everywhere his bands played. Now the crew from Houston went about the setup with the ease and confidence of long practice.

Sydney introduced herself to everyone and gave the guy in charge her cell number.

"I'd appreciate it if you could keep me up to date on the sales throughout the evening," she said.

"Sure. No problem." He grinned. "You gotta be pretty excited about your band's takeoff. Some shock, right?"

"I am. We hoped, but you know, always anticipate the unanticipated."

He laughed. "I have to say this was damn unexpected. Word of the mob at the hotel is all over the place, you know."

A girl at the table next to him looked up. "Everyone's texting and tweeting. The concert was already sold out because Deep Blue River is always a sellout here. But the box office has been slammed all day with people offering obscene amounts of money for a ticket."

Sydney's jaw dropped. "You're kidding."

The girl shook her head. "It's almost unheard of for a band to break out after the first show the way Lightnin' has. I heard the arena has hired extra security for tonight, especially for the after-party."

The guy she'd been talking to laughed. "And good luck getting people out of here tonight. Although Butch Meredith is an old hand at this. He'll manage it."

Sydney's heart pounded as she made her way back down one of the aisles. *Every publicity agent hopes the client he or she works with will turn out to be The One.* The overnight sensation. The media darling. It so seldom happened, she'd known better than to expect it. Yet here it was. Now. For her and this band.

I can't screw this up.

She was still deep in thought when she reached the steps to the stage. Deep Blue River had arrived and were now clustered around Butch on the platform. She waved at them and headed toward the dressing room area when Branch McKellar, the lead guitarist hollered at her.

"Hey, Sydney. Tell your guys, top drawer job last night. We might end up playing second fiddle to them on the tour."

She smiled. "Nice of you to say but we both know that's not happening. We're just happy at the reception we got."

"Reception? Hell, they're all over the Internet today. We're really looking forward to the rest of the dates with them. What's good for them is good for us."

"Thank you. I'll pass that along."

Excitement pulsed through her as she made her way to the dressing room. This kept getting better and better. She could only hope last night wasn't a fluke. She'd seen it happen before, too many times.

No, Sydney, it's the real deal, her little voice whispered.

Okay. She'd go with that.

Chapter Fourteen

The rest of the day turned into a roller-coaster ride, and Sydney hung onto the roll bar for dear life. Things got so busy and crazy, she had no time to dwell on the situation with Rick or her feelings for him. She monitored Internet actively on her iPad constantly as she sat in a corner of Lightnin's dressing room, out of the way. The numbers continued to climb on the downloads charts.

The Web site had crashed at one point because so many people were trying to get on to leave comments and order merchandise and Twitter was more active than an army of ants. Her cell rang nonstop, even calls from people she'd already spoken to. They wanted to make sure they were on the list for tonight and their comp tickets would be waiting for them at the box office. Her head was spinning by the time the band finished eating and began to get themselves ready for the concert.

Now she stood in the wings, Emma beside her, and watched the band move into position on the stage. The latest text from the lobby said more than half the merchandise for both bands had sold already. Sydney texted Renee back at the office to double-check the order for additional swag for Tampa. The seats were filled well before curtain time and security passed the word there was a huge crowd outside trying to get in. The local news had run some video from the show the night before, a clip they'd gotten from the network pool, and the voice-over pumped it up with the latest iTunes and airplay numbers.

The air crackled with energy and anticipation. Even the road crews and the sound and light men were aware of something extraordinary happening. Everyone was at the top of their game backstage, checking things twice so nothing fell through the cracks. The light man ran through his cues and Butch stood onstage with Lightnin', taking a few minutes to give them final words of encouragement. His posture was loose and relaxed, and she knew he wanted to ease the tension on the stage.

"I think I'm more nervous than I was last night," Emma confided, leaning closer. "I don't know how the guys do it."

"They had a lot of seasoning playing all those club and small concert dates. They're solid performers and it shows."

"Can you believe the video went viral?" Emma shook her head in amazement. "Who on earth cares about the story of how Marc and I met?"

Sydney laughed. "Are you kidding? Everyone! You have to admit it's not your usual love story."

Emma smiled back. "I guess not."

"Besides, 'Music Lady' is sort of an anomaly. A strong love song set to a high-energy tune. No wonder it's an overnight hit."

Emma was quiet for a moment. "Syd, can I ask you kind of a personal question? If I'm out of line, just tell me."

Sydney fought back the butterflies that woke up again. "I guess that depends on what it is."

"I couldn't help but notice there's some sort of, um, attraction between you and Rick. Not that it's any of my business," she was quick to say, "but do you two have something going on?"

Something going on? Is she kidding!

She could straight-out lie to Emma, or she could downplay it and set the stage for others to do the same.

"I'm not sure—I mean, there's so much...." Why couldn't she get the words out? At least to Emma, of all people. The one person sure to understand.

"Oh, Sydney." Emma touched her arm. "I hope so. He's such a great guy. He's like Marc, serious about the band and his music and a real straight arrow."

"He is," she agreed. "But there are so many things to consider. So many obstacles."

"I hear you." She sighed. "I just hope you guys can find a way around them."

"You won't, you know, say anything to anyone, right?

Emma gave her a quick hug. "Of course not. And if you need someone to talk to, I'm here for you. I want you to know that."

Sydney hadn't been so touched in a long time. In her desperation to achieve her goals, to show Janine she could be successful in a profession the woman denigrated, she hadn't allowed herself time to make friends.

Anyway, this wasn't the moment for her to get into a discussion about her past or her goals and ambitions. Or about people like Macey Shreiner who would tear her apart because of it. Or to unburden herself and unload her fears on a friendly shoulder. Thankfully, right then, Butch left the stage, the house lights dimmed, and the local radio disc jockey headed out to greet the audience.

"Here we go," the manager said, standing on the other side of Sydney.

Emma slipped her hand into Sydney's and squeezed it.

"I won't talk too long," the deejay said, "because I know I'm not the one you came to see."

"That's right," the audience hollered back, among other things they said.

"Y'all are here tonight to see a band that's been at the top of the charts for the past three years. Let's hear you say hey for Deep Blue River."

A massive shout answered him back.

"But we also have an extra special treat for you. How many out there saw the great video of Marc and Emma on YouTube?"

The answering shout shook the rafters.

"Their brand-new—and *first*—single is busting the numbers

in less than twenty-four hours."

More yelling from the audience.

"So, tonight, we're very proud to introduce to Houston a band that in less than twenty-four hours shot to the top of the music charts. Has a YouTube audience growing by the thousands every minute. Last night, they exploded onto the scene with thirty minutes of grab-your-throat music. Ladies and gents, get ready because...." He pumped his fist in the air. "Lightnin' has struck!"

"Yesss!" the audience screamed.

As the deejay ran off stage, into the wings, the curtain opened with a forceful *swish!* The lights blazed, Rick struck the opening chord of "Take the High Road," and the audience went crazy. Emma squeezed Sydney's hand even harder as the band rolled from one number to the other and each time the applause grew louder. When Rick brought Marc up to the front and had him introduce "Music Lady," the audience chanted "Emma! Emma! Emma!"

"You're on, kiddo." Sydney had to shout to make herself heard.

Emma gripped her hand one more time before she walked out on the stage to join Marc. Sydney knew the woman was shaking inside, but she smiled and waved to the audience then hitched herself onto the stool Rick brought up front for her. Her blond hair shimmered golden in the stage lights, her coloring set off perfectly by the deep purple of the long cotton dress she wore. She sat with hands folded in her lap and watched Marc the entire time he sang. When he hit the final lyrics and the song crashed to an end he bent his head and brushed a kiss over her lips.

Sydney thought the place would shake apart with the applause and the screams and foot stomps. Then, as they'd done the night before, the band played the last verse again. When the final notes hit, the curtain swept slowly across the stage and the lights dimmed.

Sydney waited to give Emma a big hug as the woman

collapsed in her arms, still beaming. The guys were soaked in perspiration but their faces split with their grins. Butch pumped everyone's hand and gave them each a man hug. The members of Deep Blue River had gathered to watch the last song and made it a point to congratulate every member of Lightnin'. A class act all the way, Sydney thought to herself, and took a few seconds to thank each one.

Butch looked like a man at the top of the world, laughing and high-fiving the members of both groups.

Sydney grinned at her band—*her band!*—as they pumped their fists in the air. She glanced at Rick, and his eyes sought hers at the same moment with a look she could only call smoldering, heated, filled with sexual desire and an emotion she didn't even want to try and name. Hot voltage crackled between them, so intense to her she wondered why no one else noticed it.

For a good ten minutes, bedlam reigned backstage before she and Butch managed to get Lightnin' back to their dressing room. In five minutes, the two reporters who had been granted brief early access would be showing up, escorted by the security guard who had their names. Sydney wanted to make sure the guys had a chance for a cold drink and a change of shirts. A pile of Lightnin' T-shirts sat on a small table with a stack of towels next to it. The band was going nuts with excitement but, with Butch's help, by the time the guard knocked on the door, they were as ready as they'd ever be.

Rick and Marc were the main objectives for the reporters, but Rick coordinated with Sydney to make sure Danny and Garrett got some cover time, too. With his usual ease of manner, Butch had helped Sydney clear the room of nonessential people by the time the River finished their first number.

For a long moment, they all stood and looked at each other. Then Rick and Marc did the fist-bump thing, hugged the other two guys, and let out a loud rebel yell.

"We did it, man." Sydney had never seen Rick so pumped up. "Holy shit! We really did it."

"In spades." Butch grinned. "Those two reporters? They

freelance for magazines like *Billboard* and *Rock On*."

Danny's eyes popped. "Did you say *Billboard*?"

Butch nodded. "Let's hope that's one of the places she puts this interview. Sydney, I'll have my secretary follow up with her because she's got some good connections. Also...." He pulled his cell out of his pocket and scrolled through his texts. "We're getting close to a million hits on YouTube and the single just hit number one on iTunes." He looked at each of the band members. "Boys, we need to book some more studio time at the earliest opportunity."

"We're ready," Rick told him. "You just say when."

"If you're all set with 'Take the High Road,' I'll look at our schedule and see when we can fit it in. After that, we need to schedule the rest of the album." He threw his head back and laughed. "Hot damn. Can I pick 'em, or what?" He looked over at Sydney. "Come over here. Take credit for what you did, too."

"I think that goes to the band," she protested.

He shook his head. "You got them here. You had the ideas. You made it happen. Take your bow, kiddo."

When Butch got ready to leave, to catch the rest of the River's set, Sydney waylaid him just outside the door.

"First this." She grinned as she showed him the texts she'd been getting from the lobby. "Sold out again."

"Music to my ears."

"Also, if we have some time after we get to Tampa, I have a couple of ideas I'd like to run by you." Her original plan had smacked her in the face when she'd heard the deejay's words tonight. "Lightnin' has struck." She wanted to capitalize on that. Use it in their promo.

"No problem. Got your phone?" He pulled his phone out and brought up his calendar. "The concert's Saturday night, but you'll be in town by tomorrow afternoon. I had Linc cancel your commercial flights and arranged for you to fly in with the band. How about meeting for a drink about four o'clock? There's a nice, quiet little bar in our hotel. That work for you?"

She removed her own cell from her pocket and punched in

the information on her calendar.

"See you then."

"Mickey's got all the info on the charter flight. I'm leaving on a commercial flight at eight in the morning so I'll see you tomorrow afternoon. I should have the air date for TMZ by then, too. After this, they'll be in a hurry to get it out there." He shook her hand. "I'll say it again. Damn good work, Sydney."

She stood outside the dressing room in a daze as she watched him stride away, Deep Blue River's music blasting from the stage. Then she closed her eyes and allowed herself a little smile.

What do you think now, Janine?

ও৪

Sydney stopped to take a breath, looked around, and thought, *This is crazy! Good, but crazy!*

The area encompassing the stage and the wings was jammed with people. At one side, two bartenders were serving people as fast as they could. Despite the fact everyone seemed to be talking at the same time, their guests had somehow managed to demolish the buffet table. Moving the media people along from musician to musician had required skill and tact. Sydney was especially protective of Emma, promising people special interviews, even if by phone.

Her goal at all times was to guard "her boys." To avoid exposing them to questions they had no idea how to answer. To make sure everyone got his or her ten seconds with someone. Linc had texted her several times, apologizing for not being able to fly into Houston and offering suggestions. But as the after-party wore on, she found herself in a groove, juggling people and situations and almost feeling comfortable.

Until a voice in her ear cut into that satisfaction.

"So, you don't plan to leave me alone with Rick, right?"

She turned and stood almost nose to nose with Macey. Tonight the woman wore a Lightnin' T-shirt with skintight jeans, a leather jacket, and stiletto-heeled boots. All the makeup in the world couldn't hide the avaricious look on her face.

Sydney dug up a smile. "I have no idea what you mean, Macey."

"Oh, don't play dumb with me. You know damn well what I mean. You can deny it all you want, but I know you've got something going on with him. Be very careful. I can destroy you with one paragraph. Get in my way and you'll never work in this business again."

Nausea rose in her throat and she had to curl her hands into fists to control herself. This woman wielded a lot of power in the industry. Absolutely everyone read her blog and her columns. Too bad she wielded that power like a light saber. What she wrote could have a great impact on the band. With supreme effort, Sydney pasted a smile on her face.

"There's nothing to write about here." She kept her voice as even as possible, trying not to shout over the loud buzz of the crowd. "You'll get your interview with Rick while we're in Tampa. In fact, if you want to fly in from here, I can arrange lunch for the three of us."

"What's the matter, Sydney?" Her smile was more cruel than friendly. "Afraid to trust him alone with me?"

Count to ten. Count to ten.

"You know one of us is always present at an interview, especially with a new band. That shouldn't come as any surprise to you."

Sydney needed to handle this and get back to babysitting the band. People were trying to hand them business cards and Danny and Garrett, in particular, had panicked expressions on their faces. And then Butch was beside her, the familiar casual grin on his face, his voice pitched in a low, easygoing tone.

"Anything I can help with here? Macey, we're sure glad you came to Houston to see us again."

The woman curved her mouth into its usual professional smile for Butch. But the look she gave Sydney said plainly enough, *I'll get what I want, with or without you.*

"Why, yes, Butch. As a matter of fact you can. I've been trying to get a one-on-one with Rick since last night, but your little assistant here seems to be putting a roadblock in the way."

Little assistant? If they hadn't been in a public place, Sydney would have smacked her.

Butch winked at Sydney. "You mean Full Moon's hotshot PR person? Hey, I'm damn glad she's assigned to Lightnin'. She's done an incredible job."

Macey looked as if she could spit nails, and Sydney had to swallow a smile.

"Oh. Well, she should know how important a piece on him in my blog would be. And my column."

"She does. We both do. I'm sure she wants to make it happen." He looked from one to the other. "I don't see a problem here."

Sydney thought if Macey moved any closer to Butch, she'd be crawling inside his clothes.

"The *problem* is I called today to set something up for tonight and she turned me down flat. What's with that, anyway?"

"Macey, you've been in this business long enough to know we wouldn't be able to squeeze that amount of time out of today's schedule. But if you want to meet us in Tampa, I know we can set something up."

"I was in the process of trying to arrange it," Sydney told him. "Lunch in Tampa for the three of us. I suggested Macey fly in from here and let me know which day worked best for her."

"And I told *her*," Macey interrupted, "that if she's busy, Rick and I can certainly handle lunch just the two of us. Don't you think?"

She had such a look of arrogance on her face that Sydney wanted to smack her.

Butch chuckled. "Nice try, Macey, but this isn't your first rodeo. You know I never let any of my clients alone with anyone from the media. Sydney needs to be there. In fact, give me just a minute here." He pulled out his cell and scrolled through his calendar. "I think it might be good for the four of us to get together. I can give you the background on how and why I signed the band." He looked at Sydney. "That work for you?"

She wanted to hug him. Swallowing a smile, she slid her own cell out of her pocket. "You bet, but do you have the time?"

He nodded. "I'll be there early to handle some business, but the charter won't land until around one." He looked at Macey. "That means lunch won't work. But Sydney and I were already planning to meet in the hotel bar at four. How about if we move it to my suite so we have some privacy? She'll let Rick know to join us and you can get your interview. Sydney? That okay with you?"

She nodded. "That's fine. That good for you, Macey?"

Stymied in her efforts to schedule the alone time she wanted with Rick, the woman looked from one to the other before dipping her head in a sharp nod.

"I've got some other interviews to do in Tampa. I can schedule them earlier in the afternoon." She shoved her phone back in her pocket. "But really, Butch, your precious little boy is safe with me."

Butch's laugh cut through the din of the crowd. "Macey, face it. None of my clients is safe with you. But we bow to your power and acknowledge your contribution to their success." He held out his hand. "Tomorrow at four?"

"At four." She watched Butch move away, the smile disappearing from her face. "Did you send him smoke signals, or what?"

Sydney frowned. "Sorry?"

"He didn't just happen to walk over here at that exact moment, missy. Oh, well." She waved a hand at Sydney. "We'll all play nice tomorrow. But understand this. I'm not finished yet. With him or with you."

She stalked away on her stiletto heels.

Sydney took a moment to pull herself together before she plunged back into the crowd. She owed Butch a debt of gratitude both for sensing her distress and for his outright support of her. But the anxiety twisting in her stomach like the start of a tornado at Macey's flip remark that this was far from over.

Tonight, Butch allowed the after-party to go on longer than usual since there was no early call for anyone in the morning. After another half hour, though, he signaled Sydney it was time to clear the decks. Both bands were exhausted from the energy they expended during the concert and coming down from the performance high would leave them exhausted.

Sydney thought her face would crack from smiling by the time the last person left the stage and the building. The road crews were still packing up the equipment for the trip the next day and the drivers Butch had on standby had carted the bands back to the hotel. He had two cardinal rules for his bands. One: no late-night partying. There would be time for that when they were off the road and in the privacy of their own homes. Two: none of Butch Meredith's bands was ever tarnished with the drugs and booze reputation other groups picked up.

"Sorry about our meeting tomorrow," Butch told Sydney when they were clear of people.

"I think it's more important for the band to get coverage from Macey," she assured him. "My ideas will keep."

"I'd like to hear them, though." He pulled up his iCal again. "Can you do breakfast the day after? At nine?"

Of course she could. Even if she'd had something scheduled, which she didn't.

"Absolutely."

"Good. Good." He paused, as if choosing his words. "I know you've been with Full Moon long enough to know what goes on behind the scenes in this industry. And I'm sure you've heard the rumors about Macey Schreiner."

She gave a short laugh. "Who hasn't? I don't understand how a woman who has such a reputation can wield the power she does."

Butch scratched the back of his neck. "This is a funny business, you know. Macey clawed her way up to where she is now, doing what it took to establish herself. She hit it lucky with a couple of entry-level bands who turned out to be winners.

People thought their success came because of what she wrote and suddenly everyone wanted a spot in Macey Schreiner's columns and blog."

"That's just so stupid," Sydney protested.

"Maybe so, but it is what it is. Anyway, she can be hugely supportive or a vicious enemy. When she sets her sights on a new objective, she makes it her business to get him. Woos him with her publicity. Plays on the insecurities practically inbred in a competitive industry like this. Usually, whoever it is she targets is seduced by her power and her blatant sexuality and not experienced enough to realize what's on her agenda."

"I don't think Rick will fall for that, Butch. He's not like your usual breed of musician. Neither is Marc."

"I'm well aware of that. And, of course, Marc is off her radar because of Emma." He cleared his throat. "But she sees you as a stumbling block in her path to Rick. She can be vicious when she attacks."

The baby tornado whirling in Sydney's stomach began to build strength. "I understand."

"Tread softly with her," he said, "and don't give her any ammunition. And if you need help, or need to run something by me, I'm as close as your cell phone."

"Thank you, Butch. I appreciate it. But I think I can handle Macey myself."

"Maybe so. Just...if there's something I need to know, don't wait to tell me, okay?"

"Okay." She grinned. "Right now I want to enjoy tonight."

"As well you should. Get a good night's sleep. Renee will be e-mailing you the overnight download and request figures and your phone will probably go crazy tomorrow."

"Okay. No problem. And...thanks for tonight."

"Sure. How are you getting back to the hotel?"

"One of the guards called a cab for me as soon as we began to clear people out. Again, thank you. For being who you are."

He pantomimed tipping his hat to her. "All part of the job."

But she knew it was more than that with Butch Meredith.

Much more. And one of the main reasons bands wanted him above almost any other manager in the business. He saw them as more than dollar signs. Cash cows. He treated them with respect unless they proved him wrong. And his clients seldom did.

With one last look around, she headed for the stage door. The guard pushed it open for her.

"Night, Miss Alexander."

"Good night. And thanks for getting the cab."

"No problem. Just part of the job."

Once more she realized it was only part of the job because of Butch Meredith.

On the ride back to the hotel, she leaned back in the seat and closed her eyes, allowing herself to relax for the first time since that morning. The tension slowly seeped from her body, replaced by pure exhilaration at the band's incredible overnight success. The day Linc assigned her to Lightnin', she'd hoped for some excitement, a mild breakout, some measurable crowd reaction. But not this. Never this.

Wow! That was all she could think.

In the next moment, Rick's face swam in her mind. Every erogenous zone in her body snapped to attention and the need for him she tried so hard to suppress swarmed through her.

The sudden stop of the cab jolted into awareness. She paid the cabbie, stopped at the front desk to leave a wake-up call, and rode the elevator up to her floor. As she walked down the hotel corridor, she scanned the closed doors and wondered which room was Rick's. As she was about to slip her key card in the lock to her room, the door next to her opened quietly and there he was, as if her mind had conjured him up.

His hair was still wet from a shower, curling at his neck. His T-shirt outlined the muscles she so familiar to her now and his old jeans clung to strong legs that had imprinted themselves upon her body. At the sight of him, her pussy throbbed, her nipples ached, and liquid soaked the crotch of her thong.

He held a finger to his lips and closed his door as he moved out into the hall. Two steps and he was so close to her, she couldn't make her brain work.

"We need to celebrate again," he told her, his lips lightly touching hers. "We did this together. All of us. The band never could have done this without you. Open your door, Sydney. I want to be with you tonight. Need to be with you."

Her heart beat so loud she was sure he could hear it. She tried to tell him she needed to be with him, too, but his touch and those few words froze her brain. She fumbled with her key card, nerves strung so taut she couldn't make her fingers work. Lips curved in a slow, seductive smile, Rick plucked the card from her fingers as he'd done the night before, swiped it in the slot, and pushed open her door. With her hand in his, he tugged her into the darkness.

"This is real, Syd. Us. You and me. Very real. Believe it."

"I do," she whispered, unable to deny it.

He cupped her face with his strong hands, eyes probing hers. When his mouth touched hers in just the softest kiss, her entire body ignited and she was lost in him. All the way.

Chapter Fifteen

*J*ust the one touch and something reached inside her and grabbed every single emotion. In one last brief flash of sanity, she realized the danger and difficulty of the situation for both of them. But then she didn't care anymore. She only wanted to be in his arms, feel his mouth on hers, his hands on her body. His cock buried so deep inside her she couldn't say where one left off and the other began.

"I wish I could find the right words to tell you how I feel, Syd." He tipped her chin up and studied her face in the semidarkness. "Hell, the first time I laid eyes on you, I knew we had something special." He grinned. "Smartass that you were."

A tiny little laugh escaped. "I was, wasn't I? It's worked to your advantage, though."

"No doubt about it. But this—this thing with us—is more than that. More than just two people coming together. This is real, Syd. You know that. Right?"

"Yes." For the first time she really, really believed it.

Just the one word, but it made him tighten his hold on her.

"It's not the high from what's going on, either. I want you to know that. This is special."

"For me, too," she whispered.

By unspoken agreement they left the lights off because, like the night before, bright moonlight streamed in through the open drapes. Sydney saw it reflected in his eyes and outlining his broad shoulders. His dark hair fell forward across his forehead, and she brushed away the still-damp strands.

She wound her arms around his neck and stood on tiptoe. As he had the night before he opened the clasp holding her hair back and tossed it to the side, fingers sifting through the loose strands. His tongue danced with a light touch across the seam of her lips in an invitation her to open for him. When she did, he slipped inside, licking and tasting every inner surface. Coaxing her own tongue to play with his, lighting a fire that surged through her body. With one arm locked, he pressed their bodies together so tightly she could feel the thick outline of his heavy erection burn against her despite the barrier of his jeans.

The kiss went on and on as they ate at each other in hunger. Only the lack of breath made them stop. When he lifted his head, she saw in his eyes everything he felt and was awed by it.

She tugged up his T-shirt and he moved his arms long enough for her to yank it over his head. His fingers fumbled with the buttons on her blouse until he managed to get it open and practically rip it from her body. With one hand, he flicked open the front clasp of her bra while the other cupped a breast in his warm palm. His thumb rasped a nipple, abrading it.

The tension of trying to restrain himself vibrated through his body but the kisses he trailed across her cheek were light as a feather. He moved unerringly to that spot behind her ear and the touch of his tongue set every nerve in her body on vibrate. He gave a gentle nip then soothed the place with a lick of his tongue. Then he was back, claiming her mouth again. He tasted her teeth, the inside of her cheeks, everywhere he could reach. Who knew gums could be such an erotic area?

Somehow he untangled their arms to pull her bra free and tossed it somewhere in the vicinity of her blouse. Her heart thumped so hard she was sure he could hear the sound of it as he nibbled his way down to her breasts. His warm mouth closed over one taut nipple, pulling it and teasing it with his tongue. A moan rippled from her throat as hot sensations danced over her skin. Her legs trembled so much she wasn't sure they could hold her upright and she dug her fingers into the hard muscles of his upper arms for support.

When he nudged her backward she sank gratefully onto the bed and gripped the edge for balance. Fingers undid the button on her slacks and tugged down the zipper. When Rick pulled the material down her legs, he followed its trail with his mouth, down one side then the other. She shivered at the delicious, hot sensations that skated through her and her pussy convulsed with need.

As soon as her slacks and her shoes were disposed of, he kissed his way from one ankle to the other. His mouth followed a path along the inside of one leg, skimmed over the sheer fabric covering the curls on her mound, and ended at her other ankle. He paid special attention to the area at the side of her knees and the crease where thigh and hip joined. The friction of his tongue across the thin silk of her thong made her even wetter and spiked her need for him. She reached out to touch him, to pull his head closer to her body, but he moved back far enough so he could stand up.

She stared down the length of her body at him and watched as he toed off his shoes and yanked down his jeans. No boxer briefs tonight. He was commando, for ease and efficiency. His cock sprang free, heavy and thick and engorged. Her hands itched to hold it and stroke it. When she tried to sit up and reach for it, he shook his head.

"Not yet."

Somehow he managed to yank back the bedcovers and move them both so she lay flat on her back. He hovered over her, his eyes so filled with passion and desire her heart clenched. Then he proceeded to torment her with his mouth and his fingers in a slow, sensuous pattern. Her breasts, her nipples, the line down to her navel, every part of her he touched received intimate attention. With incredible slowness he tasted her, nibbled, sucked then nibbled again. The touch of his mouth on her inner thighs heated her skin like the flame of a candle.

Not an inch of her body was left untouched. If she'd been on fire from the moment he kissed her, every cell now had become victim to an out-of-control conflagration. On and on it went, until she wanted to scream with need.

And with every touch, every kiss, every lick he sent her a message.

You are part of me. Mine. You belong to me.

She arched her body up to his mouth.

Message received.

He covered the triangle of silk over her cunt with his mouth and the pressure of such an intimate kiss to her body made her cry out. He closed his teeth over her clit, fabric and all, and a climax roared through her, shocking her. He kept his lips closed over that hot little bud until the tremors in her body eased and slowed. Then, with his teeth, he dragged the material down her trembling legs until it was gone. He opened the lips of her pussy, blew a soft breath on his tender skin and proceeded to lick every bit of her cream from her orgasm, so slowly and thoroughly she felt a climax build inside her again.

When he lifted his head, his lips were slick with her juice.

"Syd, Syd, Syd." He ran his tongue seductively over his lower lip. "God. You are just so amazing."

Without warning he flipped her over and began a similar assault on her back. Neck first, that place at the nape that drove her wild. Then little kisses and licks the length of her spine. When he began peppering slow kisses over her, she squirmed and pressed her hands against the bed and lifted her hips in an attempt to push herself up to him. He gave a soft laugh, a low rumble against her sensitive flesh, and tightened his grip on her hips.

When he drew the tip of his tongue through the hot crevice of her buttocks, she cried out in pleasure. She tried to move her legs apart, silently urging him to move his mouth lower but he seemed determined to torment her until she couldn't stand it anymore. As carefully as he kissed and licked his way up the front of her legs, he was even more meticulous with their backs.

She was sure flames erupted from behind her knees as he made love to them with his mouth.

"Please," she begged, gripping the pillow. "Please, Rick."

Every nerve cell was on fire, every pulse point throbbing. She needed him inside her. She watched impatiently as he dug a condom from his jeans pocket and rolled it on.

"Bend your knees," he told her.

She did and dug her heels into the bed. Then he was over her, his hands bracketing her head. His penis prodded at her entrance and stopped just inside. When his eyes met hers, she was sure he could see clear to her soul.

"Let me have all of you," he urged. "Don't deny this anymore."

The little voice inside her, told her she couldn't run away from this emotional explosion between them anymore. As much as she'd tried to fight it, there it was. He'd found his way into the thing she'd held onto for so very long.

Her heart.

And captured it.

Oh, God!

Moonlight streamed over him like some magic silver curtain.

"You have me," she said, tearing away the last barrier.

Then he rolled his hips and, with one smooth movement, thrust completely inside her. Automatically she lifted her hips up to meet him, tilting herself enough to take him deeper yet.

"Jesus!" The word whistled through his teeth.

Again he held still, staring down at her. She could no more have closed her eyes than told him to pull away.

"You belong to me." Not a question. A statement. "Don't ever try to deny it."

"Okay," she whispered.

He drew in a long breath and began a slow in and out glide, eyes still locked on hers, every thrust a punctuation of what he'd said. As he moved, he whispered to her in the darkness. Sweet words, hot words, loving words. Words that spiked right into her heart and lodged there permanently.

"I could lick you forever and never get tired of it. I want to go to sleep every night with you in my arms and wake up the same way in the morning."

"Me, too." The words slid from her lips without her even realizing it.

"I want this always, Syd. You're my heart. My soul."

The slow, torturous motion pushed her up and up to the brink of an explosion and kept her at the edge until her body screamed for release and fulfillment. She heard herself beg him. Wrapped her legs around him to pull him in tight and lifted her hips up to him. But the deliberate slide and drag never varied in its tempo.

Slow only worked for so long, though. She could tell the moment his control snapped. His rhythm sped up and he pounded into her, harder and harder. She felt the tautness of his muscles as he drove for control, determined to hold himself back and wait for her. The moment her cunt began to squeeze around him, he gave it up and let the orgasm take them both.

Sydney was sure a giant fist had grabbed them up and shook them until their bones rattled, until every muscle clenched and unclenched. It seemed to go on forever, until she had no air left to breathe, until her heart threatened to pound out of her chest. They roared through space, tumbling and twirling, wondering if the sensations would stop, praying they wouldn't.

At last, the intense shuddering subsided, leaving them both sweat-slicked with only the barest ability to breathe. Sydney was sure she'd never be able to move again. It surprised her when she had the strength to lift a hand and stroke his hair. Caress his cheek. His eyes were closed now and his breath a soft breeze against her skin. She could have stayed like this forever, satisfied and replete.

And cherished.

With every whispered word, every thrust of his body, every touch, Rick Trajean had sent her a message.

I love you.
And, silently, she answered him.
I love you, too.

ભ

The jangling of the phone on the nightstand jolted Sydney out of a deep sleep. Eyes still closed, she reached over for the receiver and listened to a recorded voice tell her it was time to get up. Her mind received the message but her body protested, big time.

Five more minutes. Just five.

She lay there for a moment with her eyes closed as she tried to unscramble her brain.

Connect with Mickey, so he knew to take the band out the back way this morning. *Check.*

Make sure he texted the guys not to go into the lobby area of the hotel. *Check.*

Pull up the coverage of last night's concert and check the overnights on iTunes, Twitter, and Facebook. *Not yet.* She'd do that on the plane. Then she could share it with the guys right away.

She shifted her body in bed and it protested in several places. The memories of the night before with Rick surged through her brain.

Oh, God! I did it again.

Forcing her eyes open she hitched herself up in bed and looked around. Of course the room was empty, a situation that left her in the momentary grip of conflicting emotions. She wanted to wake up with him wrapped around her. Have him make slow, delicious love to her. Whisper the same words so she knew they were real. A great way to start the day.

Every day!

Something had changed last night. Whatever simmered between them had erupted to a full boil. It wasn't just her body that capitulated to him. Now he had her heart. And, oh, that was dangerous.

This was all so new to her. She clutched the sheet to her, as if strange eyes in the room watched her, and tried to make sense of what she'd gotten herself into. Not in a million years had she ever expected to meet a man who rocked her world the way Rick Trajean did. Oh, sure, in the beginning she'd insisted it was sex. Nothing more. The way she'd laid it out for him after the first night. They had to be once and done.

She had spent so much of her life locking up her emotions and guarding her heart, she had no idea where to go from here. She only knew she couldn't turn away from Rick anymore. Deny the deep emotional connection between them.

Now, she wanted it all, Rick *and* The Plan.

No, Janine. He won't derail me. I'm going to show you how to have it all.

She closed her eyes and smiled when she remembered his loving words, his warm touch. As she sat there, her body hummed from the way he'd made incredible love to her last night. No, she didn't intend to run from this anymore. Going back to his room last night had been the smart thing for him to do. She could only hope no one saw him in the corridor. Time for the two of them to have a long talk about how to deal with their situation. She didn't want anything to detract from the band's unprecedented debut.

So how should they handle it? Should she talk to Linc first? To Butch? Would they pull her away from the tour and assign Lightnin' to someone else? She didn't think she could handle that. With so much of herself invested emotionally in both the band and the tour, it had become important for her to stay with them. And do her job.

Could she keep what she felt under wraps? Could he? Would a word or a gesture accidentally give it away to others? She worried the most about Macey Schreiner and others like her. They could destroy both her and the band out of sheer viciousness.

Part of your job to figure it out, Syd.

Yes. Her job. Focus on that and worry about the rest later.

She checked the clock and realized she had just over an hour to dress, eat something, and be downstairs for the ride to the airport. Then the flight to Tampa.

With the band.

And Rick.

Was he as eager to see her again as she was to see him?

God, could I sound any more like a teenager?

She ordered coffee and toast from room service then headed for the shower. Still foggy from sleep—or lack of it—her head filled with memories of the incredible night, she nearly missed the note on the vanity.

Wanted to leave this where you'd see it. Last night was about so much more than sex. You know it and I know it. I want this, Syd. We'll make it work. ILY.

PS. Text me when you get up.

Rick

She stared at the note, reading it again. *ILY.* I love you? He'd said everything but those words last night, but she hadn't really needed them. Everything else he said, everything he did, gave her proof of his feelings. They had to find a private place to talk. Work out details. She would not allow them to be fodder for gossip bitches.

Going back into the bedroom, she picked up her phone from the nightstand.

ILY2. Tlk early aftrnn?

She hit Send. In less than a minute, the reply came back.

Okay. C U on the plane.

For the first time since she began this journey, The Plan wasn't the most important thing in her life. Not that she could or would abandon it. She was a professional. She could still do her job and do it damn well.

But first, she had to get dressed.

ୡ

Rick stood in the rear service area of the hotel, stared at the text message, and swallowed a smile. Maybe they couldn't say the actual words to each other yet, but this was good enough for now. It showed him he hadn't misunderstood anything about last night. She might have fought him on it before, but last night told him she had the same feelings he did. The text certainly validated it.

So what did they do about it? He'd been so focused on getting her to admit they had something more than hot sex, he hadn't thought beyond that. He snorted. Yeah, him. The great Rick Trajean. The planner. The guy in control.

This morning, on the spur of the moment, he'd written *ILY* on the note he left her. *I love you.* Now wanted to kick himself for doing it like that instead of telling her in a proper setting. He'd promised himself he'd tell her when he believed they were both ready but, after last night, he didn't have one ounce of doubt left. He did love her. He hadn't gone looking for this, hadn't expected it. Maybe hadn't even wanted it. But there it was and he wanted to embrace it. He only hoped she didn't think he was stupid for telling her this way.

But then she texted back *ILY2* and he wanted to shout *Yes!* He had all he could do to control himself.

He wondered if she'd ride to the airport with them. They'd be in the van with the rest of the band. Could they keep the others from feeling the vibes between them? Stop themselves from exchanging silent messages? And what about on the plane, when there would be twice as many people?

Quit driving yourself nuts. You're an intelligent adult. You can handle it.

"Hey!"

Mickey Farentino's foghorn voice broke into his thoughts. He looked up from his phone and saw the rest of the band move toward the exit. Mickey had texted each of them they'd leave the same way they arrived to avoid a repeat of the day before.

"Huh? Oh, sorry. We ready to roll?" He stuck his phone in his pocket.

"If you'll move your lazy ass." Mickey laughed. "Still jazzed from last night? I don't blame you."

Mickey would be transporting Lightnin' to and from hotels and airports on this tour the same way Deep Blue River's road manager transported them. The sound men and road crews for both groups would manage the truck holding all the equipment. Rick was relieved those arrangements didn't sit on his shoulders anymore.

"I'm good," he assured the road manager as they walked down to the delivery parking area. Then he laughed. "Although I don't think any of us have taken it all in yet. Not completely."

Mickey looked over at him as Rick climbed into the shotgun seat. "Let me just say, kid, that I've been doing this more years than I'd like to admit. I've worked with a lot of exceptional bands. Dynamite bands. But it's been years since any of them came out of the gate the way you guys did. You know why? Because you've got the goods. A sound that really rocks people and songs they can't get out of their heads. Did Butch, Sydney, or anyone, give you the overnights yet?"

Rick shook his head. "No. I figure she'll go over it with us on the plane." He looked at the road manager. "She is flying with us, right?"

"Oh, yeah." He laughed. "Sydney will be sticking to you guys like glue."

Exactly how I want her stuck to me.

"She riding to the airport with us?"

Mickey shook his head. "She'll leave through the lobby and take the shuttle. It's better that way."

She was all he could think about as they rolled down the freeway. She had become so embedded in his mind, his soul, his heart in such a short time. He still had trouble processing all of it. Sydney had insisted they keep this private for now, a wise decision. And not only because of what the media reaction would be. He wasn't ready to share what they had with anyone else yet. After the tour, they could sit down and make plans. Talk about what came next for them. Discuss their future, because they damn sure had one. Together.

Lost in thought, he didn't realize Mickey was talking to him again.

"Oh, sorry, Mick. What were you saying?"

"You're either in love, in lust, or concentrating too hard on tomorrow night's concert. Which is it?"

"Oh, the concert. Definitely. What's up?"

"Just wanted to let you know you guys are already registered at the hotel again. I'll text one of the security guards Butch hired when we leave the airport in Tampa and he'll meet us at the back door with the key cards. We won't go through the lobby at all."

Rick shook his head. "I feel as if I'm dreaming this. Any minute I expect someone to punch me and wake me up. Or tell me it's all a mistake and we need to go home."

"Nah. Not happening. Butch wouldn't have signed you if he didn't think you had this kind of potential. Everything worked just right." He laughed again. "Gordo and I are really going to enjoy this tour."

Rick liked to think he didn't impress easily but driving up to a private area of the terminal sure beat standing in long lines for commercial flights. Not to mention the aircraft itself, which about knocked everyone sideways.

"Holy shit!" Danny stopped partway into the cabin, blocking the doorway.

"Get moving, idiot." Rick nudged him forward. "You can gawk all you want when everyone's seated."

But he had to admit being wide-eyed himself at the luxury of the cabin, the padded seats with tables, the flight attendant waiting in a small galley to serve them. Deep Blue River arrived seconds later so Rick moved his guys to the rear to make room for them. The members of the River grinned at Lightnin' as they piled into the plane, congratulating them again on another successful performance.

There were groups of plush leather seats in various configurations. Rick headed for one in the very back that faced the one opposite.

"Syd and I will have stuff to discuss," he told the band, "so I'll hold this for her. You okay with that?"

They were so excited to be flying to their next gig on a multimillion-dollar plane they didn't care where he sat. Nor did anyone make suggestive remarks about he and Sydney sitting together. It would be natural for them to be together and discuss business, right? He tried to relax as he kept his eyes glued to the doorway and smiled when he heard quick footsteps on the stairs. In another moment, Sydney popped breathlessly into the cabin.

"Sorry, everyone. Whew."

"You're fine," the flight attendant told her and took her luggage. "I'll put this up here with ours. Remind me to get it out when we land. Go ahead and take a seat and buckle up."

Sydney spotted Rick waving to her and grinned as she made her way to her seat.

"I left about the same time all of you did but we hit a snag on the interstate. Hope I didn't hold you guys up. As soon as I get myself together, I'll pull up all the coverage from last night's show. Butch sent me the figures on the merchandise sales, which again were through the roof. And wait until you see what's happening with Twitter and Facebook."

"Hey, Sydney," one of the River guys called. "Will you get all your followers to Like us, too?"

She laughed. "I don't think you're hurting for any, but thanks for the thought."

Rick was doing his best to keep his face expressionless but, damn, it took more effort now than he could have imagined. His eyes drank in the sight of her as she settled opposite him. He wished she'd quit pulling that gorgeous hair back in a clip but then decided it was better when it hung like a loose silk curtain around them only in the privacy of the dark. Just for the two of them.

She set her briefcase down and buckled in before she looked at him. The naked emotion in her eyes nearly knocked him sideways. He scanned the cabin with a casual glance to make sure no one paid attention to them. Then he mouthed, *I love you.*

Her eyes widened.

Jesus, Trajean. Way to find a romantic setting to say it the first time. This is as bad as the stupid note you left on the vanity this morning.

The engines turned over and the sound filled the cabin as the plane moved onto the taxiway and headed for the runway. With everyone focused on the takeoff, Sydney nudged him with her toe. When he looked up she mouthed, *I love you, too.*

Okay, then.

Somehow he would get through the rest of the day, even the interview with that shark Macey Schreiner. Tonight, after Sydney took care of whatever she had to, he'd make sure to go to her room. In the proper mood setting, he would say the words again and again. The thought made him smile. It also made his cock swell and harden. He shifted uncomfortably in his seat, adjusting his jeans as best he could. He looked at Sydney again and noted her small, knowing grin.

Great.

Again he checked the cabin to see if anyone caught the little byplay, but his guys were too busy looking out the windows and Deep Blue River was chatting in their seats at the front. So he grinned at Sydney and winked.

As soon as the plane reached cruising altitude and the word came they could turn on electronics, Sydney pulled out her iPad. He watched excitement light up her eyes.

"The reviews?"

"Look!" She leaned forward, holding her iPad so Rick could see it. "The second night got you guys even better reviews than the first. Every single one of these blogs and columns raves about last night. And a lot of them picked up that deejay's line, *Lightnin' has struck.*" She turned her head toward the rest of the band. "Guys? That list I gave you to check each day? You should start going through it. Right now!"

Elation shimmered in the air as they pulled up each Web site and devoured the words.

Alex Molina, Deep Blue River's drummer, looked back at them and chuckled. He had his own tablet out, probably surfing for the River's coverage but no one could ignore the enthusiasm Lightnin' generated.

"You rocked it," he called out to them. "Good job, guys."

"You hit Number Two on the iTunes rock chart this morning," their bass player added. "Hey. No fair. You're about to knock us off our perch."

There was a lot of good-natured ribbing, but Rick appreciated the support from one of the country's top rock bands. He'd heard horror stories of tours where jealousy ruled and the two acts barely even spoke to each other. Right this moment, excitement surged though the plane and, for the first time, he allowed himself to believe the entire tour would be successful.

"You should move over there with the other guys," Sydney whispered to him.

"Why?"

"Because they want to share this with you. You're their leader. Go on." She grinned. "I'm not going anywhere. Anyway, we have an agreement, right? Just between us."

He didn't like it but he knew she was right. They could only spend so much time together going over this stuff. The band would expect him to celebrate with them, and so would everyone else.

"Tonight," he mouthed at her. Then he unbuckled his seat belt and moved over to where the rest of the guys were seated.

The Internet provided more than enough to keep them all busy. From the corner of his eye, he watched Sydney pull up the Twitter feed and start posting. Then he turned to look over Danny's shoulder with everyone else. It was amazing to him how there could be so much chatter out there on the Internet for Lightnin'. He'd had big dreams from the moment Butch asked for a video of them and came to see them at Aftershock.

They all had. But none of them had expected an explosion of this dimension.

Butch had touched base with him that morning to remind him of the four-o'clock meeting with Macey Schreiner. He also said he'd have information on when they'd be going into the studio to cut "Take the High Road." He would discuss it with both Rick and Sydney after the meeting so Full Moon could begin the prerelease publicity.

"Damn good job," the manager told him.

Rick was sure very little in his life had meant as much to him as those words.

It hardly seemed possible more than two hours had passed when the flight attendant asked them all to buckle up for the approach to Tampa International Airport. As he took his seat again, his legs bumped with Sydney's. She looked up at him and he thought it a miracle the air between them didn't explode with visible heat. Oh, yeah. Keeping this on the down low would take some major discipline on their part. No doubt about it.

಄

Today's ride to the hotel mirrored the day before. Rick swallowed a laugh at the realization the band had become so hot, so fast, they had to sneak in and out of hotels.

Who'd a thunk it?

Mickey worked his magic again, getting them into the hotel through the delivery entrance. Deep Blue river's van was right behind them. A security guard met both bands with their key cards.

"I have one here for you, too, Miss Alexander." The man reached over two people to hand it to her. "Mr. Meredith thought you might like to make a quiet entrance. It's a mob scene out front again. He said it's just like yesterday."

Rick stared at him. "You're kidding."

The guard shook his head and grinned. "We've gotten used to it for Deep Blue River, but two bands creating this kind of response at the same time? It's nuts out there. I'm glad I get to work back here."

Service elevators delivered them to their assigned floors. Rick tried not to be too obvious about who had which room. He breathed a small sigh of relief, however, when he saw once again Sydney had the room next to his.

"What do I wear to this interview today?" he asked.

"A Lightnin' T-shirt and jeans will do it. It's very casual. Order some lunch from room service. I'll knock on your door about quarter to four, okay?"

He looked up and down the hallway but everyone else had disappeared. "How about lunch together?"

She laughed. "We wouldn't get much eating done, and we need our strength. Anyway, I've got work to do. See you at quarter till."

He'd count every minute.

രു

Sydney and Rick were already in Butch's suite when Macey knocked on the door. Butch had made sure to give Sydney a heads-up on what to watch for.

"She's a schemer, a shark, and a bitch in heat," he said, "but she's put herself in a position of power. Don't worry, though. That's why I'm here, to deflect her if necessary."

"Thank you," Sydney breathed. She'd be happy when this damn interview was over.

Butch had the minibar open and room service had delivered coffee and pastries. Despite Sydney's efforts to nudge Macey toward one of the big armchairs, the woman linked her arm with Rick's and managed to maneuver him so they sat on the couch together. The woman's eyes flashed anger when Rick slid to the opposite end of the sofa, a silent but unmistakable definition of a personal barrier between them.

Butch served drinks for everyone, including bourbon for himself he barely sipped. Sydney and Rick went for diet sodas, but Macey opted for wine. She drank thirstily from the white zinfandel he poured and held the glass out for another one. As the wine flowed through her system, an avaricious look blossomed in her eyes. She tried to move closer to Rick, then apparently thought better of it and settled for a heated look.

"I always like to get intimate for these one-on-one interviews, don't you?" She gave him a knowing wink. "Too bad it couldn't be just the two of us."

"I think this little group is just the right size." Sydney made her voice as saccharine as possible but delivered the underlying message. Macey got it but it didn't make her happy.

"We'll just have to make it work. Right, Rick?"

Sydney could have kissed him when he said, "All of this is so new to us, but you already know that. And I feel much more comfortable having Sydney and Butch along for the ride. They can keep me from putting my foot in my mouth."

"Trust me to make sure that doesn't happen." Another wink, a millimeter closer, and Macey finally pulled out her voice-activated tape recorder. At last she opened her iPad and went to the list of questions she wanted to ask.

Sydney did her best to maintain a calm appearance. She took all her cues from Butch, noting the smooth way he deflected some of Macey's questions and requests, and fleshed out some of Rick's answers to others. He also appeared to keep a close eye on Sydney's interaction with Rick. Little signals. Any indication of something Macey would sink her vicious little teeth into.

Before tomorrow night, Rick and I need to give Butch a heads-up on our situation. And assure him we won't act like goofy teenagers or let whatever this is interfere in any way with the tour.

"You know, Butch," Macey said for what seemed like the umpteenth time, "I think Rick and I have got it covered. You and Sydney must have a zillion things to do before tomorrow night."

Butch just continued to lounge in his chair, his posture

casual, a smile on his face. "We'll get them done. The two of us have a meeting right after this so it makes sense for us to hang around. Right, Syd?"

"Absolutely," she agreed. God, he did that so smoothly. She hoped one day she'd get to that point.

She expected Butch to send her some kind of signal when it was time to wrap things up, but it looked like he expected her to do it. Okay, then. Enough was enough. She watched Macey lean over toward Rick now and give him suggestive looks, not to mention a peek at her cleavage. She'd found a dozen reasons to reach over and touch him. Rick, God bless him, did his best to avoid anything Macey could misconstrue as suggestive without pissing the woman off. Either she didn't get the clues, or she deliberately ignored them. Sydney would need all the help she could get to control this situation.

She drained her glass.

"Think you've got enough now for a good interview, Macey? We're sure glad you wanted to do this piece."

"Yeah, thanks," Rick added. "Appreciate it."

"And," Sydney went on, before Macey could object, "we've got a few little things for you." She picked up the tote she'd left on the side bar. "A Lightnin' tote, one of the first. We wanted you to have it because you are special to us."

Sydney didn't know who gave off more hostile vibes, her or Macey, but she didn't care.

How long before the woman took the hint?

If she trashed Sydney in her blog, well, she'd figure out how to deal with it. Something else to talk to Butch about when she and Rick did the true confessions bit.

"Oh? Well, wow." Macey directed her smile to Rick. "Thanks."

"More key chains," Sydney continued, "a drinking cup and a travel mug, so you can take the band with you wherever you go." Finally, she pulled out was a Lightnin' T-shirt and took a silver marking pen from her pocket. "And, as requested, Rick will be very happy to sign it for you."

Macey arranged her face in a pout, directing it at Rick. "I was hoping you'd do it while I had it on." She winked at him yet again. "Maybe across the front?"

"He can get a smoother place for his signature this way," Sydney told her, ignoring the evocative suggestion and laying the garment out on the coffee table. "Rick, make it nice and big, okay?"

Rick barely hid his grin as he took the pen from her and wrote *To Macey, with special thanks, Rick Trajean.*

"Here you go," he told her. "A one of a kind." He stood up before he handed it to her, easing away from her.

"Oh. Thanks again." Her smile was that of a marauder hunting the kill.

"Always the joker," Butch said. Sydney knew he'd been through this many times before with Macey and was sure he'd have to do it again. He pushed his chair back and rose. "Thanks, Macey. Once more, we really appreciate this."

"I'm sure we'll be seeing you again on the tour," Sydney added.

"Oh, most definitely. Have laptop, will travel. I'm going to try and hit most of the tour stops." Macey rose and gathered her things. "Thank you so much for the goodies." She lifted the tote. "You know I always like to be first with new things." She glanced at Rick as if expecting him to say something, then shrugged. "Okay, then. Will there be a backstage pass for me tomorrow night? As usual?"

"If you're still in town," Butch told her. "Syd will put you on the list."

From the corner of her eye, Sydney watched Rick tense.

Butch rested his hand on the younger man's shoulder, a silent signal for him to relax. Everything was under control.

"Of course." Sydney held out her hand, a business card between two fingers. "I'm more than happy to take care of that. And, certainly, you should feel free to call me any time you want information. I'm always available."

"I'll just bet you are," the woman said under her breath.

"Looking forward to seeing you again." She opened the door to the hallway.

The smile Macey gave her was one part bitchiness and two parts hostility. "Oh, me, too. Of course."

In a pig's eye.

They watched her walk away, hips in an exaggerated sway. She stopped, turned slightly, and blew a kiss to Rick. Then she disappeared down the hallway.

"Why do I feel like I need a bath?" Rick asked when the woman was out of earshot.

Butch laughed. "I often feel that way myself after a meeting with her. Okay, let's all relax and discuss studio time and our plan for the release. Our next stop is Atlanta. That means backtracking, which I don't usually like to do. However, I've had the date for the River there for some time. Tampa came up after we booked Atlanta so we'll just make it work."

"We can handle it," Rick assured him. "But that's a lot of driving for the road crews."

The manager nodded. "Fortunately, or unfortunately, they're used to it. However, the schedule also means we have four days before we hit the Carolinas. There's a great recording facility in Atlanta I love using, so we're going to take advantage of it to cut 'Take the High Road.'"

Sydney opened her Notes section on her iPad and began entering items.

"What will you need from me?" she asked Butch.

"Short media releases that tease the recording session. And put in a reference to when the rest of the album will be cut. Which, by the way, won't be for another three weeks."

"Yeah," Rick said. "I looked at the dates and noticed we come back to San Antonio after the Carolinas before we head out again. Does that mean our part of the tour is over then?"

Sydney waited just as tense as Rick for the answer. The original contract dates spelled out a fairly short tour. What would happen now? Would Butch make changes? She hoped?

Butch grinned at them. "Oh, hell, no. I should smack myself

for not at least anticipating what's happened." He looked from Rick to Sydney. "You always hope you'll get that one band that explodes on the scene. When I got the sales figures from the first night alone and saw the iTunes downloads, I realized I'd have to do some juggling."

Sydney wet her lips. "That's why you want to get the album done now?"

"You're right. Originally I planned to tease the public with a release now, then another in a few weeks and slowly work on the album. But like last night's deejay pointed out, Lightnin' has struck. We need to take advantage of it, pronto."

"Will the tunes come from their show performance?"

"Without question. The public is screaming for more so we're going to give it to them. Syd, I'll text you the info for the studio in Atlanta. You need to sit in on the session."

Sit in? Sit in?

She wanted to pump her fist and shout, *Yes!* Not that she hadn't observed sessions before, but this was *her* band and therefore special.

"I'll be there. That's a given."

She avoided looking at Rick, afraid the shared excitement would be underscored with the ever-present heat that blazed between them. Tonight she'd talk to him and make arrangements for them to have a sit-down with Butch tomorrow. Her nerves snapped and fired as she thought about what they'd say and Butch's reaction, but she also was smart enough to know, especially after today, how valuable Butch's input and experience would be.

"When we get back to Texas, folks," Butch continued, "I want the band to have one week of rehearsals before we hit the studio. And I'll use the time to contact the venues for the rest of Deep Blue River's dates on this particular tour. Let the managers know we're keeping Lightnin' as the opening act." He finally took a healthy slug of his bourbon. "I don't want to jinx us but with the reception so far, the sales of merchandise, and the downloads of the single I can see adding an extra night in some places." He grinned at them both. "So buckle up, you guys. We're gonna be in for a wild ride."

"What about Emma?" Sydney asked. "She'll have to get back to work after Tampa."

"I plan to sit down with her and Marc this evening. With the dollars Lightnin' generates, it's worth my while to put her on as an assistant, pay her a salary, and make sure she's at every show."

Sydney's jaw dropped. "You'd do that?"

"Hell, yeah. I'd be a fool not to." His face sobered. "I just hope they don't think I'm trying to buy them."

"The fact is," Rick interjected, "Emma can't wait to quit that job. She has another career in mind, so I don't think she'll mind too much. Is it okay if I kind of pave the way with them?"

Butch nodded. "You guys have been friends for years. I think that would help. Thanks."

"I'll go over this other stuff with the rest of the band, too," Rick assured him. Then he frowned. "Deep Blue River won't get upset we're horning in on them, so to speak, will they?"

"Are you kidding? They've been in your position before, done it, got the T-shirt to prove it. Anyway, they like you guys a lot, as well as your music. And they're smart enough to see it's a good blend with them. Rick, you and your guys are handling yourselves really well. You're probably freaking out, but I'm proud of how you're all dealing. You too, Sydney."

"Thank you. I appreciate hearing that from you."

Butch looked at his watch. "I need to get going. I'm meeting some people for dinner. Rick, you and Sydney need to take the band out for dinner tonight. She'll put it on her agency credit card. It's all worked out with Linc. But no Lightnin' T-shirts and find some out of the way place. If we're going to have a mob scene I'd like to have it tomorrow night. Okay? We good to go?"

They both nodded.

"Will you have any time available tomorrow?" she asked. "I know I'll have a couple of things to run by you."

"Sure. How about right before the soundcheck? We can

meet in the lobby around one and catch a quick lunch here. And be ready for the calls you'll be getting from the media you contacted here."

She held up her phone. "Already got a bunch today. I told everyone I'd get back to them after our meeting. Did you want to sit in on any of the interviews? I know you'll use your judgment about how to handle things so it doesn't interfere with the soundcheck or anything. So just have at it."

"No. It's your ball game, and you're doing very well. Set up the interviews you think will be the most advantageous. Just make sure to e-mail me which ones so I know what to track."

"Works for me," she told him. "And thank you."

He opened the door and shook their hands. Then they were out in the hall. As they waited for the elevator, Sydney stared at Rick. She was sure she had the same stunned expression on her face he did.

"Holy shit," he said at last.

"In spades," she agreed.

They stared for another long moment.

Then Sydney cleared her throat. "I'm going to check out some places for us to eat tonight. Maybe the concierge has some suggestions. We'll have to leave and return by the service entrance again. You know that."

"If you asked me before this tour started whether I thought we'd have to avoid huge mobs at the various hotels, I would have told you you're crazy."

She laughed. "Maybe I am. Maybe we both are. But it's a good kind of crazy." Then she sobered. "Rick, after the meeting with Macey today, it might be wise to get out in front of our situation before she does some real damage. We want the publicity coverage to be about the meteoric rise of the band, not Rick Trajean and Sydney Alexander."

"So what are you suggesting?"

"I think we need to clue Butch in on this and assure him it will not interfere with what's going on. I don't want him blindsided. That's why I asked for the meeting tomorrow."

He blew out a breath. "I guess you're right." He leaned forward. "If I didn't think it would cause some real problems and take the focus away from the band, I'd be happy to shout it to everyone. You know that, right?"

"Me, too."

One corner of his mouth kicked up in a crooked grin. "Big change of tune for you, Miss Sydney Alexander."

She looked down at her hands. "I'm so mixed up inside, Rick. I never expected this to happen. At least not while all of this is going on. And you have to know I tried hard to fight it in the beginning."

Rick took one of her hands in his, turned it palm up, and rubbed his thumb slowly over the skin. "Yeah, me, too. Probably all the baggage we tote around."

"Hah! You don't know the half of it."

"Same goes. But maybe when we're in Atlanta, if there's time, or when we're back in San Antonio, we can start unloading it. Sound good to you?"

"It does."

He stroked her cheek with his fingertips and said in his slow drawl, "Then we'll make it happen."

&#x03;

The concierge recommended a good steakhouse for them and assured Sydney they'd be way out of the mainstream.

"We have bands here all the time." She grinned. "A fun part of my job is figuring out ways to hide them in plain sight. This place is very casual and your guys will be able to relax."

The excitement level at the dinner table zoomed into the stratosphere, especially when Rick gave the others the news about the stepped-up recording sessions.

"Holy crap!" Garrett blurted out.

"But wait!" She held up her index finger. "There's more. Rick, you want to give them the rest of the good news?"

"Our tour as the opening act for Deep Blue River isn't going to end in San Antonio," he told them. "Butch is already making calls to let the promoters know we'll be continuing on to the rest of the dates."

They were all yelling and screaming now, bumping fists, grinning like maniacs. Sydney was laughing herself but she had to remind them they were in a public place. What if people got curious, asked the hostess about them, and the mob suddenly descended?

"So, let's just dial it down a little, okay? For now?"

"Syd's right," Rick added.

"You'll have lots of time for this when we get back to the hotel," she explained. "Meanwhile, order thick steaks for yourselves and keep the alcohol to a minimum."

"I'm sure you must have noticed," Rick told her, "that we really have a lid on alcohol when we're working. Even in the dressing rooms, most of the liquor and beer is for the guests."

"I did," she agreed. "Smart move."

Danny had his phone out, texting his family and his flavor of the month. Marc and Emma kept grinning at each other. Rick had told her before they left for dinner he spoke with them about Butch's idea and they were on board. Sydney did her best to appear relaxed and make sure everyone enjoyed themselves in this brief respite before tomorrow.

Somehow she managed to sit next to Rick throughout the entire meal and not show her impatience for it to be over. She couldn't wait to be alone with him. To lock out the world for a very little while and make incredible love. To tell each other, even in whispers, how they felt. To deal with those brand new feelings so shocking and unexpected. Feelings they were allowing themselves to explore.

Dinner finally over, everyone's excitement level now manageable, they cabbed back to the hotel. They all keyed the entry to their individual rooms and disappeared inside. Instead of helping her with the lock tonight, Rick slid a sideways glance at her and mouthed, "Ten minutes."

Ten minutes. Time enough for a quick shower and to shave

her legs. For a wild moment she wondered if Rick liked his women shaved *everywhere*. Then she went back to spreading scented lotion everywhere. Thoroughly. A walk through a mist of perfume, a little lip gloss and mascara. Done.

Although she'd packed only a carry-on suitcase, at the last minute she'd optimistically tossed in a pale green shortie silk nightgown. A frisson of anticipation brushed her skin as she slid it on, the fabric so smooth and light against her body.

She opened the drapes to let in the brightness of the full moon and wondered if she should turn on the corner lamp to its lowest setting. No, moonlight had worked for them the other times and gave an air of seclusion, of privacy. She took one last look in the mirror just as a knock sounded on her door. Three quick raps. Pause. Three quick raps again. They hadn't arranged some kind of signal yet, but it could only be Rick. Sure enough, she looked through the little peephole and there he was, hair still damp from his shower, wearing jeans and a T-shirt. Butterflies beat an accelerated tempo in her stomach as she opened the door.

He slipped in quickly, closed the door, and turned the lock, then threw the safety bar in place. Sydney stood there, waiting, the beat of her heart trip-hammering. With slow deliberation he licked his lower lip while his eyes tracked every inch of her from head to toe.

"Do you know I could eat you up with a spoon? Lick every inch of your body. Every part. And still not be satisfied." His rich brown eyes darkened to the color of espresso. "Come here, Syd."

On legs that trembled, she moved the few inches separating them. When their bodies were nearly touching, he slid his palms up the length of her arms before he slipped them around to cover her ass. His hands squeezed the rounded globes, gently, as if they were two peaches. She wasn't sure which one of them moaned at the contact. She stood on tiptoe and licked the hollow of his throat. Felt his heartbeat echo inside her.

His lips touched hers in a feathery caress. Against her

mouth, he murmured, "Moonlight again. Good. But one of these nights I think I'd like to have all the lights on. Just so I can see every inch of you in minute detail."

"Okay. But for now, I love the moonlight. It highlights every thought reflected in your eyes. So, what did you tell the guys? I'm sure they wanted to party in your room."

"That we might feel like a big celebration tonight but we have an important show tomorrow. That they needed to chill out and focus in on giving the best damn performance. That they should spend the night in their rooms with their tablets, enjoying all the great press we're getting."

"And they didn't give you a hard time about it?"

"No. They're used to me not being a party animal. Never have been, so it's not out of character for me."

"Good." With a bold stroke she ran the tip of her tongue against the seam of his mouth before delicately licking each corner.

He stroked his fingers through the thick strands of her hair before tilting her head to give him better access to her mouth. On a hot slide, he pushed his tongue into her mouth, tasting her everywhere. He took the kiss long and hard and deep, holding her head captive while he drank greedily. He tasted of sin and sweetness and the promise of something new and delicious. They broke apart only when both of them were air starved.

"Sydney?" His mouth was on her jawline, her neck, then across the slope of her breasts.

"Mmm?" She had to cling to him for balance because that kiss alone made her weak in the knees.

One arm banded around her, anchoring her to him, while the other cupped her chin. "I want to say this when I'm cold sober, when there's nothing around to take away from it and you won't think it's because of all the great hot, sweaty, dirty sex that turns both of us on."

She tried to read his expression but it was impossible with just the moonlight. "Will I hate it?" She flashed a quick grin at him. "If so, let's just get right to the hot, sweaty, dirty sex."

He just kept looking at her face, his body plastered to hers. The thick ridge of his erection fought the restraint of the thin denim of his jeans.

"Sydney." He said it like a caress. "I don't know how this happened, but I love you." He gave a half grin. "And I don't have to make some excuse that when I wrote it earlier, I was only joking with you." The expression on his face was sober. "I'd never joke about something like this. It's not who I am. You believe me, right?"

"I do. Oh, yes. I do." Her heartbeat stumbled. "I love you, too, Rick. And let me just say this wasn't even on my radar. Not you. Not any guy. Certainly not falling in love."

Rick brushed her hair away from her cheek and sprinkled her face with lazy, tasting kisses.

She went up on tiptoe again and touched him everywhere she could reach.

His low chuckle promised hot sex in all the meanings of the phrase. He lifted her up in his arms, carried her to the bed, and held her just long enough to sweep the covers back. Then he placed her so she knelt on the mattress, facing him. He lowered his head to lick a line from one shoulder to the other, a line that traced her collarbone, a contact so light and tender it made her entire body shiver.

He gnawed her lips with a gentle pressure of his teeth, then moved to close his mouth around one taut nipple, thin fabric and all. Sydney sucked in a deep breath at the hot, moist contact. She tried to tug Rick's T-shirt over his head but he was so focused on laving her breasts, on cupping them in his palms, she couldn't seem to distract him. Somehow she found the energy to push herself away from him and the nipple popped out of his mouth with a *plop!*

She grabbed handfuls of his T-shirt in desperation. "Off," she panted. "Take it off. Now."

Unsteady and wobbly on her knees, she nevertheless froze in place when the bright moonlight blazed in like quicksilver and illuminated his hard pecs and abs, the fine dust of hair across his chest and the dark brown, flat male nipples. She did what the sight of his bare chest always tempted her to do. Clutching his upper arms for support, she leaned forward, took one hard nipple into her mouth, and dragged her teeth against it budded surface.

"Jesus!" he hissed through his teeth.

Aroused by his response, Sydney nibbled and licked the nipple before moving to the other. Laving the hard ridges of muscle between them, she dragged her mouth down the center of his body until she reached the point where the thick arrow of hair disappeared into his jeans. Letting herself fall back on her heels, she popped the top button on the denim and, as slow as molasses flowing upstream, she lowered the zipper. And gasped when her fingertips encountered no other material.

She looked up at his face and grinned. "Commando, again?"

He gave her his crooked half smile. "Figured the less I put on, the faster I could get it off."

"A good plan."

Her hands shook and even her voice wobbled as she pushed the jeans down to the middle of this thighs. Her eyes popped as the moon cast its silver beams onto his broad, swollen cock and the thick nest of curls surrounding it. Wrapping her fingers around the thickness of it, she stroked up and down in smooth strokes. Her other hand slid between his thighs to cup his heavy balls in a sac covered with soft, fine hair. She noticed a thick bead of fluid had emerged and tempted it from the slit of the head. Without even thinking, she brought him to her mouth and, in a movement designed to tease him with its slowness, lapped it with the flat of her tongue.

She had never been a fan of oral sex with her too-few previous partners. Maybe because she hadn't been into them that way. Didn't want to pleasure them because it meant giving a part of herself away. She had goals. Ambitions! The Plan! Perhaps it was her disinterest that drove them away each time, her unwillingness to sacrifice everything on the altar of The Plan. Maybe after she reached that point, after she'd virtually spat in Janine's face....

No! That couldn't be it. Because, plan or not, she wanted to do everything to and with Rick Trajean. And have him do as much to her. Every sexy, erotic, dirty thing he could come up with.

Love you, too.

She couldn't get the words out again because she was so lost in the sensual intimacy of what she was doing. What *they* were doing. Her hand squeezed his balls rhythmically as she took him deeper and deeper into her mouth.

Rick laced his fingers through her hair to tilt her head this way and that, to accommodate his size. She, herself, was dripping wet. Her essence clung to her inner thighs and cunt, demanding attention. When he tried to pull away from her she just shook her head slightly. Every so often she glanced up at his face through her lashes. The image of his magnificent body moonlit like some magical warrior made her redouble her efforts.

"Damn, Sydney." His voice was ragged. "Let up or I'll come in your mouth."

"Mm-hmm," she agreed and continued on with her steady stroking and sucking. She knew the exact moment he reached the point of no return. In the next second his orgasm hit, he lost all control and gave himself over to the pleasure of the climax. He came in thick spurts, his semen hitting the roof of her mouth and, as she tilted her head slightly back again, sliding down her throat and into her body. They were inextricably blended now. Inseparable. One.

He bowed his head and rested his forehead against hers.

"Amazing doesn't even come close to what I just felt. Holy shit, Sydney. That was a whole lot more than just sex."

Her lips curved in a secret, self-satisfied smile.

She slid her hands from between his legs and slowly eased his cock from her mouth. When she looked at him and licked her lips, he gave a strangled cry.

"I love you, Syd. I love so many things about you. Who you

are. The things you do. But this is going to become one of my most-favorite fantasies. Of all time."

His hands were trembling, and he curled them into fists, a visible sign of his effort to reach for control of his body. She sat up and gave herself enough balance to push his jeans down around his ankles.

Thank God he's not wearing any shoes. I'd hate to be struggling with those right now.

Chapter Sixteen

Rick kicked his clothes, or what there was of them, to the side. He took a moment to fish condoms from a pocket and toss them on the bedside table. Jesus, he needed her naked. Now. In desperation he yanked her gown up and over her head. He couldn't stop himself from taking a soft swipe with his tongue across her dusky-rose nipples before arranging her on the bed and joining her there.

His thighs bracketed her body, and his cock pointed at the top of her mound. He rested back on his heels and drank in every wonderful inch of her. The need to touch every inch of her at once consumed him and he had to dig his fingers into his palm to restrain himself. Body still weakened by the climax she had quite literally wrung from him, he was obsessed with giving her the same pleasure.

"I love you, Syd," he whispered to her, stroking her cheeks with his knuckles. "You're..." He searched for the right word, but his brain had turned to mush. "Everything."

She opened her mouth as if to speak, but he bent low over her and nipped her lower lip. With the weight of both breasts in his palms, he tightened thumbs and forefingers around each nipple. When he squeezed them hard before scraping the edge of his thumbnails over the pebbled surface he drew a ragged moan from her throat.

"You taste like hot sin," he murmured as he danced his tongue over the spot where he bit her lip, then created a trail the length of her body.

He paused often in his sensuous journey from the hollow at her throat to the tempting valley between her breasts. He released his grip on her nipples as if giving up a treasure, which they were to him, but not before one last, hard final pinch that made her twist beneath him. Her skin, as he worked his mouth down her body, felt like the smoothest silk or whipped ice cream and he felt like a cat lapping at a treat.

He left no inch of her body unexplored—the tiny curve of her tummy, the crease where thigh and hip bone joined, her knees, her ankles. Sitting back on his haunches again, he lifted one elegant foot and pressed soft kisses to the graceful arch. The sweet little sounds drifting from her mouth fueled his hunger.

Rick didn't know who he tormented more, himself or Sydney, as he took a slow journey to every part of her body. At last, when he'd tasted and nibbled every inch of her skin, he held her hips in his hands and lifted her to his mouth.

Jesus! She smells so damn sweet. And sexy.

With slow strokes he drew his tongue over the smooth, slick flesh of her pussy. He loved the flavor of her cream, a sweet-spicy blend he couldn't seem to take into his mouth fast enough. If there weren't so many other things he wanted to do with her and to her, he was sure he could have spent the rest of the night with his mouth and tongue worshiping her cunt. The taste reminded him of a decadent dessert. Best done slowly to savor each bite and not so fast the incredible experience was over too soon.

He rimmed her opening with the tip of his tongue, slow, lazy circles that elicited delicious cries of pleasure from her. Flicking it back and forth across her clit drew more of those little moans he loved to hear, sounds that made him hard. Made his balls ache.

He pulled the sensitive bundle of tissue into his mouth, closed his lips over it, and slid two fingers into her waiting channel. Sydney almost levitated off the bed. And, holy shit. She was so wet and ready for him. His exhausted cock reacted, hardening and thickening again.

With slow, rhythmic movements he stroked her clit and rubbed his fingers in and out of her. With each thrust, her whimpers grew until they became one long sound. Soon her body moved in measured cadence with his tongue and hand. She tensed, pushed herself into his touch. Her inner flesh gripped him and clenched around his fingers.

Moving his hand so he could grasp her hips, he sped up his movements until with one long, deep cry, she came. He sucked harder on her knotted bundle of flesh and curled his fingers inside her to reach her sweet spot, drawing her release out as long as possible. Aftershocks had not quite subsided when he freed his fingers and rose up over her.

"Open your eyes, Syd." He could hear the hungry rasp in his own voice. "Look at me."

When her eyelids fluttered open, he used careful, unhurried strokes to lick away every bit of her essence.

"Now we'll each carry a part of the other."

He reached for a condom and rolled it on, his fingers unsteady with desire. Now. He had to be inside her *now*. When she'd finished using her mouth on him, he was sure his dick would be limp until the next day. But watching her as he brought her to climax changed all that.

He knelt between her thighs, lifted her legs, and draped them over his shoulders. With just a moment to enjoy the sight of her spread wide before him, he guided his cock to her entrance.

"Please," she begged, even as she tried to recover from the orgasm he'd just wrung from her.

He rolled his hips and, with one strong push, he drove into her.

Oh, sweet Jesus!

He stilled, eyes closed as he took a moment to enjoy the feel of her surrounding him. She was so hot and tight, and the residual tremors in her pussy squeezed his shaft for all it was worth. Then, because he couldn't wait any longer, he pulled back slightly and drove into her again. He took it as slow as he could, stunned that he'd reached the point of no return so fast.

He set up a cadence, in and out, watching her eyes for a sign that she was on the roller coaster again. He found her clit and rubbed it again and again, his fingers moving with every stroke of his cock.

There. There she was. He could see it in her eyes. Feel it in the clutch of her cunt walls. He accelerated the tempo and then she was with him. Faster. Harder. The orgasm hit them both at the same time with unexpected force. They rocked together as intense spasms overtook them and hurled them both into an erotic black-velvet space. He fell in great jerky movements, holding tightly to Sydney so she was anchored to him.

Then, it was over. Heart galloping, lungs dragging in air, he steadied himself as he lowered her legs to the bed. He had no desire to withdraw from her. He wanted to extend the intimacy of the moment as long as possible. The world outside ceased to exist and it was just the two of them.

He caught himself on his forearms so he wouldn't bury her beneath his weight. Limp and drained, he rolled them to the side then adjusted himself so she was on top of him. He could still see her pulse hammering at the soft hollow of her throat. Her eyes were glazed with passion, her breathing unsteady.

"Tell me," he insisted in a low, hungry tone. "Tell me, Syd."

Bracing herself on his body, she leaned forward so her hair formed a thick curtain around them. And in that moment of seclusion she whispered to him, "I love you."

He whispered back, searching for just the right words to tell her how he felt. They murmured to each other, hot words, erotic words, emotional words. It was so strange to him that, for a songwriter, at such a critical moment in his life, words deserted him.

In those quiet moments, when only the two of them existed, they shared their secrets. He told her about his family and the desertion of his father. She spoke to him of her Aunt Janine, the genesis of her desire to prove herself. To succeed. About The Plan. In the dark, everything was so much easier and they opened their hearts.

They lay there, wrapped in each other's arms, for what seemed like forever. At last, he forced himself to get up and deal with the condom. When he came back into the bedroom, she stood by the glass doors to the balcony, silhouetted by the ever-present moon. He wished he could make time stand still, freeze it for eternity, a moment when the rest of the world couldn't intrude.

He walked over to where she stared outside the room and wrapped an arm around her.

"Putting on a show for the world?" He chuckled. "I think that kind of show should be for me only."

"The lights are off. I don't think anyone can see us. Or is even looking." She leaned her head against his shoulder. "Wouldn't it be nice if we could shut out the world completely? Have it just the two of us?"

"You bet." He tightened his arm around her. "Too bad we have to deal with tomorrow. On the other hand," he laughed, "there is the tour."

"Speaking of which...."

"I know. Talk to Butch about us. You're really worried about this, aren't you?"

"You've been involved in this world for a long time. So have I. I see what happens on the other side of the curtain. Rick, you have no idea how vicious some of these people can be. What they can write. Everything is great right now because the performances are outstanding. 'Music Lady' has captured everyone's attention and the single is selling in astronomical numbers."

"I hear a *but* coming."

"Yes. But. There are people out there, as in every industry, who make it their business to knock people off their pedestals. They think being negative is what makes them experts. I don't want that to happen to Lightnin'.""

"Neither do I." He stroked her way with gentle movements of his fingers. "Why does this have to be so complicated?"

"Maybe because we're both complicated people?"

He chuckled, "That we are. Okay, we'll talk to him together first thing tomorrow."

"I'll text him as soon as I get up. Maybe we can all have breakfast together."

"Meanwhile, we need to get out of the line of vision," he joked. "We look like we're posing for an adult magazine."

"And you need to get back to your room. Okay?"

"Yeah, I know." He let out a long breath. "But I don't have to like it."

"It won't be forever," she promised, hoping she was right. "We'll brainstorm with Butch on the best way to let it leak. That is, if we have his support after we talk to him."

He nodded and pulled her against him for one last, very long kiss. He insisted she wait by the door until he was out in the corridor so she could throw the locks right away. But he couldn't resist turning to wink at her before walking on bare feet to his room next door. Idly he noticed the door to the room across from him was open a tiny bit, as if someone had used the security lock to prop it open.

Weird.

Even stranger was the itchy feeling along his spine, almost a warning he'd missed something. But what?

Then he was inside his room, already missing the feel of Sydney against his body, her hands stroking every inch of him.

⊰

For Sydney, the day started with a bang. She checked her iPad before she even brushed her teeth and found more rave reviews about the concert, as well as a lot of traffic on the social-media platforms. Renee sent her a text with the latest sales figures on merchandise from the Web site and the local distributor assured her the additional goods had arrived and would be at the venue by early afternoon.

A text from Butch suggested breakfast in his suite to avoid any lurking media or wild-eyed fans and also gave her the latest rankings on the single. Her phone chimed constantly while she dressed: people who wanted a pass to the after-party, media who wanted more skinny on the band, a local deejay who wanted a short phone interview with Rick, which she scheduled.

With the meteoric rise of "Music Lady" and the craze for Lightnin' paraphernalia she now had major publications and music shows calling for some time with the band. She set up a tentative phone interview with some of them, pending Butch's approval.

Their Facebook Likes and Twitter followers were at astronomical numbers. Not to mention even the lesser-known blogs were all about the band, shouting *Lightnin' has struck!*

"I think we need to revise the T-shirts," Butch told them when they met. "Let's capitalize on the slogan."

"I'll take care of it." Sydney texted Renee even as they spoke. She nodded when the response came back. "Okay. She's good to go. She'll get onto the graphics people, get the new design, and send it to me on my iPad later today."

"We can still sell what's left with the original design," Butch said, "but I really want to push the hell out of this one."

"It means changing the logo on every type of swag," Sydney pointed out.

"I know. Renee will get me the costs, and I'll figure out the best way to handle it." He refilled his coffee cup and leaned back in his chair. "So what's really on your mind, kids? I can tell something's up."

In the end, it surprised them how easy he made their explanation.

"I had a sense something was up with you two. You can't fool an old dog." The words had a warmth to them and his approval was obvious.

"You might want Linc to send someone else out," Sydney

began, her voice and her posture both stiff.

Butch shook his head. "Not at all. You're both professionals, and you've behaved accordingly on this tour. Sydney, Linc didn't just pluck you out of your cubicle to do this. He and I spent some time going over who we thought would be the best person to handle this and we agreed it was you."

Was that a blush she felt creeping up her cheeks? "Um, thank you, Butch. That means a lot to me."

"You know how important this is," he added, "and I don't expect either of you to do anything to endanger it."

"I can promise you that," Sydney assured him. "And thank you."

"Just be ultra-careful around Macey Schreiner. I don't have to repeat what she is and the damage she can do. And let's brainstorm about how we're going to leak the news ourselves, maybe while the band is cutting the rest of the album. We've got some time to talk about it."

"I want to assure you," Sydney said, "that this isn't my normal behavior pattern."

Butch laughed. "If it was, you wouldn't be handling Lightnin' or traveling on the tour with us. Be sure you read Linc in on it but I'll talk to him myself."

"Thanks for the support," Rick put in. "You know we won't let you down."

"We'll do our best to be extra-careful," Sydney assured him.

"But some things are beyond are control," Rick added.

They spent another thirty minutes looking at the situation from all angles to make sure they had answers for any questions that could pop up. Sydney holed up in her roof for the rest of the day with her iPad and cell phone. She reviewed the list for the after-party, fielded calls from the media, worked the social-media platforms. At four, she again rode to the soundcheck with Butch and checked on the merchandise. Then Emma arrived and they shared the catered dinner with the band.

Sydney brought them up to date on all the latest reports. It was fun briefing them. They were so stunned by their unexpected success, they were like kids in a candy store.

When she followed the guys from the dressing room to the stage she sensed a difference in the air around them tonight. Lightnin' was everywhere in the media, the reviews of the concert had been killer so far, and the single was rocketing out of sight. She had managed to get most of the phone interviews scheduled for the next couple of days and some high-powered folks were added to the after-party list.

Beyond the curtain, the voices of the audience drifted back to them. Everyone in the wings had a feeling of anticipation. Of expectation. Energy just crackled in the charged environment.

Sydney stood to the side with Emma and watched the band members take their places on the stage.

"I can hardly believe this," Emma told her. "I feel as if we're living a dream."

Sydney grinned. "You are, but it's one that won't end. At least for a long time."

Butch appeared next to them out of the backstage darkness.

"Merchandise is selling like crazy," he told them. "Good thing we increased the order for this stop."

Sydney just grinned at him.

At last it was show time.

The house lights dimmed and a local deejay walked out onto the stage. An earsplitting roar rose from the crowd and people began chanting for the band.

Rick hit the opening notes, the curtain slid away, and they were on.

The performance just knocked it out of the park. For both bands. The Marc-Emma thing with "Music Lady" brought the crowd to its feet and then Deep Blue River followed up with one of the best performances they'd ever given.

At the after-party, the sensation of riding a roller coaster still clung to Sydney. Conversations were layered over conversations and everyone jostled for face time with the members of both bands. Sydney was in constant motion, doing her best to keep things under control for Lightnin' while Butch did the same for the River. She wondered as she shook yet another hand if she'd ever be as comfortable about this as Butch was.

She was just congratulating herself on all the juggling she'd been doing when she happened to glance at a corner of the backstage area.

Damn it to hell, anyway.

Macey Shreiner stood so close to Rick there was barely room for a sheet of paper to slide between them and her hand rested possessively on his arm. Her mouth was curved in a hungry smile while Rick wore a look of panic.

Sydney excused herself from the small group she'd been chatting with and headed right for that spot. If the woman had a gun, Sydney was sure she'd be dead. Macey Shreiner was not used to being thwarted in anything. Right now, she wanted Rick and she didn't intend to let Sydney stand in her way.

"So glad you could make it again tonight, Macey." She put on her best professional smile and voice. "This gives me a chance to ask when your interview with Rick will run."

"I think that depends on whatever incentive I have to run it sooner rather than later." The look she gave Sydney was equal parts cunning and irritation.

Sydney counted to five. "Just let us know whatever we can do to facilitate things for you."

"Well, for starters, you could convince Rick it's okay to join me for a drink later. That would help a lot."

Patience, Sydney.

"I'd love to, but we have a really tight schedule. In fact," she glanced to her left, "I see Butch beginning to wind things up right now." She looked back at Macey. "You know how he is about his 'boys' getting in a party mode."

"Butch Meredith needs to remember who butters his bread," Macey snapped. Then, reeling herself in with obvious effort, she looked up at Rick with that same greedy smile. "I'm hoping my guy here can make you understand how much he'd like to do this." She looked back at Sydney. "No keeping all the goodies for yourself, you know."

Sydney just stared at the woman. She was searching for the right words when Butch moved into place beside her.

"Thanks for coming tonight," he told the reporter. "You know we're always honored to have you at our events and appreciate all the good words you write about my clients."

"I could write better words if I could get some time alone with them, Butch."

He laughed, although Sydney could see the lines of irritation around his mouth. "Nice try, Macey. Let me ease the loss for you by giving you an exclusive on what we're about to do with the new logo. We're already revising it. I can make sure you get the first sketches."

Exerting firm pressure on Macey's arm, he guided her away from Rick.

"Whew!" Rick looked down at Sydney. "What a barracuda. How does she get away with it?"

"The most common answer is she slept her way into prominence with high-profile placements for her blog, used that to get her syndicated column, and then took raw young bands and worked them the same way." She snorted. "I guess she must be damn good in bed."

"Well, that's for others to find out. Not for me or any of Butch's bands." He lowered his voice even more. "Butch wants a few minutes with both bands in his suite after this, but then I'm all yours for the rest of the night."

Her body went liquid at his words, heat pouring through her. "Then I'd better make sure we wind things up here and get you up to the suite."

She turned away from him to give Butch a hand and stopped dead in her tracks. Macey Shreiner stood partway to the stage exit, staring at both her and Rick with pure hatred on her face.

Crap. She didn't need a sign to tell her trouble lurked on the horizon and she'd better be prepared for it.

Chapter Seventeen

Sydney was still zonked out when the shit hit the fan. Rick managed a couple of hours in her room after the meeting with Butch, and they'd made the best use of it. Afterward she'd been too excited to sleep. The tour had changed so much of life for her, including the details of The Plan. She'd discovered her niche in the publicity world was guiding a band that exploded on the scene. And that it was okay to fall in love with a man who returned her feelings. She wasn't in any mood to face the world so early.

The alarm on her phone was set for seven a.m. so she'd have time to dress, order coffee, and check the overnights before the trip to the airport. But it wasn't her alarm that woke her up so rudely. It was the ringtone she'd assigned to Butch. Struggling to sit up and gather her scattered wits she pressed Answer.

"Morning, Butch."

"Fifteen minutes," he told her. "In my suite."

Oh, hell. What had happened?

She was headed toward the bathroom when her phone sounded with Rick's special tone.

"Did you get a call from Butch?" he asked without even a hello or good morning.

"I did." Her nerves were doing a sudden tap dance. "What's it about, did he say?"

"Nope, but I can promise you it isn't good. Meet you there."

Sydney looked at the cell phone in her hand. Whatever residual excitement she might have retained after the great concert and even great night with Rick disappeared like smoke.

Macey Shreiner. That bitch has done something. I just know it. I never should have allowed myself to get involved with Rick.

Oh, yeah? Like you could really stop what you feel? Or what he feels?

She threw on a pair of jeans and a Lightnin' T-shirt, opened her door, and found Rick outside the door to his room. He looked more somber than she'd ever seen him.

"You should have just gone on ahead," she told him.

"Uh uh." He took her hand. "Whatever this is we're in it together."

Neither of them spoke as they rode the elevator to the next floor. Butch opened the door to his suite at their first knock.

"Come on in." He, too, was dressed down and along with his jeans and shirt he wore a grim expression on his face. He waved at the room service cart by the window table. "I ordered coffee. Help yourselves."

"I'm good," Sydney said. She didn't think she could swallow anything at the moment.

"None for me, either," Rick added.

"Sit. Sit." The smile Butch gave them was tired but not angry. "We have some strategizing to do."

They took seats across from him. Beneath the table Rick reached for Sydney's hand again.

"Okay, kids. We have a problem." He looked at Sydney. "Before I say anything else, I want you to know that you both have behaved as you should on this tour. The situation between you has not affected your work, Sydney, or yours with the band, Rick. Like the saying goes, shit happens."

"I just want to say—" Sydney began.

Butch held up a hand. "Not yet. Our friend Macey Schreiner actually called me this morning to tell me to check her column and her blog." He turned his iPad so they could both see it.

"She's really gone over the top this time."

Sydney took a look at the screen and nearly passed out.

Tidbit from On the Scene

Who is the latest toy in Rick Trajean's toy box?

Could it be neophyte publicity agent Sydney Alexander?

How lucky can a newbie get to ride the tour with Butch Meredith's new breakout band, the one everyone's talking about? Just ask Sydney. She's been glued to Trajean's side since before the tour kicked off. On the Scene *hinted at this right after opening night. One wonders exactly what made her the agent of choice since she's never soloed before. Oh. Could it be the* extra service *she provides for Trajean? And what about the rest of the band? Do they get to sample her talents, too?*

Maybe Butch needs to take a closer look at why this newbie works so hard to keep the media away from her precious boy toy. After all, the man has a reputation for keeping everything about his bands squeaky clean.

Hint to Sydney: Not the best way to make friends in this industry.

Will Full Moon have the guts to admit what's really going on and yank her home before she does real damage to the band?

Stay tuned.

Included in the body of the item were two photos, one of the two of them on her balcony and one of Rick leaving her room in just his jeans. Although the balcony shot was blurry because of the darkness, the suggestion of two naked bodies was evident.

"Some asshole had to help her," Rick spat out. "One of them outside watching Syd's room and the other hiding in a room across from us."

For a moment Sydney was sure she was going to pass out. Or throw up. Or both.

"You can always find some sleazebag who will do anything for a buck," Butch said. "At least I wasn't blindsided. Thank you for cluing me in yesterday. I appreciate it. Too bad we didn't have time to deal with this ourselves."

"She was really ticked off when I hauled Rick away from her last night," Sydney told him. She glanced at Rick.

"Can she do this?" he demanded. Anger vibrated from his body in waves. "Just print crap like this?"

"Unfortunately, the industry has allowed Macey to build her power base, even knowing how she did it. People kiss her ass because she wields the kind of influence she does. And she loves to brag that when a new band hits the scene, she bags the hottest guy for herself. At least until the next one comes along." Butch took a swallow of his coffee. "Usually her hints are pretty harmless and we've all gotten used to them. But apparently, Rick, she's well and truly pissed off she couldn't make you her newest conquest. And she's got a hard-on for Sydney, who she sees as the stumbling block."

"But—"

Butch shook his head. "Whatever you're going to say, I agree with. The woman's a venomous bitch drunk on power, and the rest of us can take the blame for letting it happen. But it does present a problem."

"I can take whatever she dishes out," Rick said. "But it's just wrong that she slams Sydney like this." He shook his head. "What a bitch."

"I agree." Butch refilled his coffee cup, took another swallow. "But she's created a situation we need to deal with. Rick, the band is hot out of the gate. Far greater response than any of us even hoped for. We can't let something derail that."

"All this because I wouldn't let her haul me off alone to some dark corner?"

"Yeah," he agreed. "And it sucks."

"So what happens now?" Rick wanted to know. "Do we put out a statement of our own? Should Syd and I just go public and tell our side of the story?"

Sydney wanted to say something, but she couldn't seem to get any words out. She was hot and cold at the same time, and so light-headed she was afraid she'd pass out in the chair. Whatever was coming she was sure it wasn't good.

"Does Linc know about this?" she finally managed to ask. She saw her career and The Plan shattering into little pieces around her.

This is what you get for falling for a man.

Janine's words were so loud in her head, the woman might have been in the same room with them.

I never should have let myself fall in love with him. I should have stuck to The Plan. Now it's all going to be ruined. Everyone will blame me.

"He does," Butch answered. "I rousted him as soon as I saw this." He leaned forward in his chair. "Sydney, this is nothing against you. I want you to know that. I told Linc that you've been doing a damn fine job."

"I should go home. Right now. If I'm gone, Macey can stop playing her games." She wet her lips. "None of this should have happened."

"You're right," Butch agreed. "Unfortunately, you're the victim here, and we both know it. But we think it's best for the band and the tour if Full Moon sends someone else out for the rest of the dates on this part of the tour. Give you the chance to step back a bit."

Sydney shook her head. "Going home, yes. But not just for a bit." She looked at Rick. "I knew this would never work. Now it's going to hurt you and the band and that can't happen."

"No." Rick nearly shouted the words. "Wait a minute here. Damn it, Butch. That's not fair. We haven't done anything wrong."

"I agree. And Sydney, let's not go overboard. All we need is a little breathing room to get things back on track. We'll reevaluate during the three-week break."

"That just stinks," Rick argued. "Sydney, you can't turn your back on us like this. We have something special here."

She wanted to put her head down and cry. "It's not special when it hurts so many other people. I know this business. That picture of us will never die. Every time you walk on stage, people will think of it. Every time I talk to a media person, they'll be picturing me naked with you. That's just the truth." She looked at Butch. "I want to get out of here. Now. Can you get me a flight home? And tell Linc he'll have my resignation first thing in the morning."

Butch frowned. "Slow down, here, Sydney. We need to take a step back, but please don't do anything drastic. Give Linc and me a chance to handle this."

"And what about me?" Rick asked. "About us? Are you just going to toss it away so easily? Or doesn't it mean anything to you?"

"Of course it does." She twisted her hands together. "But I'll just be an albatross around your neck. And Butch's. And Full Moon's. I'll be the promo slut who got naked with the band leader. You don't need that spilling over onto you."

"Don't do this." His voice was low and rough. "Please." He looked at Butch. "I don't think Syd should get all the blame for this," Rick said. "I would never have given Macey what she wants, no matter what. It's not me."

"Nor would I expect you to," Butch said. "I've had problems keeping her away from musicians before, but she's never gone off the rails like this. I think she focused all her venom on Sydney because she saw her as someone who challenged her authority. The obstacle. It's all about jealousy." He pushed away from the table. "Meanwhile, we have a lot of damage control to do, I need to talk to the others and, Syd, we need to get you out of here."

Yes. Get out of here. Now.

"How soon can I leave?"

He glanced at his watch. "You take off in two hours. Linc already made a reservation for you. Get your things together. I've already got a car coming to pick you up. Someone will meet you on the other end."

"No." She shook her head. "I'll get a cab after I land." She let out a shuddering breath. "I don't think I can talk to anyone right now."

This can't be happening. My life is turning into a nightmare because I fell in love.

"Text me as soon as you land," Rick said.

She turned to walk out of the room but Rick grabbed her hand and pulled her back to him.

"This isn't over. We'll fix it and go on from there."

Then, before she could protest, he wrapped his arms around her and gave her a soul-searing kiss.

"Think about that on the way home."

She just shook her head and swiped at the tears that suddenly blinded her.

Butch took her down the back way to where the car waited for her, gave her a reassuring squeeze as he handed her over and, less than two hours later, she was on a plane flying home. The thought of never seeing Rick again, never being in his arms, never sharing what they'd found together, made her sick to her soul. A deep-seated pain invaded her bones.

And the gossip. She could just hear it now. Sydney the slut. Sydney who could only get to the top by sleeping with a client.

And what would it do to Full Moon? Surely some of the dirt would spill over onto the agency and Linc.

She exited the plane and made her way to the baggage-claim area like a sleepwalker. She heard someone call her name and was stunned to see Linc himself waiting for her.

"It's probably not a good thing for you to be seen with me." She gave him a wobbly smile.

"It takes more than a little dirt to cause me any problems." He rested his hands on her shoulders. "We'll talk about this after we get out of the terminal. Come on. Let's grab your luggage. And, Syd? Falling in love with someone isn't a crime. From everything Butch tells me, you and Rick behaved in the best manner possible. That bitch just painted a target on your back."

"You'll have my resignation in the morning," she told him as soon as they were in his car.

"What makes you think I even want it? Let's not go crazy here. Besides, that would give Macey Schreiner more power than she needs."

She shook her head. "I can't do this anymore. I'm not even sure I want to."

All she could think was, *I did this. I put Rick and the agency in a bad situation. It's my fault.*

Linc spent most of the drive on his cell. Sydney leaned back in the seat, eyes closed, deliberately shutting out the sound of his voice. If it was about Lightnin', she didn't want to hear it just yet. If it wasn't, at the moment, she didn't care.

She'd texted Rick when she got to the airport in Tampa and again when she landed. His answer to her was simple and direct.

Butch fixing. ILY.

How could he love her when she'd damaged the thing he'd worked so hard for? She didn't even know what to say to him so she just ignored the message.

Finally, they reached her place and Linc followed her inside, carrying her suitcase.

He nodded at her living room. "Let's sit down and chat a little."

"If it's all the same to you, I don't think I'm up to much conversation right now."

He studied her face. "Don't do anything rash, Sydney. I've been in this business a long time and ridden out a lot of rough spots." He looked at his watch. "I have some things I need to take care of right away, but tomorrow we'll talk. And, Sydney? This will all work out. Count on it."

"Can you just answer a question for me?"

"Sure. Fire away."

She curled her hands into fists. "How come I never heard of Macey Schreiner doing this kind of thing before? I've worked for you for a long time. Assisted other agents. Wouldn't I have heard something?"

"Butch and I have been back and forth on this. We've spoken to some other managers and publicity agents this morning and we all agree on one thing. The woman has been a pimple on our ass for a long time. I'm sure you know there's a lot of sex behind the scenes in the entertainment business. As long as it doesn't screw things up, no one bothers about it." He rubbed his chin. "But she's never used her power as a weapon like this before. You got under her skin."

"I'm sorry." She didn't know what else to say.

"No. Nothing to be sorry for. But we can't allow her to ruin anyone just because her sex-for-publicity plan was thwarted. And we won't. That's why I'm telling you not to make any rash decisions."

"I appreciate that very much, but I think I'd better take a really big step back here. Reexamine my priorities. All this isn't doing the agency or the band any good. Or me." She stood up. "So I thank you for everything, but I think I need to move on."

"Tomorrow," he insisted. "We'll talk tomorrow."

She just shook her head and, with as much courtesy as she could muster, ushered him to the door. She knew he could spin this so it wasn't so bad. But that didn't mean it would go away. The Plan suddenly didn't seem quite so important, not when a bitch like Macey could derail it with a few words. And Rick? Right now, that all seemed like a dream. She'd allowed herself to believe in the fairy tale. To think she could have it all.

What a joke.

No matter what Linc said, it would be weeks before this died down. Before those pictures of her and Rick stopped circulating. And who knew when they'd pop up again?

She held it together until she closed and locked the door. Then she simply collapsed on the floor and let the tears come.

໖

"She won't answer my calls or even my texts." Rick sat opposite Butch, holding his cell phone, watching it as if he could literally make it chime.

"She's been hurt and embarrassed," Butch reminded him. "She was living a dream she worked very hard to realize and someone came along and threw mud on it. That's not easy to take. On top of it all, she feels she did damage to you and the band."

"The band will survive," he insisted. "This isn't the first so-called scandal in the business and it certainly won't be the last."

"True. But this was Sydney's first solo gig as an agent. The success is beyond anything anyone could have predicted. Just as Lightnin' has had their goal for a long time, she's had hers. She thinks she's ruined it by allowing herself to get involved with you."

"There are two people in this," Rick pointed out. "She didn't do it all by herself. And by the way, I had to do a lot of convincing to break down all those walls she'd built around herself."

"I understand. But, right now, she's taken all the blame on her shoulders and you won't be able to reason with her. We need to let the dust settle."

"My feelings haven't changed, and I don't think hers have, either."

"Despite all our efforts, those pictures are still popping up here and there. Especially the one at the balcony window. That's not easy to get past."

"Damn it." Rick pushed himself out of the chair. "She's the innocent in all this. They should blame me. I was the one who convinced her we could have it all. Stupid, stupid, stupid."

"You *can* have it all." Butch spoke in a very calm voice. "It will just take some getting there. And the new rush of promotion is a big help. 'Take the High Road' was an instant hit, just like 'Music Lady.' The numbers are great. Merchandise sales are zooming. And you know how well the concerts have done."

"She worked damn hard on this," Rick reminded the other man. "Now she doesn't even get to enjoy it."

Butch shoved his hands in his pockets. "Syd's been with Full Moon since high school when she worked as an intern. I don't know how much you know about her family history—"

"I know about her folks and her aunt," Rick broke in. "And what a bitch the woman was to her."

"Everything Sydney got, she worked twice as hard for as anyone else, in an effort to prove herself. Now she sees herself as a failure. Let her have some breathing room. At the moment we need to focus on the band. I promise you this will all work out."

"Yeah, yeah, yeah." He stared out the window, wondering how he would get past the pain in his heart. Or if he ever would. "We'll be home in another couple of days, right?"

Butch nodded. "And in the studio to cut the rest of the album."

"I want to see her."

"I understand. But she thinks she's doing the right thing by staying away from you. Linc and I have a plan. Give us a chance to put it in place, okay?"

For Rick, though, every day he was separated from Sydney was agony. He hoped whatever plan the guys had would work. Soon. Because, without Sydney, the rest of this meant nothing.

ભ

Sydney hadn't realized a week could pass so slowly. Maybe if she'd been able to sleep or do something to occupy her time, it would have helped. But every time she closed her eyes, images of her nights with Rick rose up to haunt her. She could feel his skin next to hers, taste him on her lips. Her body and her heart cried out for him and she couldn't seem to make the pain go away. Rick called and texted constantly, but she couldn't bring herself to respond to him.

She had begged Linc not to call her any more. Her decision was firm. She'd faxed him her resignation, and she was done. Of course she had no idea what she would do with the rest of her life. She was probably poison in the business. Maybe she could change her name. Or something.

Emma called and texted and even came by a couple of times, but Sydney didn't have the energy to get involved in a discussion.

"He loves you," Emma told her the last time she stopped by.

"He's absolutely miserable."

"He'll get over it. He doesn't need me around to remind everyone of that stupid photo."

"Sydney, you're the only one hung up on it right now," Emma protested. "Butch and Linc are handling everything. And the band is just doing killer."

"I should have listened to my aunt," Sydney told her. "She said you had to make a plan and stick to it if you wanted to be somebody and 'not let some man push it off the rails.'"

"Ohmigod!" Emma threw up her hands. "Rick didn't do anything here."

"No, I did, but it happened because I let myself fall in love with him."

"Do you hear yourself?" Emma argued. "*Let* yourself fall in love? There's no letting. It happens. And you're going to turn your back on the best thing to happen to you. For what?"

Sydney turned on her in anger. "Don't you get it? That picture will never go away. Everyone will think of me as a slut. They'll always believe Rick could have done better, and the agency will suffer the fallout."

"I don't believe this."

Emma had left, at last, and apparently figured she'd done her best because she stopped calling.

When Rick, too, stopped texting or calling, she knew they'd reached a milestone.

She surfed the web daily, hungry for news of the band. Devoured every tidbit. Their concerts drew rave reviews again. "Take the High Road" was headed for the top with "Music Lady." Whoever Linc had sent out to replace her, it seemed had things under control.

See? They don't need you after all.

According to the entertainment reporters, Lightnin' was back in the studio and the contracts had been signed for them to join Deep Blue River on the rest of the tour. She scoured every site for any publication of the photos but apparently Linc had worked some kind of magic because, like magic, they disappeared. Instead all the chatter was about the hot new band. About Lightnin' and their exciting music. About their two singles zooming up the charts.

Someone at the office continued to handling the social-media platforms. She checked them every day, thrilled at the amount of traffic and sad that she was no longer a part of it. At least, she thought, she'd stopped crying every five minutes. That was something. At some point she'd have to decide what to do with the rest of her life. She couldn't spend it hiding at home. She just needed to wait long enough that the whole nasty episode had completely died.

Although she wasn't sleeping, getting up in the morning was becoming harder and harder to do. Yet, lying in bed didn't do anything except depress her even more. She was standing in the kitchen one morning in the old shorts and faded T-shirt she'd dragged on, hair pulled back in a messy ponytail, when the doorbell rang. With a halfhearted swipe at the stray hair on her cheek, she opened the door and nearly fainted.

"Hello, Sydney."

Shock immobilized her. She was sure every bit of blood had drained from her body and, for a scary moment, she thought she might faint. Then she wondered if she was hallucinating. She hadn't had a face-to-face with Janine in ages. Years, maybe. Not even a telephone conversation. The woman looked nearly the same as Sydney remembered her, well put together, every hair in place, makeup meticulous. But age had carved lines in her face and her eyes were filled with regret.

For a long moment Sydney was speechless, unable to do anything but stare. What was going on here? "How did you find me?"

"You are listed in the phone book, you know." Janine gave her a half smile. "However, a friend of yours gave me the address." Her fingers tightened on her purse. "It wasn't easy for me to come here, Sydney. May I come in?"

"Oh. Um, yes. Of course." She stepped back from the doorway. "Would you like a cold drink? Coffee? Tea?" What did you serve someone who had made your life so unpleasant you'd had to carve them out of it? And who then showed up out of the blue.

"Nothing, Thank you." She walked into the living room and sat down. "Come sit with me, Sydney. I have some things to say to you. Things I should have said a long time ago."

Here it comes. Raking me over the coals for what happened. I'm no better than my mother. Blah, blah, blah. Just what I don't need.

"If it's all the same to you, I don't think I'm up to a confrontation right now. You were right. Is that what you want to hear from me? Okay, I've said it. Now you can go."

"That's not what this is about. I promise. Please. Sit."

Sydney perched on the edge of one of the armchairs, her body rigid. "Okay, I'm sitting. I have no idea why you're here."

Janine studied her, a sad expression on her face. "To offer an apology I should have given years ago."

Apology? Did she hear that right?

"I don't understand."

"I'm sure you don't." Janine stared out the window. "I've lived with bitterness for so long, I can't seem to get rid of it. And it seems I've poisoned your life, too."

"What—"

Janine held up a hand. "I know you've heard me more times than you can count tell you the story of your mother and father. And me. The problem is, I was so very bitter, so angry, I never stopped to realize what your father and I had wasn't the real thing. And I hated it when I saw him with your mother. I was insanely jealous. I thought I had my revenge by turning you against happiness, just as I'd turned myself."

"But you always said—"

"I know what I said. I was wrong and I've had to live with it all these years. It robbed me of the pleasure of a relationship with you and probably of ever letting love into my life." She sighed. "You have some very good friends, Sydney. A woman named Emma and the people you work for. They care about you a great deal. I wish I had someone who cared about me that way. It may be too late for me but not for you."

Sydney frowned. "I don't understand. Do you know what happened?"

Janine made a face. "Of course I do. Some worthless piece of trash is trying to kill your reputation and your romance. Do not let that happen."

"Excuse me?"

"It seems you have the opportunity for both things that I didn't—a successful career as well as a man who loves you. Not one you just expect to love you. The people you work for think very highly of you. And your young man sent someone to plead his case very well."

Her jaw dropped. "Rick came to see you?"

"No. A young lady named Emma did. I wish I had a friend who cared as fiercely for me as she does for you."

"But you always said—"

Janine waved a hand in the air. "I know what I always said. It's taken me all these years to admit I was wrong. Everything came so easy to your mother. She was smart, beautiful, people loved her. I had to work twice as hard at everything."

Sydney frowned. "I don't understand."

A look of utter sadness washed over Janine's face. "No, I don't suppose you do. From the time we were kids, I had it in my mind I had to compete with her. Our parents certainly didn't make me feel this way. I don't know why I felt that way, but I just did. When I met your father, I thought, at last, someone who wants me first. But then he met your mother and I never had a chance."

Sydney was puzzled. "Didn't you ever meet anyone else? You're smart. Good looking. Savvy. I don't understand."

"No, I guess you don't. It took me a lot of years to realize the competition between Beth and me was all in my mind. You look just like her, you know. When you landed on my doorstep, that just made it worse. I drove you away because of it and you have no idea how often I've wished I'd handled things differently."

She rose stiffly. "I've said what I came to say. Perhaps, in time, you'll be able to forgive me for the way I always acted toward you. But whatever you do, don't walk away from what's waiting for you. You'll regret it forever."

Sydney just stared at her.

"You're going to get a call today," Janine continued as she moved to the front door. "From your friend Emma. I suggest you listen to her and do what she asks."

"Wait, wait, wait." Sydney hurried over to her. "Are you just going to leave like this? Walk out of my life?"

Opening her purse, Janine extracted a slip of paper and pressed it into Sydney's hand. "My phone number. I'm sure you've wiped it from your mind by now. I know I don't have any right to ask but I would really like it if you'd call me. Get things in order, Sydney, and then we'll see where we go from here."

She opened the front door and walked out, closing it gently behind her.

And then she was gone. Sydney stood there, stupefied, staring at the piece of paper.

What the hell?

⌘

"I'm not going." Sydney fisted her hands in her lap. "Please, Emma. I can't do this."

"Yes, you can." Emma spread out cosmetics on the vanity in the bathroom. "You managed a face-to-face with your aunt, didn't you?"

"Exactly how did you set that up, anyway? I can't believe the old bat even talked to you, much less came to see me."

Emma tossed the empty cosmetics bag she was holding onto the vanity and stuck her hands on her hips.

"Okay, old bat? Yes, she was. And she totally admitted it, if you can believe that. But, Syd? After she got over the shock of seeing me she nearly broke down in tears. Don't you think everyone deserves a second chance?"

Sydney sighed and nodded. "Yeah, you're right. It was just such a shock seeing her. And having her tell me she'd been wrong all these years. I still can't wrap my mind around it."

"We all make mistakes, you know."

"I still don't think my leaving the agency was a mistake, if that's what you're leading up to. And, in case I didn't mention it, Linc has stopped calling."

"Maybe he's just waiting for the right moment. Like tonight. Besides, it's a hometown concert again only, this time, they're big rock stars."

Sydney shook her head. "How did I let you talk me into going? I can't do this, Emma. If I walk in there, everyone's going to look at me and that picture will pop into their minds. Along with Macey Schreiner's rotten column."

"I don't think you give people enough credit. Where would Marc and I be if I hadn't gone back to the club that night?"

"That's different."

"No. It's not. Besides, have you even seen a hint of that picture lately? Has anyone written anything about it? In case you hadn't noticed, Macey Schreiner's column is among the missing."

Sydney raised her eyebrows. "Who managed that?"

"Linc Forrester and Butch Meredith wield a lot of clout in the industry. And there were tons of other people who were plenty tired of her. Besides, you can only have the power as long as you used it wisely. She didn't and it bit her in the ass."

"But still." She was so afraid of making a mistake again.

"But still, nothing. If you don't have the guts then say so. But if you love Rick, you have to do this. For both of you. The guy is miserable, Sydney." She leaned against the vanity. "If we get there and it's too awkward, we'll both leave. I promise."

"But a concert? With everyone there?"

Emma laughed. "There's safety in numbers. Now shut up so I can do your makeup."

Big mistake, big mistake, big mistake.

Sydney repeated it over and over to herself during the ride to the venue. As they showed their passes at the stage entrance, her stomach tied itself up in giant knots. And when they walked into the wings, she was sure she'd throw up any minute.

"The band is already on stage, waiting," Emma whispered in her ear. "Come on. Over here."

Sydney let herself be guided to the spot in the wings where she usually watched the shows. When Linc Forrester moved away from one of the equipment cases and silently gave her a hug, she was afraid she'd cry.

"You belong here, Sydney," he told her. "We were afraid we'd have to hog-tie you to get you here."

Then Butch was next to her, slinging his arm around her, telling her how much they'd missed her.

She was still trying to pull herself together when the house lights dimmed, a voice from the sound booth said, "Okay, everyone. Here we go. The band you've been waiting for. San Antonio's own." Pause. "Lightnin' has struck!" She heard the familiar intro to "Take the High Road" and electricity crackled through her system. There they were. Her band. In their eye-catching T-shirts, playing better than they'd ever played before.

She clutched Emma's hand as the audience screamed their approval after each number. Although Marc had caught Emma's eye between two songs, Rick had yet to look in her direction.

Maybe he didn't want me to come at all. Maybe Emma was wrong. Maybe I can get out of here before it's too late.

"I need to go," she shouted in Emma's ear over the roar of the crowd.

"Not on your life." She nodded toward the stage. "Pay attention."

She saw Marc standing at the front of the stage, holding his hand up for silence. Okay, it was time for the Marc and Emma thing. She'd leave after that. Get a cab and just get out of here.

"This is the time in our show when we always do 'Music Lady' for you," Marc said to the audience.

"Yes! Yes! Yes!" the crowd chanted.

"But, tonight, we have something even more special for you.

If you've been following Lightnin', you know that a lot of our success is due to the hard work of Sydney Alexander of Full Moon Productions."

Sydney froze, a chill racing over her skin.

"What you don't know is that she is the very special lady of our leader, Rick Trajean. So, tonight, we want you to be the very first to hear the song he wrote just for her, 'You're the One.' And, tomorrow, we hope you'll be downloading it on iTunes and nagging deejays to play it." He turned and motioned to Rick. "It's all yours, my man."

Marc moved back as Rick stepped up to the mic and picked out the opening notes of a song Sydney had never heard before.

You walked into my life and brought with you the sun.

I took one look and knew you were the one.

You brighten up my days.

In a million different ways.

For me, You're the One.

Sydney felt her throat tighten and tears clog her eyes. She could hardly catch her breath.

Just the touch of your hand and I feel it in my heart.

I love you in a hundred different ways when we're together or apart.

The taste of you that lingers with me.

The scent of you that never leaves me.

The feel of you against me that makes me come alive.

For me, You're the One.

It was so quiet in the hall that Sydney could hear herself breathe. She stood, motionless, fingers pressed to her mouth.

"Go on," Emma said and gave her a shove toward the stage.

At that moment, Rick turned to look at her, and the tears began in earnest. Someone else nudged her again. Like a sleepwalker, she moved out onto the stage, barely heard the screams of the audience or saw Marc motion for silence. All she saw was Rick and the heat and love in his eyes. How had she ever thought she could walk away from this, from him, no matter what?

He held out his hand and she somehow made her feet move to where he stood.

No matter which way the wind blows or how the music flows.

In the darkness and the light, in the day or night.

Miles apart, you're still in my heart.

Because for me, forever, ever, You're the One.

His beautiful bass voice held the last note as the band played the final chords of the song. For an endless moment, there was complete silence, just as there had been at the first concert performance of "Music Lady." Then, like that other time, the audience was on its feet, screaming, yelling, cheering, whistling. Rick took off his guitar and rested it on its stand before pulling her into his arms. The kiss he gave her would be burned into her memory forever. She wound her arms around his neck, realizing she could never let him go. Whatever happened, they'd work it through together. There would be other tough times ahead but they'd handle them.

Vaguely she heard the audience chanting, "More, more, more."

Rick released her, pulled his guitar strap over his head, and launched into the final verse again. She saw lights popping at the foot of the stage and realized photographers were crowding each other to get pictures. Someone finally pulled the curtain closed, and Rick wrapped her up in another hot kiss.

"Don't ever leave me again," he whispered in her ear. "I love you."

"I love you, too." She was laughing and crying.

Then Butch and Linc were both on the stage, shaking hands with everyone. The road crew moved into place to make the equipment change and gave them the thumbs-up.

"It's our own aftershock," Butch told them and winked. "The effect or repercussion of an event. I think this qualifies, don't you?"

But Rick was paying no attention to him or anyone else. He held on to Sydney as if he'd never let her go.

"You're the one for me," he kept repeating. "I can't make it without you."

"And you won't have to." She brushed her lips against his. "I'm yours. For always."

"Just as soon as we can get out of here, I'm going to show you. And then we have plans to make." He glanced over at Emma. "I owe you big-time."

Sydney saw the other woman grinning like an idiot and smiled back at her.

"Thank you," she mouthed.

Emma just kept grinning and gave her a thumbs-up.

Someone touched her shoulder and she turned to see Linc standing there. "We need to have a talk. I think we've wasted enough time. My office. Ten tomorrow morning. No arguments."

She managed a smile. "Yes, sir. I'll be there."

Rick pulled her against him as tight as he could, as if afraid she'd disappear. But she wasn't going anywhere. Not anymore. Never again.

"I'm yours," she told him.

"Believe it. Because for me? You're the one."

~ About the Author ~

Desiree Holt's writing is flavored with the rich experiences of her life, including a long stretch in the music business representing every kind of artist from country singer to heavy metal rock bands. For several years she also ran her own public relations agency handling any client that interested her, many of whom might recognize themselves in the pages of her stories. She is twice a finalist for an EPIC E-Book Award and a winner in 2014, a nominee for a Romantic Times Reviewers Choice Award, winner of the first 5 Heart Sweetheart of the Year Award at The Romance Studio as well as twice a CAPA Award for best BDSM book of the year, winner of the Holt Medallion, multiple winner of the Whipped Cream Book of the Week Award and is published by five different houses. *Romance Junkies* said of her work: "Desiree Holt is the most amazing erotica author of our time and each story is more fulfilling then the last."

You can visit Desiree at:
www.desireeholt.com

Joy Ride

Emma, the good girl poster child, is running from a life she suddenly sees as gray and suffocating—a life where she's successfully buried all her hopes and secret dreams. Until the night she wanders into Aftershock and is immediately drawn to the hot bass player. The electricity of his performance, the powerful music he coaxes from his guitar, the heavy vibration of each note reaches out to something deep inside her and wakes an Emma she didn't even know existed.

Marc doesn't much care for the groupies who hang around the band. He needs a woman he can create a future with that's a counterpoint to the craziness of the rock music business. When he sees Emma for the first time, something inside him cracks wide open. Just one sizzling glance between them, and he's sure he has found the woman to complete his life.

www.ingramcontent.com/pod-product-compliance
Lightning Source LLC
Chambersburg PA
CBHW051418170626
46809CB00006B/2210